To Krystal, with Best Wishes & Happy Reading! Deb Marlowe

Murder on the Mirrored Lake

THE KIER AND LEVETT MYSTERY SERIES
BOOK 3

DEB MARLOWE

ARE YOU SIGNED UP FOR DRAGONBLADE'S BLOG?

You'll get the latest news and information on exclusive giveaways, exclusive excerpts, coming releases, sales, free books, cover reveals and more.

Check out our complete list of authors, too!

No spam, no junk. That's a promise!

Sign Up Here

www.dragonbladepublishing.com

Dearest Reader;

Thank you for your support of a small press. At Dragonblade Publishing, we strive to bring you the highest quality Historical Romance from some of the best authors in the business. Without your support, there is no 'us', so we sincerely hope you adore these stories and find some new favorite authors along the way.

Happy Reading!

CEO, Dragonblade Publishing

Chapter One

London

“ARE YOU GOING to listen? Or are you going to stare at that barmaid's bosoms all night?”

Sally Doughty watched the big man shrug in answer.

“It cannot be helped. 'Twas a long voyage.” His foreign accent was heavy and his tone unrepentant. “A man has thirsts of all sorts. They need slaking.”

“Yes, well, slake your thirst and do it quickly. Our friend is traveling even further, and I suspect he'll want us to be ready and focused when he arrives.”

Sally stared through the smoke circling through the taproom. The second man was definitely English. He sat facing away from her, but she could tell he was also tall and powerfully built. She thought she detected the slightest hint of an accent. Something about how he spoke reminded her of her granddam, who spoke the Gaelic. He had the slightest tint of red in his hair, too. Irish in his ancestors, perhaps?

The foreigner drained his pint and waved for another. His gaze left the barmaid to drift across the crowded taproom. Sally pressed herself against the column at her back and focused a sultry smile on a bloke at the bar. She could feel the foreign man's gaze linger on her.

The man at the bar, dark and dressed like a dockworker, raised a brow at her. Definitely interested. She smiled again, and the foreigner's attention moved on.

"Do you think he'll show up with the twenty thousand?" The foreigner sounded thoughtful. Now, the way he spoke—it reminded her of Prince Albert. She'd been at the Crystal Palace with her mistress a few weeks ago and heard the queen's husband give a speech at the end of the Great Exhibition.

"He'd better," the Englishman answered grimly. "I'm taking serious risks for the League."

"We all are," the foreigner growled.

"We've done our bit. The groundwork is nearly complete."

"Nearly," the foreigner said significantly.

"I'll have it. And in plenty of time. There's no worry there."

"There had better not be." The foreigner shook his head. "We need a spark. Any would do, if you ask me, but that's not how it's played out. That request is very specific—and you are the one who promised to hand it over."

"I said I would get it. All of it. And so I shall." The Englishman sounded exasperated now. "That's not the worry. The worry will start if our friend doesn't come with the money. That's all we need now, to get in the last supplies and to light the fuse. That's their contribution. Conflict costs money. Our efforts will fizzle out without it."

The foreigner shrugged. "Perhaps. Perhaps not. There are other ways to fan the flames."

"Ways that will be more difficult to start and impossible to control. We'll do better sticking to the plan we've got." Shifting in his seat, the Englishman glanced over his shoulder. "Is someone watching? I've got that feeling at the back of my neck ..."

Sally darted her glance away. The dockworker at the bar had got to his feet. She curled her finger at her waist and beckoned him, even as she waited breathlessly for the foreigner's answer.

It was several long moments coming. The dockworker arrived before he spoke. "You waitin' fer someone?" he asked, moving in close.

"Waiting for you," Sally told him. "Took you long enough to get the hint, didn't it?" She stood on tiptoe and pulled him down for a kiss.

"Nah," the foreigner answered at last. "Everybody's about their business."

"Good." The Englishman drained his drink. She saw it out of the corner of her eye. "Let's move on. We'd better get all your cravings taken care of, so you can focus on the plan."

Sally kept kissing her dockworker, though he tasted like onion. His hands left her waist and climbed higher as the two men pushed through the crowd toward the door.

Sally pulled away. "Why don't we wet our whistles with a pint?" she asked with a grin. "Before we move this someplace more private."

"How 'bout we drink after?"

"Now, now. A girl has needs," she purred, taking her cue from the foreigner and his thirsts. "Wetter's better, ain't it?"

Heat flared in the dockworker's eyes. He turned toward the bar. "I'll be right back."

"Hurry," she urged.

She had eased through the crowd and stepped out the door before he ever got the tapster's attention. Walking out into the night, thick with the river's stink, she grinned.

Yes. *The League,* he'd said. And the way he'd said it—it showed the importance of it. Money. Foreigners. Conflict. This was all something she could use. Her lady knew at least one of those men. That Englishman. Sally had seen him before, more than once. She'd known there was something going on. Well, now her lady would have to listen. Sally would get her position back, any way she had to. And she did have to. She ached for it. For her mistress. For the confidences and the intrigue. For the sort of connection that she'd never felt before. For that feeling of being … special.

A watchman up the street called out the hour. Sally straightened her shoulders. Tonight. The ceremony. She would go tonight and get it all back.

Hurrying away toward a busier street, she used a few precious coins and caught a hack to the station. She made it just in time for the train heading west. When she disembarked at the village, she knew she had the correct night. There were two wagons waiting outside, when normally, this late, there would be none.

"Just you, young miss? You must surely be the last one. Be sure to tell them all that we'll be waiting to take them back. Last train heads back to London at midnight."

She nodded, but kept quiet. The young man kindly offered to let her ride on the seat with him, but she perched at the back, letting her legs dangle while she carefully planned how she would approach her mistress and what she would say.

The wagon left the village and navigated dark country lanes.

"Here it is," the driver called, pulling the cart to a stop. "Sure you can find your way in the dark?"

She handed him his coin. "I've been before."

He leaned down toward her. "What is it the lot of you are doing in there? Strange rituals? Are you all witches, then?"

Sally shot him a disgusted look. "It's a group of women gathered together, asking for guidance on major decisions, for blessings on births and children, looking for a bit of the mystic in their lives, and adventure in their souls."

"Don't sound too Christian, if you ask me. Heathens, are you? The whole lot?"

"No, curse you. But it's women, and they are doing something you ain't heard of or seen before, so I suppose there's no convincing you they aren't a bunch of dark pagan witches, then."

He shrugged. "S'pose not."

"But you'll offer your service and take their money," she sneered.

"Sure and I will, then." He tugged off his cap and scratched his head. "We'll be here when you are done."

She set out on the slight trail that led to the lake. Sally had to admit, it sent a thrill down her spine, being out here in the dark wood, with the last leaves rustling and the scurry of small animals sounding loud in the undergrowth. It was a fine thing, to be able to escape the city with the other members of the club, to feel the connection with the ancient women who had trod paths like this, for similar reasons.

The sound of chanting rode faintly on the breeze as she drew closer. Sally shivered, both with the chill of the night and with the sheer, dark splendor of it all. She was glad she'd been here before and knew what to expect. It was unnerving enough, even with the knowing.

She stepped quickly, listening for any sound of someone ahead of her on the path, but she encountered no one. Her memory held, and she recalled enough to stop at the right spot, at the edge of the trees, before the sky opened up over the still lake and the cleared edges around it.

She stood a moment, breathing quietly. Like magic, it was, staring out at that cold, star-filled sky. Their faint light reflected in the mirror of the lake. She heard the quiet lap of water and felt the slight stirring of the chill wind on her face.

The chanting started up again, slow and even. It came from the right, from the far edge of the lake. The women must be in the same spot they had used the last time. She didn't approach, though. She would stay here and watch. Wait until the ceremony was over. Until the mood was light and the women happy. She would confront her mistress then.

A bright light flared. She shrank back into the shadow of the trees. Another light came to life, then another, low to the ground, like stage lights in a theatre. Lit by linked fuses, seven lights in total illuminated the women gathered in their white ceremonial gowns, done in the style of the ancient Romans. The chanting grew louder before it abruptly stopped.

A figure stepped forward to the edge of the lake. Her gown was edged in silver embroidery and her dark hair piled high on her head, topped with a shining tiara. Emelia. The founder and reigning leader of Lake Nemi. She began to speak, low and slow. A prayer.

Behind her, torches lit, one by one. The light picked out the vivid colors of the flowers the women wore in their hair. Another woman stepped forward, holding a tray of offerings. Sally knew they would be carved tablets, bright ribbons, and rich fabric. Offerings to the Goddess Diana.

She stared at the woman who held the tray and set it down on a pedestal at the front. Her gown was also different from the others. The bosom was underscored by vivid scarlet and gold beads that Sally had painstakingly applied herself. She wore a scarlet cloak, too, the gold embroidered hood pulled over her hair.

Hungry for any indication of mood or attitude, Sally watched her closely. The woman's head bowed. Her shoulders slumped forward. The hood fell forward to completely cover her face. She kept her hands clasped modestly before her.

Wait. That wasn't right. Sally took a step closer to the edge of the trees. Her footstep sounded loud in the quiet wood, but she narrowed her eyes …

No. The fit of that gown was not right, nor was the posture. She knew it with a certainty. That wasn't—

She gasped suddenly and rose straight onto her toes. Pain bloomed low in her side. Her breath went out of her in a rush, and she gasped again, trying unsuccessfully to pull air in.

"It's your own fault." The voice grated, sounding harsh in her ear. "Should have kept your nose in your own business, girl."

He pulled her head back, and she stared up into a shadowed face. She couldn't see his features in the dark. Her heartbeat raced, then began to trip wildly. She couldn't breathe. Why couldn't she breathe?

"I'd slit your throat, but you are already dead."

He let her go, then pushed her forward. Sally fell against a tree and slid down, still fighting desperately for air. The pain faded, and she felt, suddenly, very cold. No matter how hard she fought, she could not pull breath into her lungs.

The chanting started up again, and Sally's last thought was that she hoped that the goddess was listening, and that, in her aspect as the Huntress, she would avenge her death.

Chapter Two

The Following Day
Hyde Park
London

"THERE'S NO NEED to subject yourself to this."

Miss Kara Levett smiled at her old friend. "I know, Eleanor. I do believe you, you know."

"It's hardly likely that there are two wealthy women running about Town with the name Malina. It's not exactly as common as Mary or Jane, is it?"

"I know you are right. But I must see it with my own eyes."

"Well, keep watch on the path, then. London might be thin of company at this time of year, but when the autumn session of Parliament is in, there's always a bit of Society to be had. And though the viscountess is in mourning and cannot partake of most events, she is sure to drive through the park every day at the fashionable hour, all alone and in her widow's weeds, in her open landau. So affecting," Mrs. Eleanor Braddock said in disgust.

"Wait. Look. There." From her perch in Eleanor's high gig, Kara had an excellent view of all the people who had come to see and be seen in Hyde Park. "Good heavens. It is her. It truly is."

Kara sat, stunned, as the beautiful woman drove by, nodding

and waving as if she were a member of the royal family, gifting the populace with a glimpse of her.

"A viscountess," Kara whispered.

Niall Kier was her friend. A fellow artist. A partner in the last months, as they had first cleared her own name of a murder charge, and then a friend's. And he was more than that, as well. Kara had feelings for the tall, handsome Scotsman, and he returned them. They had confessed as much to each other, right before he told her he had to go into hiding for a while. Right before she discovered that he'd had a wife, in the past. A wife of sorts, in any case, as they'd been handfasted, but never sealed the vow.

And now she'd discovered that Niall's previously handfasted mate had married again. That she was now a viscountess. How could she have missed this? Blinking, she tried to absorb the shock of it.

"A small matter that he might have mentioned," Eleanor said wryly.

"One would think."

"Unless, of course, it didn't matter to him."

Kara could feel the careful weight of Eleanor's gaze. "He did radiate relief, more than anything else, when he spoke of their separation."

"Well, there you have it," Eleanor declared. She eased her gig past a couple of riders that had stopped ahead of them.

"He might have mentioned the fact that it was her husband's murder that his name had been linked to, though."

"Perhaps he wasn't overly concerned about that, either. He did have an undeniable alibi, didn't he? He was here in London, with an inspector from Scotland Yard, when the viscount was killed in Dover."

"Oh, he was concerned," Kara said. "He's hiding somewhere, isn't he? And I am concerned, as well. She specifically gave Niall's name to Scotland Yard. Why? If they don't mean anything to each other any longer, why would she name him as a person of interest in her husband's murder? Especially when it was so easily disproven?"

"Spite? Jealousy? Perhaps she's ignored him until now because he's never before cared for another woman." Eleanor's tone softened. "Not the way he cares for you."

Kara flushed. "Perhaps. Maybe she wanted to damage his reputation? Or perhaps she wants something from him and meant to use the suspicion as leverage?"

Eleanor considered. "You might be right. But what could she want from him?"

Sighing, Kara lifted a shoulder. "It's just another thing I do not know. There are so many of them. You know she's been hanging about the club?"

"The club of Lake Nemi?"

"Yes."

"Why would she risk it? If Society finds out she's socializing so soon after her husband's death, they won't look kindly on it. Or her."

"Perhaps she doesn't care what Society thinks."

Eleanor tossed her a look.

"Well, *we* don't care what they think," Kara reminded her. "Not much."

"Yes, well, *we* are not looking for husbands or to rise higher in the social ranks, whereas she does seem like the social-climbing sort to me. And those types must care about what the gossips have to say." Eleanor looked thoughtful. "I'd say she must have a good reason for risking it. What could she be hoping to accomplish at your women's club?"

"I would guess she just wants to annoy me, but instead she avoids me. She avoids everyone, except for Emelia Naronne, the founder of the club. They hide away in Emelia's rooms, for the most part. And I haven't heard even a whisper of gossip among the members or the staff about her being a viscountess. Is she trying to hide her identity? What does she *want*?" Kara sighed in frustration. "There is so much I don't know!"

Eleanor pulled her horses up as all forward progress ground to a halt. There was a bottleneck of wheeled traffic ahead, as two open carriages had halted beside one another so the occupants could speak, and another had paused while a groom checked one of the horses. Foot traffic and riders continued on and around, but Eleanor and a few other drivers were forced to pull up and wait.

Kara noticed a pair of ladies walking together, coming from the other direction. They stepped around the grouping of carriages blocking the way. One of the ladies looked their way and paused. She leaned in to say something to her companion, then left her to approach Eleanor's gig.

"Mrs. Braddock," she called as she stepped closer. "Good day to you."

Eleanor glanced around and smiled when she spotted the lady. "Miss Wilkes! How lovely to see you!" As the woman stopped next to the vehicle, Eleanor gestured toward Kara. "I hope you will not mind if I introduce my friend? Especially as you both share an interest in science."

The lady raised a brow, and Kara studied her as Eleanor made the introductions. She was of African descent, with lovely, smooth skin and eyebrows that arched and gave her a quizzical look.

"I am happy to meet you, Miss Levett," she said congenially. "I saw your work at the Exhibition. I found it quite impressive."

"Thank you." Kara smiled. "What area of science do you favor, Miss Wilkes?"

"Chemistry is my main interest, but I do branch out here and there."

"I met Miss Wilkes at Mrs. Lindsay's salons," Eleanor explained. "We bonded over our scorn for the demonstrations of a phrenologist."

"Oh dear," Kara said with a laugh.

"Such a waste of our time. Trying to tell me about my personality and my life based on the bumps on my head? I have no patience with pretend science." Miss Wilkes gave a shudder. "But I do enjoy the salons. They are so calm. Orderly. It's restful to one's nerves."

"I find my work to be calming in the same way, sometimes," Kara told her.

"Yes. Order. Rules. Balance. They are to be found in the laboratory. Some of the ladies will sometimes exclaim when I mention working with volatile substances, but I tell them the harshest chemicals are not so dangerous as humans. If I know the properties of the ingredients I am working with, I am rarely surprised." Miss Wilkes lifted a shoulder. "And if I am careless and accidently cause a small explosion now and then, at least I know it was my mistake."

Kara laughed. "I know just what you mean. People can be so unpredictable."

"Exactly." Miss Wilkes raked Kara with a thoughtful look. "You know, Mrs. Braddock, we should talk to Mrs. Lindsay about inviting your friend to give a lecture at one of her salons. I find your work a fascinating blend of art and honest science, Miss Levett."

Kara flushed a little. "What a lovely compliment. Thank you."

Miss Wilkes inclined her head, and then she and Eleanor spoke a little about the upcoming scheduled topics to be covered at the salon. Kara let her attention drift. A little frisson of awareness went down her spine, and she looked up to find Miss Wilkes's friend watching her.

The woman nodded. Kara returned the gesture. She looked a little older, perhaps nearing forty years. Her hair was dark, as were her eyes. Her gaze felt ... intense. She wore a plain gown of dark brown, with minimal trim, but even from here, Kara could tell the quality of the material. The woman's gaze did not flinch. At last, Kara looked away as the coaches ahead began to move again.

Eleanor lifted the reins. "We'd better move on. So nice to see you out and about," she said to Miss Wilkes.

"It was lovely to meet you," Kara said as Miss Wilkes stepped away from the gig.

"And you as well. Perhaps we shall see each other again." With a regal nod, she turned away and headed toward her waiting friend.

"Well, that's enough of the park, wouldn't you say?" asked Eleanor.

"I would," Kara agreed.

Eleanor urged her team on. "There is one more thing I should likely tell you."

Kara's mouth twitched. "That I've yet another stain on my reputation, being seen with you as you drive your own gig in the park? I saw the scandalized looks some of the high sticklers were giving us."

"Let them look," Eleanor said with a snort. "Setting all their wicked tongues to wagging is just an enjoyable side benefit of the pleasure of driving myself. You should bring your little chaise to the city. We could start a trend."

Kara laughed.

Eleanor's voice dropped to a confidential tone. "No. It's one last thing about Malina. I heard from a reliable source that the viscountess has told the trustees of her husband's estate that she is with child."

Kara considered this news. "Well, it would certainly be better for her, if she were. They will delay the passing of the title and estates until they find out if the child is a boy. If the babe is male, he will inherit. As his mother, she will likely keep the houses, the other estates, and considerable influence, in his name."

"There will be trustees, though."

"Most likely. And do you doubt her ability to wrap them around her finger?"

"I don't doubt she would try. And I know she would hate for the nephew to inherit it all, while she is pushed off as the dowager viscountess and shipped away to a dower estate somewhere."

"I should imagine she would hate it with a passion," Kara mused.

"Well, I do know something else as well," Eleanor announced. "I know you need a treat. A diversion. What shall it be? Tea? Ices? An afternoon at the museum?"

"No, thank you." Kara gave her friend a smile. "I really must get back to Bluefield Park. I'm nearly finished with the automaton I've been working on, and the client is most anxious to receive it."

"And how, exactly, do you propose to do that?" Eleanor glanced pointedly at the sling on Kara's right arm.

"Turner has been recruited as my stand-in. I direct him, and he acts as my left hand, as needed."

"Good heavens." Eleanor looked horrified. "Poor Turner. Well, if there is a man alive on the planet who could survive your hovering at his shoulder and bossing him about, it's him."

"Oh, he's quite looking forward to the day this sling comes off. And it should be soon, the doctor says."

"Good. It ruins the lines of your gowns."

Kara laughed.

"Are you sure you cannot be tempted to wile away the afternoon with me?"

"Someday soon," Kara promised.

"Very well. But you owe me a sumptuous tea. With pastries."

"With all the best, most decadent pastries," Kara vowed. "Soon."

>>><<<

"I THINK YOU should use the magnifying glass," Kara said patiently.

Turner, her butler, lab assistant, and friend, grumbled under his breath. "You have young eyes."

"And we have tools to help yours. Why not use them?"

"Very well."

Over the last few weeks, Turner had become adept at using the smallest tools of Kara's trade. Now he tightened a tiny screw on the Hooke's joint she'd adapted for this project.

"Ah, there!" he said, triumphant.

"Very good." She paused. "Only twenty-four more to go."

"What? Twenty-four?"

"There are a lot of joints on this particular piece. Here, I'll hold one end steady while you make the connections."

They kept at it until the last was done.

"That should do it," she said, cautiously optimistic. "Give it a crank. Let's see how it goes."

He did, and the sea turtle came to life, moving its head and flippers as if it were at home in the water, its body turning and tilting as if it followed the currents of the sea.

"It's magnificent," Turner breathed.

"With thanks to you," Kara said. "Mr. Vestry will be thrilled not to have to wait much longer. Thank you, Turner."

A noise sounded from the corner of the lab before he could answer. They both stilled.

Another soft *thunk* came from the same direction, followed by a scrape.

"The tunnel," he whispered.

Kara's heart lifted. No one knew about the tunnels, save for the two of them, her head gardener ... and Niall Kier. She started moving toward the hidden entrance. Turner followed, but she noticed he took up a heavy metal rod as he came.

In silent accord, they stood behind a rolling rack of coiled wire. Waiting, they watched the section of wall that contained the secret door.

Slowly, it opened. Kara held her breath.

Niall stepped out of the shadows.

Kara moved out from behind the rack. Their gazes met. Niall's countenance brightened, lighting brilliantly, but only for a moment. He quickly schooled his expression to sobriety.

Kara drew in a long, shuddering breath.

Behind her, Turner set down the metal rod. "I'll just go, then," he whispered.

Before she was aware of moving, Kara had thrown herself into Niall's arms.

He enfolded her in warmth and welcome. Burrowing her face into his neck, she inhaled deeply. Citrus and cedar, but no trace of smoke. She'd missed it. But that small lack didn't keep her from feeling like she'd just stepped into the comfort and joy of home.

Niall exhaled deeply, his breath rustling her curls. He held on, his touch communicating relief and demonstrating how he'd been waiting for this, just as she had.

For long moments they stayed locked together, but at last he heaved a sigh, kissed her brow, and set her back. "Are you well?" He ran a finger along the soft fabric of her sling. "Healing?"

"Well enough. I'll be free of this soon. After that, I'll just have to be careful not to strain the shoulder."

His eyes closed. "Thank heavens. You cannot know how I've worried."

She bit her lip. "Actually, I believe I can, Niall." She raised a brow. "Did you discover anything about the viscount's death?"

His face stilled even as his grip on her arm tightened. "Who told you it was the viscount who died? Stayme?"

"No." She snorted. "Stayme warned me off right after I was injured. I've seen neither hide nor hair of him since."

"I'm afraid he's being kept busy right now. Things have quickly become complicated."

She held her silence at that, turning toward the table set up before the fire. "Have you eaten? There are muffins and honey left from tea. I can send for a fresh pot—"

"No. Cold tea is fine." He'd followed her. Holding out a seat, he waited until she was settled before dropping in beside her and falling on the food. "I don't want anyone to know I am here," he said after he'd had his first bite and sighed in bliss.

"Not even Gyda?" Gyda Winther was Niall's forge assistant

and close friend. She'd been staying with Kara for the last several months. Since Niall had left, Gyda had the forge here at Bluefield Park to herself.

He shook his head. "No. Our association and friendship is well known. Gyda must be able to deny any knowledge of where I am."

Kara waited, letting him finish his first muffin before she made her bald announcement. "I had a visitor soon after you left. Malina showed up to confront me."

Niall froze. The second muffin in his hand dropped to his plate.

"She came in the night, to the White Hart, after my injury and before I was moved home. She took great pleasure in telling me she was your wife."

"She is *not* my wife."

"I know. I quite spoiled her fun when I recalled the traditions behind handfasting. She was disappointed when I didn't fall apart at the thought of your marriage."

"Spiteful little chit," he growled. "Handfasting is a trial. It is temporary unless you choose to make it permanent. She was long gone before we would have married, after a year and a day."

"I knew that. She was quite shocked you'd even mentioned her to me. I don't think she liked it."

"You haven't seen her since, have you?"

"I have. She's been hanging about the club at Lake Nemi. Apparently, she and Emelia have grown close. They are often in each other's company, usually behind closed doors."

"She hasn't bothered you? Poked at you?"

"No. I've kept my distance. But we did have our first ceremony out at the new lake several weeks ago. I specifically asked Emelia not to bring her."

He looked interested. "How did it go off?"

"Swimmingly. The members were enchanted. They arranged another, a couple of nights ago, but Emelia specifically requested permission for Malina to attend, so I stayed away."

"Wise decision."

"She's not using her title at the club. I didn't discover that she was a viscountess until yesterday." Kara specifically didn't mention the woman's possible pregnancy.

"I'm sorry," Niall said with a sigh.

"Turner and I dug a little deeper into her background, then. Once we had a solid place to start."

He came alert. "What did you find?"

"Nothing untoward. She and the Viscount Marston appear to have had a typical Society marriage. Perhaps with a few more spats than most, and less time spent in London, but their financial situation looks stable from the outside. The family have not spoken much about the new viscountess's background, and there was some gossip amongst the matrons of Society about her. Whispers of a common background. She wasn't exactly taken in by the upper crust, but the family title and estates were all in order."

"She wouldn't have liked that," Niall mused. "That was one of the things she crowed over, leaving me. A place in the rarefied world of the aristocracy."

Kara burned to know more. To hear the details of how he and Malina had met and what happened to end their handfasting.

But Niall did not speak of his past. He scarcely ever did. He'd told her only that he held secrets that he must keep, and she had vowed not to ask, to let him come to her at his own time. She knew it was the right thing to do, but the questions surged, flaring like fire in her chest. She waited a moment to let the scorch of curiosity subside.

"Everything was in order until the viscount's recent death, of course," she continued at last. "The title and property will go to his heir, a nephew who is still an adolescent." Kara pressed her lips together. "Malina is expected to be immersed in mourning, and instead she's refused to leave for the country estate. She's still in London, hanging about Emelia incessantly, tooling about the park, and implicating you for her husband's murder. All of which leaves me wondering—why? Why is she bothering you—and me—now?"

He started to speak, but she held up a hand. "Do not tell me it is out of spite or jealousy. I've known enough women of her stamp. She wants something, Niall. What is it?"

He heaved a long sigh and bowed his head. When he looked up again, there was a tightness around his eyes that had not been there before. "I want to tell you, Kara—"

"Then tell me."

"I dare not! It isn't safe for you. There are things about me, things that no one knows. That no one can know."

"Except for Lord Stayme?" she asked pointedly.

"Well, yes."

"Things you've done?" she probed.

"No! Nothing I've done, I assure you. But it is altogether safer for you not to know. You need to be able to deny knowing anything at all. It's one of the reasons why I've gone into hiding. I don't want anyone thinking you might know things about me."

"But Malina knows?"

He shook his head. "She doesn't *know*. But somehow, either she or her husband came to suspect something, to think they knew something about me that they surely do not. Marston started looking about, prying into my past, and now he's dead—and not by accident." Both hands came down hard on the table. "Malina didn't kill her husband. She must have brought someone else in. What has she told them? And why kill the viscount? Damn it, Kara! I've got to discover what they think they knew and squash it before anyone else gets hurt. And before they stir up a hornet's nest. It could all turn very ugly."

Kara shot to her feet and began to pace around the table. "You are infuriatingly frustrating, Niall Kier."

His mouth twisted. "I know."

"I am positively on fire with a thousand questions!"

He nodded.

She stopped. "I won't ask them, though."

His eyes closed. "Thank you."

"Even though it might kill me."

He managed a grin. "You are not a cat. The curiosity might burn, but it will not kill." He sobered. "Truly, though, Kara. I appreciate your patience."

"You should. You know it doesn't come naturally."

"Kara," he said quietly. "With Marston's death, I'm wondering if there aren't those who just might find it easier to kill me, as well, rather than have certain secrets come to light."

She stopped walking, stricken.

"If they think you know anything, they could kill you, too."

Determination stiffened her spine. She knew how to live under threat. And she knew how to fight back.

"No," he said, reading her correctly. "This is not your fight. If you want to help me, then go about your normal routine. If anyone asks, tell them I accepted that invitation to Oslo, to consult with a client about a large collection of work."

"Surely there is *something* I can do?"

"I don't know who these people are. I don't know how dangerous they might be. I cannot have you involved. It isn't safe."

She wilted in acceptance. "Will you be back? Will you keep me updated?"

"I will, if I can do it without endangering you. And Kara?"

She waited.

"I promise, I will tell you all, when it's safe to do so."

"Yes, yes," she grumped. Better to set his mind at ease. "But what will you do now? How will you proceed?"

He only gave her a look.

She sighed. "Very well. But at least tell me where you will stay? You should not go back to the White Hart."

"No. There are people looking for me. I discovered that much in Dover."

She set off pacing again. "They'll be watching the Grove too, then. All of your usual haunts."

"Don't ask me to stay here," he cautioned.

"I wouldn't. The maids would sniff you out within the day."

He laughed.

"But you can go to my building near Hyde Park. Not even Scotland Yard has figured out the situation there. Go to the coffee house and ask Rachel to give you the key to the other side, the one they don't know I own. She knows I trust you. And she most certainly knows how to keep quiet."

"Thank you." He gripped her hand as she passed and pulled her down onto his lap. "I shouldn't have come. I know it. But I had to see you."

"I'm glad you did."

They gazed at each other, and the world narrowed. If only it could stay like this, just the two of them in a bubble of heat and awareness and possibility. The cadence of their breathing slowed and evened. Matched. Eyes locked, she breathed out as he breathed in. Shared breath, shared energy, shared anticipation.

A knock sounded on the door, breaking the spell. It opened and Turner peered in, his expression solemn. "There are police at the house, asking for you," he said to Kara.

Just like that, all the trouble and peril of the outside world swept back in.

Niall set her aside and stood. "Do they know I'm here?"

"It doesn't appear so."

"Don't tell them. Not even Wooten should know I've been here."

"It's not Inspector Wooten. It's another pair of detectives. You should perhaps keep hidden in the tunnels until dark, sir. They don't appear to be at all friendly."

Chapter Three

KARA ENTERED HER parlor with a smile. "Good afternoon. I am Miss Kara Levett. Mr. Turner tells me that you gentlemen are from Scotland Yard?"

The two men surged to their feet. "Indeed, Miss Levett," the older man said. "I am Detective Everett Frye. This is my colleague, Detective Tom Caden."

"Please, sit. Tea will be here shortly. What can I do for you?"

"We are here to ask about a purchase of land you made recently." Detective Frye wore a fine suit of brown. All of it brown, save for his linen shirt, and all of it almost the same shade as his hair. He looked startlingly monochromatic, except for the fine gold watch chain that hung at his waist. "You bought a tract of land from your neighbor, Mr. Camleigh at Wood Rose Abbey?"

Kara hid her surprise at the question. "Yes, I did."

"And that land has a lake upon it?"

"Well, a good-sized pond is more accurate, but we have named it Lake Nemi, in honor of the ancient site used by the Roman women who honored the Goddess Diana."

"We?"

"Excuse me?"

"You said *we* named it?" Detective Frye repeated. The sour look on his face appeared to be permanently fixed.

"Oh, yes. I am a member of a women's club called Lake Nemi."

"Wait!" Frye held up a preemptory finger. "Is the club called Lake Nemi? Or is the pond called Lake Nemi?"

"Both are, sir. I bought the land specifically because of the pond, so that it might be used in our ceremonies."

Detective Frye's gaze sharpened. "What sort of ceremonies?"

Kara raised a brow. "*Private* ceremonies, sir. May I ask why you are so interested in Lake Nemi?"

He didn't answer her question, but countered with one of his own. "Do you perform sacrifices at your ceremonies, Miss Levett? Offerings to the goddess?"

"Good heavens, no. The ladies offer up carved wax tablets, pretty ribbons, candles, and fabric in hope that their prayers and wishes might be heard. There are no beheadings of chickens or any such thing. Even in the ancient temple in Northern Italy, there were no such offerings. Diana is a protector of women. She blesses childbirth and advocates for care of the young. She rules over crossroads and is known as the Goddess of the Hunt. She protects the countryside and all who dwell in it. She is not associated with blood sacrifice."

"She condemned that lad, Actaeon, didn't she?" Detective Caden spoke for the first time. He was younger than his counterpart and far larger. Tall and broad and powerfully built. "Just for watching her bathe? She turned him into a stag, and his own dogs mauled him."

"You are well versed in the classics, Detective," Kara said with a nod.

"I just brushed up on this bit," he clarified.

"Again, may I ask why?"

"Are you saying that you do not practice human sacrifice at your ceremonies, Miss Levett?" Detective Frye flung the question at her like an accusation.

"Don't be absurd," she said sharply, but then she paused. "Human sacrifice? Why would you ask such a thing? And in such a manner? Has something happened?" She gazed between the two men as they shared a look.

"Your club held a ceremony at your Lake Nemi just the night before last, didn't they?" Detective Caden asked.

"Yes."

"Were you there?" Frye barked.

"No. I didn't attend." She stared. "What has happened?"

"It appears a young woman was killed at the site of the ceremony, Miss Levett." Detective Caden delivered this news gently. "While it was ongoing or shortly afterward."

"Oh, no," she breathed. "Someone drowned?"

"No." Detective Frye scowled.

"I see. Was it a member of the club?"

"That has yet to be determined."

"Do you know the poor woman's name?"

Detective Caden consulted his notebook. "We believe her to be a Sally Doughty. Apparently she's stayed in the village before. The innkeeper knew her well enough to identify her. Did you know her?"

Kara shook her head, puzzled. "No, I don't recognize the name."

"Do you know every member of your women's club?" Detective Frye's tone conveyed his low opinion of both the club and of her.

"I believe I know most of the regular attendees, but I suppose there must be some members I have yet to meet. Did the others see it happen?" she asked, suddenly struck. "Did it occur during their ritual?"

"No, the girl was some ways away from the site where the others gathered, at the side of the lake. It appears she was alone in the wood, near the trail that led out there."

"Might she have interrupted someone spying on the ceremony?" Kara mused.

"Or might someone have slipped away to do her in, while the others were distracted?" Frye asked, watching her closely.

Kara was shocked. "I hope you are not considering any of our members as suspects, sir."

"I should think, given your recent history, Miss Levett, that you would know a woman is as capable of murder as a man."

"I do know that, unfortunately. But the women of this club are dedicated to learning and to travel. To literature and to science—"

"To interests beyond a woman's sphere, you mean?" Detective Frye said derisively.

Kara straightened. "A woman's sphere is what she makes it, sir."

The door opened, and Turner carried in the tea tray. The hostility in the room lessened a bit as Kara carefully poured tea and passed around Cook's melt-in-your-mouth madeleines with one hand.

"Thank you, Turner," she said as the butler made to leave.

Detective Frye grunted. "Turner, you say?" he asked after the door closed.

"Indeed. I must surmise from your question that you are aware of my history, sir." Kara lifted her chin. "And yes, Turner has been with me since I was a child. Since before he did what Scotland Yard could not, and rescued me from my kidnappers."

The man didn't answer. He also did not appear to approve of her mention of her childhood abduction or the police force's failure in solving it. He shoved another madeleine in his mouth and smirked at her.

Kara turned to Detective Caden. "How was the unfortunate young woman killed, sir?"

Frye's cup rattled as he hastily set it down. "We are not sharing that information, Miss Levett," he said thickly, swallowing as quickly as he could. "I am aware of your past and your feelings about how the police handled your kidnapping—"

"And the subsequent attempts," she interjected.

"I also know Inspector Wooten has given you a bit of free rein recently in a couple of his enquiries. But Wooten is busy elsewhere. He has been assigned a special task by the commissioner. And this is *my* case, young woman. I won't have you mucking about in it, beyond answering my questions." He took out his notebook. "So, you say you were not at the ceremony the night before last?"

"No."

"Where were you, then?"

"Here at Bluefield Park. In my laboratory."

"Alone?"

"No. Since my injury I have required Mr. Turner's help with my work. He was with me. The maids brought our dinner there and came back to clean up afterward."

"I will wish to confirm that."

She nodded. "Also, you may check with the postmaster. He knew I was waiting on a delivery, and he sent his boy out that evening to bring it straight to me. The lad can verify our presence there."

"I'll check with them, as well."

She inclined her head.

"Now, to your knowledge, was Mr. Niall Kier present at the ceremony the night before last?"

She blinked. "No. He was not."

"How can you be certain, if you were not there?"

"Mr. Kier is in Oslo. Or perhaps he might still be on his way, depending on travel conditions, I suppose." She told the lie without hesitation. There was nothing that could make her believe that Niall had been lying to her—and she was convinced of the need to conceal his whereabouts.

"But he is associated with the club?"

"Yes. Although it is largely a women's club, they have made exceptions for a few exceptional men."

Detective Caden made a note. "Do you know why he went to Oslo?"

"Yes. He made a contact with an art collector from there, during the Great Exhibition. The gentleman wished to commission Mr. Kier for several pieces, all based on Nordic history and folklore."

"Are you aware of what date Mr. Kier departed?"

She frowned. "I don't think I know the exact date, but it was soon after I was injured." She gestured toward the sling. "Several weeks back, that was." She named the date.

Detective Frye eyed her closely. "It has been suggested that Mr. Kier might have been involved in this girl's death."

Kara gave a short, incredulous laugh. "Balderdash."

"Balderdash?" Frye repeated indignantly.

"Indeed. Utter nonsense. Even if Mr. Kier was in the country, it would be completely alien to his nature to harm a woman." She stopped short. "Wait. The woman who was killed, it was not the Viscountess Marston, was it?" She paused. "No, you said her name was Sally Doughty, did you not? Was the girl somehow connected to the viscountess?"

The two men exchanged glances.

"We believe Sally Doughty was once employed as the viscountess's lady's maid," Caden answered.

"Well, that explains that, then."

"Explains what?" Frye asked irritably.

"It explains the ridiculous notion of Mr. Kier's involvement. The viscountess appears to have a strange fixation on the gentleman. Did you know, her husband, Lord Marston, also recently died? She named Mr. Kier as a possible suspect for that enquiry, even though he had spent all the relevant day in the company of Inspector Wooten." She shook her head. "I understand her fascination. Mr. Kier is exceedingly attractive. But honestly, if she does not curb her excessive interest in the man, the truth about their past is bound to come to light. And I am not sure how kindly Society will view her, if it does."

Frye's mouth dropped open. "What truth about their past?"

"They were once handfasted, but the relationship fell apart before the traditional sealing a year and a day later." Kara pursed her lips. "I suppose thinking of an old love is natural, in a time of stress, but making two absurd accusations in a matter of weeks?" She shook her head.

Detective Caden looked thoughtful. "What would Society think of her, should that background become widely known?"

"Well, having such an intimate relationship before her marriage is unusual. And most of Society does not approve of anything different." She gave a wry laugh. "Ask me how I know."

Caden smiled. "Indeed."

"If I were you gentlemen, I would be wondering why two people close to the viscountess have died in mysterious circumstances." Kara stood, signaling the end of the interview. "I am sorry you were sent on a wild goose chase, Detectives. I certainly hope you find that girl's killer."

Frye gave a nod, snatched up his hat, and stalked out.

Caden paused. "Thank you for your help, Miss Levett."

"Of course. I wish you good luck in your enquiry."

Kara waited until they had climbed back into the hack that had brought them and set off down the drive before she went to find Turner. "Call for the chaise," she told him grimly. "We are going to Wood Rose Abbey."

❯❯❯❮❮❮

ONE OF THE other rooms that Bluefield Park's secret tunnel system gave out into was a storage room deep in the bowels of the house, containing old, heavy furniture covered in dust, ancient linens, and trunks of clothes long gone out of fashion. Niall had once taken the initiative to hide a portmanteau there, inside an old trunk. He'd consulted with Turner and included a few things that might be useful for both him and for Kara. Now, he took out the blanket they'd added, wrapped up, and settled down to rest.

He had to admit, it felt good to be back at Bluefield Park, even hiding in the shadows. It shouldn't. After he left Scotland, he'd thought it safer to keep wandering. To not get attached to any one place. Or person.

But he'd already made his decision to change all of that. He'd thought long and hard, weeks ago, after Kara had been hurt and before he'd snuck off to try to find what happened to the Viscount Marston. He'd almost convinced himself to go, to leave her behind where she'd be safe.

But he'd known what it would do to her. She'd made that clear. Stated it right out loud, in that direct fashion that he loved about her. And he'd known what it would do to him, too. Contemplating another leave-taking, another starting over—this time it had felt *wrong*.

He'd realized for the first time—he didn't want to be alone. Not any longer. Not after having a taste of what might be between them. What they might have together. He'd decided it was worth fighting for.

And now it was to begin. Purposefully, he cleared his mind and curled up to sleep for a few hours. After it grew dark, he snuck back into the tunnels and left them in plenty of time to reach Hammersmith and the last train back to London.

He did not, however, go to Kara's building by the park. He went instead and knocked upon his friend Ansel Wells's door. The artist welcomed him with wine, cheese, a promise of silence, and a few hours' sleep on his divan.

Niall was up well before dawn and walking through the wide, sleeping streets of Mayfair. Berkeley Square lay quiet as he stopped before Lord Stayme's door. Pulling a narrow strip of tartan from his pocket, he contemplated the viscount's slightly naughty door knocker. Two dancing nymphs formed the circle, their arms entwined at the top and one leg each entangled below. From between their knees leered a wizened, grinning face. Niall tied the tartan where the garish countenance's neck would be. Watts, Lord Stayme's faithful butler, would find the strip of cloth. He would take it to the old man, who would know what to do.

Niall turned away, then found a station and caught the train to Camden Town. The streets here were already wide awake, busy and noisy. This was the terminal spot for the Western Railway, where goods were loaded off the rails and sent onto the roads of London. The expanded function of transportation hub had transformed the semi-rural, solidly middle-class area into something decidedly different. It was far noisier and more polluted now—and crowded, as cheap, hurriedly constructed cottages were still being erected to house a great many railway employees.

Niall dodged people, wagons, and a number of the two hundred and fifty thousand workhorses housed here as he headed south for the Edinboro Castle Pub. He settled in at a table in the corner and ordered breakfast. A sleepy-looking serving girl brought it, and Niall tucked in, content to listen to the familiar and distinctly Scots accents that swirled around him.

He waited quite a while before the pub door opened and the slim, still-spry figure of Viscount Stayme entered. He came and sat across from Niall, shooting him a look of resentful resignation.

"You were far more biddable when you were young, boy."

Niall grinned. "There are plenty who would beg to differ."

"You always obeyed me back then."

"Well, I was in awe of you," Niall confessed.

"And are you not still?" the old man demanded.

"Even more so now. And my care and appreciation for you have grown as well, sir."

Stayme's habitually hard expression softened, but it didn't last. "Had you a care for me, you would have been long gone and out of the country by now." When Niall would have spoken, the old man raised a hand. "It's too late now."

The viscount's acceptance of his presence surprised Niall. "How so?"

"Things are afoot, boy. We are on the precipice of something, and my gut tells me these stirrings involving you are in some way entangled in it."

"What? Surely not?"

Stayme didn't answer right away. He hailed the drowsy server and ordered a coffee. When it was steaming in front of him, he frowned over at Niall. "The Edinboro Castle? And why does everyone here sound like they might have just actually come from Edinburgh?"

"The place was built for the Scottish railway workers. There's also a Windsor Castle, Pembroke Castle, and Dublin Castle pub, for the English, Welsh, and Irish workers. The railway owners figured out if each group got their own pub, there were far fewer employees unable to report for work each morning due to nasty pub brawls."

"Well, that's one way to keep business going, I suppose."

"And who is it that is keeping this meddling going, do you suppose?"

"I've yet to find out, but that is the next order of business. There are rumblings of discontent in the city. Things are heating up. I've lost two of my watchers, trying to ferret out just what is happening in those buildings around Boyd's Yard." Stayme took a sip of coffee and watched Niall over the rim of his cup. "And I've had word from Scotland. From Jedburgh. Men have been rummaging about there, asking questions."

Niall stilled. "They cannot have learned anything."

"Perhaps not, but they knew enough to make their way into Hartrigge and ask about you there."

Worry—and fury—hit him hard. "It must be Malina."

"I cannot think of anyone else." Stayme sighed. "God knows, I made sure there was no one else. But these are not her men. This is bigger and more organized than that silly chit could manage. She's talking to someone, it seems clear. But whom?"

"Does it matter? It couldn't do them any good to ask questions up there. No one knows anything."

"We have to face facts, Niall. Someone—someone with money, resources, and some sort of agenda—suspects something. Even if they don't quite know the true facts, they must be damned close, or they wouldn't be pursuing the matter so hard.

Now, they are looking for proof."

"Odin's *arse*," Niall cursed. "Why now?"

"I told you why. Something serious is brewing."

"Don't think to order me off again," Niall warned.

"Oh, no," Stayme said softly. "It's too late for that. It's time we changed tactics."

"To what?"

"Ready yourself, my boy. We are going on the hunt."

Chapter Four

KARA'S SPINE HELD stiff and defiant as Turner drove her little chaise up to the main entrance of Wood Rose Abbey. Niall had forbidden her to interfere with his quest to find the unknown men looking for him, but he hadn't said anything about the known enemy in their midst—the Viscountess Marston. He hadn't even known about the new charge the woman had leveled against him. Kara felt confident that she wasn't breaking any promises in discovering what she could about this poor girl's murder.

And as for Detective Frye's order to stay away from his case?

She owed him, and all the arrogant specimens like him, absolutely nothing.

A maid opened the door. The surprise on her face indicated she recognized both Kara and Turner. "Miss Levett! Do come in. I'll just run and see if the mistress is at home."

"Thank you." Kara smiled at her. "I am not here to see Mrs. Camleigh, but her husband."

The girl looked startled.

"In his capacity as magistrate."

Flustered, the girl paused. "Oh, but miss, perhaps you hadn't heard." She leaned in and whispered, "A girl's been killed."

"I had indeed heard. That's why I must speak with Mr. Camleigh."

The maid looked dismayed. "Oh, but the coroner's jury has only just departed. The master spent the morning with them, examining that poor girl and going out to see the spot where she was murdered. He's come back and shut himself into his study, and has asked that he not be disturbed."

"Very well. I will wait."

"Oh. I ... Ah, of course. Please, come into the sitting room, and I'll send word as soon as he emerges."

"Thank you, but no. While I wait, I would like to see the body of the girl that was murdered. I'm assuming she is being kept here, somewhere?"

The maid's mouth dropped open.

"Well, is she?"

She started nodding and kept on. "She is, yes, miss. In a tack room next to one of the barns."

"Good. You shall take me out there." Kara turned to Turner. "I assume you won't mind a chance to visit with Mrs. Canning?" Her butler's slow and steady courting of the abbey's housekeeper was the stuff of local legend and longtime gossip.

"I would be happy for the chance," he assured her.

"Very well." Kara turned to the maid. "Shall we go?"

"I know the way downstairs," Turner told the uneasy girl, and headed for the green baize door set in a nearby passageway.

"Do we go out the front, then?" Kara asked. "To reach the correct barn?"

"No, miss," the girl said faintly. "It's easier to go through the library."

Kara followed her outside and down a shelled path that led toward the stables. The maid pointed toward a small building attached to the barn, then bobbed a curtsy. "If you'll excuse me, I must get back to my duties."

"Thank you," Kara called after the girl as she hurried away—most likely to immediately report the visitors to her mistress. She figured she had better hurry before someone was sent out to run her off.

Opening the door, she found herself in a tiny office with a desk, stacks of breeding manuals, stud books, and ledgers—and a woman crying, heartbroken, into her handkerchief.

"Oh! I do beg your pardon ..." Kara stopped, suddenly shocked. "Emelia! Whatever are you doing here?"

Emelia Nardonne, the tiny, dark-haired, vivacious founder of Lake Nemi, looked up in surprise. "Oh, Kara! Thank goodness you have come!" She stood up, stumbled over, and fell weeping onto Kara's shoulder.

"Emelia!" She held the woman steady. "What is it? Why are you here?"

"Oh, K... K... Kara!" the woman wailed. "You must help! That poor girl. I knew her. She did not deserve this." She lost herself in another round of harsh sobbing. "I blame myself! I have nursed a viper at my bosom!"

"Please, Emelia. Be calm." Kara took the woman's shoulders and set her back a little. "I am here. We will discuss this. Sit down. Calm yourself. Is the girl's body inside?" She gestured toward the door that led further into the building. "I must see her, then I will come back and we will talk."

"Oh, yes. Yes! You must see it too. But hurry! The coroner has decreed a dissection is called for. He is in there, right now, getting ready to begin."

"I'll be right back." Kara stood at the door and knocked briskly.

"Look at the wound," Emelia whispered loudly as the door opened. "Be sure to look at the wound!"

"Yes?" A gentleman in spectacles peered out at her. "What is it? I am really very busy."

"Good afternoon. I am Miss Levett. You are the coroner?"

"Yes. I am Dr. Engle."

"Excellent." She pushed past him into the tack room. The space was small, the walls covered with highly polished tack and gear. The air hung thick with the smell of leather ... and death.

"What's this? You cannot ..." The man looked shocked at her audacity. "Young lady, this is highly inappropriate!"

The body was laid out on a long table in the middle of the room, covered to the shoulder with a sheet. The girl had been turned on her stomach. Her head was turned toward Kara. She looked young, but her face was distorted into a frozen grimace, as if she'd fought the onslaught of her death. Kara did not recognize her.

"The poor thing," she breathed.

"Who are you?" the coroner demanded.

"I am Miss Levett, sir. You have ruled this girl's death as unnatural?"

He stiffened. "I have, though I'm sure it's no business of yours."

Kara drew in a deep breath. "She was murdered, then, and it happened on *my* land."

His surprise clearly showed. "Your land? I took the coroner's jury out this morning to the spot where she was slain. Mr. Camleigh led us. It's not so far, and I assumed it must be his property."

"No longer, I assure you. More than that, I bought the land specifically for the use of a ladies' club that I belong to. And now I find that this girl was killed not far from a group of members who had gathered at the lakeside for a blessing ceremony."

"A blessing ceremony?" The coroner looked interested. "Mr. Camleigh intimated that it was pagan rites."

Kara sighed. "He would, I suppose. But it is all harmless enough, I assure you, sir. It is a women's club. We explore many kinds of learning. Literature, science, the classics. A group of our members have been exploring the lore surrounding the Goddess Diana. She is a feminine deity, who bestows blessings on childbirth, and on those who have reached a crossroads in their lives—"

"And on the hunt," he said, as if in recall.

"Yes. They went out to reenact the pilgrimage to Lake Nemi,

in Northern Italy, where worshippers came to offer garlands and bright threads and tablets inscribed with prayers."

"Fascinating. I never heard of women studying the classics in such a way."

"Our club encourages learning—about any subject that interests the members. But now I find that this girl was killed on that night? Very near to the ladies I invited to use the land? You must understand the responsibility I feel. I must know what happened to her."

The man stared at her as if she was some sort of newly discovered insect.

"Please, sir?"

"This is all very irregular. I am the coroner for a sizeable region. Nothing like this has ever happened in Fulham, Chelsea, or Putney."

"This is our village's first murder, I believe," Kara told him. "I'm sure we don't know how to behave. But please, I have an obligation. I must be sure something like this doesn't happen again."

"Oh, very well." He appeared to tire of the argument. "It will all come out in the inquest, in any case." He straightened as he approached the body, and his tone became clinical. "The girl was stabbed. The assailant knew what he was doing. The knife went in through her side, pierced her kidney, and drove up to rupture her diaphragm, making it difficult or impossible for her to breathe. She could not have survived it. Either the blood loss or the lack of air would get her. Or, at least, those are my predictions based on the signs left to be observed on the body. I am about to confirm them with a dissection." He gave her a frank look. "I don't think you'll wish to be here for it."

"No. I shouldn't. But is there something odd about the knife wound?"

He took a step back. "How did you know that?"

"The woman outside said so. May I see it?"

"Oh, yes. Another one. She shuffled in behind the jury, and I had to have her removed. Who is *she*, then?"

"A friend of the poor girl. May I see the wound?"

"I suppose there's no harm to it, though it isn't a pretty sight."

"I promise to alert you, should I feel faint."

"Do that, please." The coroner pulled a portion of the sheet up, being sure to preserve the dead girl's modesty. Or perhaps Kara's. "As you can tell by the extensive bruising, she was stabbed with a good deal of force."

The knife wound looked small to Kara's eye. Edged in red, it gaped a little. She paused. "What are those darker marks on either side of the laceration?"

"They appear to have been caused by some sort of ornamentation on the hilt edge of the knife. She must have been stabbed with some force, for the imprint to have been made."

She stared, trying to understand. On one side of the knife wound there were two marks, a small one near the top of the cut and a larger one near the bottom. On the other side of the wound was the largest mark, centered between the two others. All of the marks had small lines flaring in a circle from the center. She struggled to envision what could have made such a distinctive pattern. Those lines were almost like rays of the sun ... or a star—

She abruptly straightened.

"Are you all right?" The coroner sounded alarmed.

"I'm fine. Thank you. Were there any other marks on the girl's body?"

"None. Perhaps you should step out for some air." The man was clearly anxious to be rid of her.

"Yes," Kara answered faintly. "Air. Fresh air might help. Thank you, sir, for explaining how the poor girl died."

He nodded in response.

"Good afternoon."

He closed the door firmly behind her, but Kara stood staring grimly at Emelia.

"You saw it?" the other woman asked.

"I did." Her brain was spinning. "Come," she said curtly.

"But you saw it! The knife!"

"Not here," Kara said sharply. "Come with me back to Bluefield Park. We need to talk to Gyda."

⫸⫷

THEY FOUND GYDA Winther in the forge, with the doors flung open. She sat in the sunlight, painstakingly etching designs in an axe head.

"Gyda," Kara said breathlessly. "We need to speak with you."

The woman looked up, her fine features looking delicate in the sun and totally at odds with the power in her slight frame and the force of her personality. She blinked when she noted the woman at Kara's side. "Emelia! What a fine surprise."

Emelia let out a sob and sank down into a chair near the cold forge.

Gyda raised a questioning brow at Kara.

"Wait a moment," Kara said. "Is there anyone about?"

"No. It's just me."

Kara took the precaution of going to the wide doors opened on both sides of the small building and checking, just to be sure. Coming back, she pulled a folding chair near to her friend. "Did you know Sally Doughty?" she asked.

Gyda's expression darkened. "Well, I know of her. She's Malina's personal maid." She straightened. "If either of them are bothering you, I will put a stop to it."

"The girl is dead," Emelia declared, sniffing loudly.

"What?" Gyda looked shocked. "Sally, do you mean?" She looked to Kara.

"Sally Doughty was killed at the pond. In the woods at the edge of the clearing. Likely sometime during the ceremony, or soon after."

"Good heavens." Gyda's eyes widened. "You were not there,

were you?"

"No. Were you?"

She shook her head. "I had an engagement in Town." Gyda breathed out. "I can scarcely believe it."

"I should never have become mixed up with that woman," Emelia moaned. "It has all led to this!"

Kara raised a brow at Gyda. "What do you know of the girl? The maid?"

"Only a little. For a while it seemed as if Sally was always at the club." She shot Emelia a look. "While you and Malina were cavorting, the maid was always skulking about, prying, asking question after question and generally making a nuisance of herself."

"Yes. Questions. Always the questions!" Emelia agreed. "Malina wanted to know everything about everyone. Every bit of gossip. But she had so many questions about Niall." She frowned at Kara. "And then about you, Kara." Her face crumpled. "I listened to her evil whispers. I let her turn me away from you."

"Don't worry about it now, Emelia," Kara told her. "We have to concentrate on the maid and her death."

"But then, suddenly, not so long ago, Sally wasn't about anymore," Gyda continued. "Malina began to bring a different maid along."

Emelia buried her face in her hands. "She let the girl go. They got in a spat. Over me. Because Malina and I had grown close." She looked up. "I do not think things between them were as usual for an English lady and her maid."

Kara and Gyda exchanged glances.

"I will admit, I was glad to see the back of her," Gyda confessed. "Sally had a mean streak. She habitually upset Beth. On purpose, as far as I could tell."

Kara knew Beth. She was a young girl, timid and retiring. She had taken refuge at the club. Kara didn't know the details, but it was obvious the girl had fled some sort of abusive situation. She jumped in terror at loud noises or sudden movements. Once she'd obtained one of the club's permanent boarding rooms, she'd barely set foot outside. Many of the women in the club had made it a point to be kind and encouraging to the girl, but Gyda had taken her under her wing.

Gyda set her tools aside. "Who would have killed the maid? Sally may have been more than a bit of a bully, but she didn't deserve to die."

Emelia straightened at these words. "Tell that to your precious Beth, then, Gyda. For Sally Doughty was killed with Beth's own knife! The very one you made for her!"

Gyda sank back into her chair. "What?"

"I'm afraid it's true," Kara said. "Or, at least, that was my first thought. We saw the stab wound that killed her." Kara cast about, then went to Niall's desk and rummaged about for a pencil and paper. "It looked like this." She thrust a sketch of the wound and the three marks at Gyda. "It reminded me of—"

"The Pleiades." Gyda took the sketch and stared at in shock. "I ... It truly looked like this?"

Kara nodded and squeezed her hand.

"That knife," Gyda whispered. "I crafted it especially for Beth. She was so frightened all of the time." She looked up. "You recall, Kara. I asked you about strong feminine symbols I could use to decorate the blade and hilt."

"I do remember," Kara said gently.

"I thought having something of her own would make her feel better. It was meant to be symbolic. A sharp blade to keep in her pocket, so she would know she was no longer helpless. Something to show she was no longer alone."

"The seven sisters," Kara said. "The stars in the constellation. It was one of the symbols you used on the knife."

"Yes. Seven stars, seven sisters, spending eternity together, safely tucked up and away from the man who so relentlessly pursued them. I had the stars made of paste, but they still sparkled finely." Gyda ran her finger over the paper. "These three on the face of the hilt, on either side of the blade. The others spread across the bolster." She pointed out the two marks Kara had drawn on one side of the wound. "These two—in the stars, they actually represent the parents of the girls. I included them because Beth's parents were good to her, while they lived. She'd had them in her past, and now she has her sisters at Lake Nemi. For her future."

"Did you make another knife like this, Gyda?" Kara asked quietly.

"No. It was special. Meant just for Beth. And I thought it had done the job, for a while. Didn't you? She seemed stronger. More confident than she had before."

"Confident enough to kill?" Emelia asked in a whisper.

"No. I cannot believe it of her," Gyda insisted. "Although I noticed she'd grown quiet again, lately. Skittish, again."

"Was she at the ceremony?" asked Kara.

"She meant to go," Gyda answered quietly.

"We need to get into Town and speak with her," Kara said. "Now."

Chapter Five

NIALL WOULD HAVE expected the Viscount Marston's London home to be an old family relic, tucked up in some fashionable corner of Mayfair. He was surprised to find, instead, that the man had invested in the newer and more newly fashionable area of Knightsbridge. A lush and tranquil retreat for the viscount, perhaps, but it made watching the place a damned tricky business.

Situated on a corner of an oval arrangement of houses, the house faced a lovely garden in the middle of the development. It also boasted direct access to a larger, private garden behind and to the side of the house, carefully planted and enclosed by wooden posts connected by draping iron chains.

Easy enough to sneak into the garden, but not to actually set up anonymous surveillance. After a bit of thought, Niall returned to Ansel's home, borrowed an artist's smock and an easel from his friend, tucked his distinctive hair up into a loose hat, and headed back to set up in a spot where he could observe both the front and the back entrances of Malina's lair.

All day he sat and sketched with charcoal, while children and their nurses and young couples strolled and frolicked around him. He started on a depiction of the garden, with the stone and brick houses in the background. But as the hours passed, he found himself flipping pages and drawing dark eyes, bright with interest and laughter. Slim fingers at work with gears and clockwork. Ebony locks curling about bare, creamy shoulders.

Truthfully, he needed the distraction, for the knocker was off the door at Marston's house and the strictures of mourning appeared to be in full observance. No one came to the front, and only authentic-seeming vendors and deliverymen approached the back. As the afternoon sun began to sink low in the sky, Niall made a show of packing up his supplies and departing. He ducked into a thicket of plane trees that still held their leaves, providing a separation of the garden from the road. Wrapping the easel and supplies into a bundle, he tucked it all under some shrubbery. He peeled off the smock and added it, too. Underneath, everything he wore was black or charcoal gray.

Seeking out a comfortable spot, he sat and watched again, waiting for dark. Perhaps, if Malina had unsavory accomplices, they would come when they had the least chance of being noticed.

The sun set in a blaze of glory, and darkness moved in. Before the moon could rise, Niall left the wood and moved closer to the house. On the garden side of the back of the house, a terrace stretched out and invited residents to a narrow stretch of manicured plantings and a roundabout walk. This pretty section ended up against a hedge that separated it from the practical side of the yard, including a small kitchen garden, stacks of wood and crates, and the privy. But the hedge ended just short of the property line, and between the two halves of the garden sat a small shed.

Niall tried the door. Unlocked. He took one of the crates in with him and settled down, with the door cracked open, to wait.

The moon rose. Hours passed. Slowly, inevitably, doubt tried to creep in. He pushed it away. Stayme had not been convinced this was a viable means of discovering anything, but Niall knew better. Whatever was going on, Malina was tangled in it. She had been at the start of it, he suspected—at least at the start of this looking into his secrets. But Niall had to wonder if, whatever she had begun, it hadn't started to slip out of her control. Presumably, it would have been her suspicions that set her husband to lurking about London and Paris, asking questions about miniatures and the long-ago friendships and the travels of Lord Stayme. But who had killed the viscount?

Niall and Stayme were the logical suspects. They had secrets to protect, and Marston was nosing about, dangerously close. But neither of them had done it. It didn't make sense that Malina would send her husband looking, then kill him before he found the answers she wanted.

Who had done it? And why were they now looking for Niall? He'd discovered in Dover—the hard way—that there was a bounty on his head. And it wasn't the government who had set it. But who? Who else thought they knew his secrets? Why kill Marston? And what did they want with him?

He had no answers, only questions and a gnawing frustration eating away at his gut.

Around him, the neighborhood quieted. Lights went out. Fires were banked. Malina's house grew dark. Heaving a sigh, Niall shifted on his crate and told himself to stay awake.

It must have been an hour later when he heard slow footsteps coming along the garden walk. He stood to peer out. A man approached the house, crossing right in front of the shed. Niall drew back into the shadows as he passed, then watched him walk through the kitchen garden to the back door.

He was big. As tall as Niall himself and nearly as thick through the shoulders. Niall slipped out and followed silently as the man went down the stairs to the kitchen door and knocked softly.

The door opened immediately. Niall crouched down behind the stack of crates. In the scant light that came from the house, he could see that the fellow's scuffed leather cap didn't match the better quality of the rest of his clothes. An attempt at a disguise? And though the suit was of decent quality, the loose and boxy fit of his coat over his shoulders betrayed that it hadn't been bespoke.

Curious. Which part was the disguise?

After speaking quietly to whoever had opened the kitchen door, the man entered the house. Niall backed away, looking up and watching the windows. He breathed a sigh of relief when a light shone in the parlor just off the terrace. Moving silently, he crept up onto the stone surface.

Malina had come into the room and begun to light a few candles. Her visitor followed and positioned himself near the cold hearth, his back to the terrace door. Niall crouched into a corner near the French-paneled doors to watch.

Neither of them looked happy. Heated words were being exchanged. Slowly, painstakingly, Niall reached up and turned the latch to the closest of the double doors. He cracked it open just enough so that he could hear the argument going on inside and kept his hand on the latch to keep the door from opening further or making any noise.

"I'm telling you, they do exist," Malina was insisting. "I saw them myself. Held them in my own hand."

"Then where the hell are they? Why can I find no trace of them?"

"He's a damned tricky bastard! He caught me at it, as I told you. He saw the miniatures in my hand. Obviously, he moved them afterward. You need to keep looking. The papers were there, too. I didn't know what I was looking at, at the time. But now I know what they were. Put them together, and it's all you need."

Odin's arse, but Niall knew what she was talking about. She was talking about *him*. Silently, he cursed his own youthful stupidity. For once caring for this woman. For thinking she needed saving. For thinking *she* could ever care for anyone but herself.

"Damn it all!" The man struck the mantel with the heel of his hand. "I don't think you understand the importance of this! This is my contribution to the plan. Do you know what they will do to me if I don't cough up what I've promised? I will have no value and far too much knowledge. I'll be a dead man. And I have no doubt but that you'll be right behind me."

"Don't be absurd." She tried to laugh.

The man snorted. "Do you think because you're sleeping with—"

A soft step sounded behind Niall. Without hesitation, he let go of the door and rolled away, just before a loud *thunk* sounded and a knife struck the frame of the door, right where his wrist had been.

The blade quivered and the door swung inward.

"What the hell?" The cry rose from inside.

Niall was up and facing the man who'd thrown the blade. He was small. His eyes looked white and wide in the moonlight and contrasted with his dirty, thin face. He took an instant to look over Niall's frame, then uttered a curse and turned and ran.

Damnation! Niall set out after him.

He was fast, damn him. The little man was quickly out of the viscount's garden and into the larger, adjoining space. Niall sprinted after him across the open area and into the wooded border. The knife-thrower ran without seeming to tire, but he forgot the hanging iron chains between the fence posts. He hit one going full speed and went sprawling.

Niall ran faster and gained ground, but his wiry prey betrayed a familiarity with the chase when he hopped up and ran on without so much as a glance behind him.

At this narrow end of the garden, a dirt lane lay beyond the trees. Niall's quarry took off down the center, moving fast. He ducked into a connecting alley that ran behind a row of tall brick homes, erupted onto a wide street, crossed it, and hopped a tall fence.

Niall followed, hesitating at the top of the fence to see what he was getting into.

It was another garden, vast and neatly organized in boxes and rows. It held groups of many different specimens, each planted together. A nursery garden, perhaps? Across the vast space, he could see a variety of shapes and sizes—and his prey, sprinting down a long row of ankle-high shrubs, but heading for a corner lot of well-grown fruit trees.

Niall did not want to lose him in the cover of the trees. He put on a burst of speed, but the knife-thrower got there first and disappeared into the protection of the grove.

Niall slowed as he entered, trying to control his breathing and listen. It was darker under the canopy of branches, with the moonlight coming through in lines and stripes, lending an otherworldly quality to the space. He scanned upward, not wanting to be attacked from above. But no, he heard a step ahead and saw a shadow dart into another row of trees. He stepped his way carefully in that direction.

He saw and heard nothing else. Following the row of fruit trees to the end, he found a cleared space beyond. It held a collection of wheelbarrows and garden carts, an assortment of glass cloches, stacked burlap sacks full of fertilizer, from the smell of it, and a decent-sized glasshouse.

The door stood open. It was an invitation he didn't mean to take. Instead, Niall continued on around the house to the opposite side. There was a door there, as well. He opened it and peered in.

It appeared to be a fernery. Lush and gorgeous specimens in varying shades of green hung from hooks and covered benches and the floor. The air was warm, moist, and heavy. Two paths wound their way through the dense greenery. Stepping inside, he made the mistake of pausing to choose which way to go.

He heard the swish of air and tried to duck, but he didn't move quickly enough. The heavy cloche struck him on the shoulder instead of the head. He spun and stumbled, getting caught between two great ferns at his feet. Dazed and unsteady, he went down backward, crashing through the ferns and landing in a pool of brackish water.

The knife-thrower was on him in an instant, another blade

pressed to Niall's throat.

"Cor, and ye're a persistent one, ain't ye?" he said harshly. The blade pressed closer as Niall struggled to lift himself. "No. Hold still. Now, hold up yer hand, guv."

Niall slumped back a little. The back of his neck rested on the edge of the pool. Bracing himself, he lifted his hand—and tried to grab the man's arm.

"No!" The wiry man easily evaded him. "I'll be switched, but ye're troublesome." He gazed down at Niall, assessing. "They are askin' fer ye alive, 'tis true, but if ye mean to be difficult, then I'll slit yer throat and take the gamble they'll offer a dead bounty." Grabbing Niall's hand with one of his, he slipped a loop of tubing over it. "Now, give me the other, nice and slow-like." He chuckled. "I knew if I followed the big man, he'd lead me 'round to ye. He always keeps the best fer hisself, don't he? Well, I don't care if he is—"

A shot rang out, and they both jumped in fright as the bullet splashed into the water just at the little man's side. He yelped and stared wildly about, yanking at Niall's hand. "Hurry up, then, and give us the other one—"

Another shot. That one ruffled the man's hair as it breezed past his head.

"Damn ye to hell, ye big bugger!" The assailant dropped the tubing and pulled back the knife. "Keep him fer yerself, then! But this won't be the last ye hear of me!"

Niall sat up as the smaller man backed away and eased out of the glasshouse door. He stood and stepped out of the pond, dripping water and staring deeper into the fernery, where the foliage hid whoever it was who had fired those shots and set him free.

"Who is it? Who's there?"

But there was no answer. And though he searched the glasshouse from one end to the other, he found no one.

>>><<<

THE LATE-AFTERNOON SUN warmed the townhouse in London that housed the Lake Nemi women's club. Inside, all lay quiet. Kara, Emelia, and Gyda went first to Beth's room, but found it empty.

"She likes to help in the kitchen," Gyda said.

They trooped downstairs and found the cook/housekeeper pulling fresh loaves from the oven. "The lass is upstairs in the laboratory," Mrs. Umbers told them. "She and Lady Alina were talking round and round about the spinning of the Earth." She paused. "No pun intended, of course. In any case, they went upstairs so Lady Alina could demonstrate."

The three women climbed to the third floor, where a large room had been converted into the laboratory. A group of the members were dedicated to science and the latest technological advancements, and this was their lair. High windows lit the room, where several tables placed about held an assortment of books, notebooks, beakers, burners, and other equipment. Lady Alina had set up a pendulum in her space. Beth sat beside her, frowning as she listened.

"Monsieur Foucault proved his theory this past February, in Paris," Lady Alina Standham was saying.

Kara had heard the earl's daughter was fascinated with science, but had been forbidden to pursue her interests at home, as her mother was convinced it would sour her suitors. Undeterred, Lady Alina had forged a bargain with her matchmaking mama, promising to uncomplainingly attend all the balls, routes, breakfasts, and parties that a young debutante was supposed to, as long as she was allowed a few hours a week at Lake Nemi to pursue her scientific studies.

"But what does that swinging ball have to do with the Earth spinning?" Beth asked, perplexed.

"Think of the pendulum," Lady Alina explained. "It moves

back and forth, in the same motion, in the same direction, along the same plane. Now, what if it made a mark while it traveled? Foucault used sand, but we can use paper." She placed a sheet under the pendulum and made a mark along its path. "The pendulum's motion is fixed. But the Earth, beneath it, is rotating." She turned the paper. "See? Now the pendulum has not changed, but the mark has." She turned the paper again, rotating it slowly. "So, we can see that the Earth is actually spinning."

Beth frowned. "But if we're all spinning, why don't we feel it? Why are we not all dizzy? Why is the wind not always rushing along at us?"

"Excellent questions," Lady Alina said, her manner encouraging.

"But the answers must wait, I'm afraid," Emelia said firmly. "Beth, would you please come along with us, *cara mia?*"

The girl looked around, startled. "Yes, ma'am." She appeared nervous as she followed them down a floor to Emelia's lush sitting room.

Kara looked around with interest. She'd never been in here before. She noted that some of the art from the club's distant origins, decidedly carnal, had made its way in here.

Beth took a seat on the sofa. Gyda sat beside her, while Kara and Emelia claimed two seats across a low coffee table.

"Beth, we understand you had some difficulty with Sally Doughty," Kara said gently. She'd told the other women she wanted to ease into questioning the girl and not give her a fright.

"Well, we didn't get on, it's true."

"Will you tell us about it?"

Beth looked from one woman to the other. "She was frightful mean to the staff here. She always complained that they were slow and lazy, acting above them, even though she was but a maid herself." The girl shrugged. "But a lady's maid is not the same as a lady."

"She wasn't kind to you, either, was she?" Emelia asked sadly.

"Well, no. I saw her drop a tray of food once, all on purpose, just after the kitchen maid passed it to her. She gave a great hue and cry and accused the girl of making her drop it. She got real angry when I stood up for Lucy. She never left me alone after that." Beth sighed. "But it's been better, these last couple weeks, when her mistress started bringing a different girl along with her to the club. The latest one is not so friendly either, but at least she doesn't pick at anyone."

Gyda sat straighter. "We need to ask you about the knife, Beth. The one I gave to you."

The girl's face abruptly crumpled. Tears sprang forth. "I'm so sorry," she cried. "I didn't mean to!"

The women all exchanged glances.

"Didn't mean to do what, Beth?" asked Kara.

"I didn't mean to let her have it," Beth sobbed. "I know I should have been brave. I know I'm supposed to learn to stand up for myself. I should have said no and meant it, no matter how she pinched me or twisted my arm. But it just … It reminded me …" She dropped her face into her hands. "She was so set on having it. She meant to have it, and she wouldn't let up. I got so tired of being scared, of watching for her and knowing she was going to jump out at me and start up again. So, finally, I just … let her take it." She looked at Gyda with agony in her expression. "I know you are disappointed in me."

Gyda shook her head and took the girl's hand. "Who took the knife, Beth?"

The girl blinked in confusion. "Sally did. Did I not just say so? I thought you must know, and that's why you were asking."

"Sally Doughty took your knife?" Kara repeated.

"Yes. I know why she wanted it. Her mistress was that angry with her. Sally thought that knife might get her back in the lady's good graces. A gift, it was." Beth's lip trembled. "Sally gave it to her, right in front of me, in the parlor." She darted a glance at Emelia. "Her ladyship knew it was mine, too. She looked over at me and took it anyway."

Kara sat straight, suddenly struck. "Her ladyship?" she said sharply. "You knew about her title, Beth?"

Surprised, Beth nodded.

Kara glared at Emelia. "Did everyone know? Everyone but me?"

Emelia's countenance fell. "It's my fault, Kara. Malina quite despised you, you know. I didn't know it at first. I met her at Kew. I like to go there to walk among the myrtles and the cypress. They remind me of home. She was so beautiful and so interested in me and in everything we have accomplished here." She fluttered her hands. "You know how I am, Kara! I fell quickly. We began to spend a great deal of time together. She had many questions about Niall, but I didn't think anything of it. He is the only man you see around here with any regularity, and he is ..." She waved a hand again. "You know. Beautiful. But she kept asking, more and more, and when she found out your name had been linked with his ..." Emelia shook her head. "I knew then. I know what jealousy looks like. I tried to turn her away, but she kept coming back, with presents and sweet words and promises."

Kara sighed.

"It wasn't until after your injury that I realized how much she disliked you. You were gone for a while, and when you came back, you seemed determined to avoid her. I just told everyone not to bring her up. To avoid the subject with you. Honestly, I could feel her pulling away, especially after she let Sally go. Her interest was elsewhere. I could feel it. I thought she would end things and we wouldn't have to worry about her any longer."

"Instead, she stole Beth's knife. The knife that was used to kill the maid she let go, and then she sent Scotland Yard after me as a suspect for the murder." Kara let her exasperation show.

Beth gasped. "Killed the maid? Sally? Sally's dead?"

"Yes," Gyda said. "She was killed in the wood near the ceremony the other night. Were you there?"

"Yes! She was killed with my knife?"

Kara nodded.

"But her ladyship could not have done it. She was in the

ceremony herself. She presented the offerings. I stood right behind her the whole time."

"And after the ceremony? Did she stay with the others?"

Beth frowned, thinking. "Yes. After the ritual, we lit a big fire and all sat in a group along the shore, enjoying the night, until we had to leave to catch the train. I remember seeing her there, and seeing the moonlight shine off the gold embroidery of her cloak."

"And you, Beth? Did you stay with the group?" Gyda asked. "For the entire evening?"

Beth nodded, then suddenly gaped at her friend. "You don't think that I ..."

"No," Gyda assured her. "But the police will ask, once they hear about the knife. Were you with anyone? Can any of the other women assure them that you didn't wander off?"

"Yes. Lady Alina can. She missed the first ceremony out there, because she had to attend a ball. She wanted to be sure to make this one. Lily stayed close to us, too. She was interested in all the things that Lady Alina could tell us about the old ceremonies, back in Italy, so long ago."

"Miss Lily Broadchurch," Gyda told Kara.

"Yes, I've met her. I read the article she wrote for *The Lady's Companion*." Kara looked to Beth. "They will both back you up? Assure the police that you stayed with the group the whole evening?"

"I'm sure they will."

"Well, what do we do now?" Emelia demanded. "Malina will never answer our questions about the knife."

"No." Kara straightened. "But find me a paper and pen? I believe I know someone whose questions she will have to answer. I'll arrange a meeting for first thing in the morning."

Chapter Six

K ARA WATCHED DETECTIVE Caden pause in front of the pie shop from her seat at a table inside. Watching the light way he moved gave her a pang, as it reminded her of Niall. Unusual in a man so tall. Of course, he did not have Niall's uncanny grace, nor quite his breadth, but Caden was a fine figure, nonetheless.

He opened the door and came in, sizing up the place in a glance. Reminded of her purpose by thoughts of Niall, Kara nodded at the detective and indicated a seat across from her. He approached, and his face lit up at the sumptuous spread she had ordered.

"Good afternoon, Miss Levett." He removed his hat, damp from the misty rain outside. "I see you know the way to a poor bachelor detective's heart."

She laughed. "I do know your work sometimes keeps you from enjoying regular meals."

"Unusual choice," he remarked, as her friend Maisie hustled over with fresh tea. "For a clandestine meeting."

"Well, I have friends here, and truthfully, you cannot find a better pie in London, savory or sweet. The apple turnover is especially good today." Kara took a sip of her tea. "I would have invited you to Carlisle's, except I wished to speak with you alone."

"You know Carlisle's?"

"Enough to know the risk of others from Scotland Yard coming in was too great. And that I quite enjoy their pastries."

He took up his cup. "Why did you wish to see me alone, Miss Levett?"

"Because I found your compatriot, Detective Frye, to be quite repugnant."

"Well, you wouldn't be alone there."

"And because I have information about the death of Sally Doughty."

He set down his tea. "I'm all ears."

"I will tell you, but first, I require your promise to take me along on the interview that the information will lead to."

He sat back. "That is not something my superiors will approve of."

"Nevertheless."

"Will it be dangerous?"

She considered. "I doubt it. Unpleasant, perhaps. But not dangerous."

"Will it lead me to the killer?"

"Honestly? I doubt that, too. But it will lead you a step closer. And, in my opinion, perhaps to someone who conspired with the killer."

"Are you sure you won't just—"

"No," she interrupted.

He thought a moment. "I might agree to your terms, if you will answer a couple of questions for me in turn."

Kara hesitated. "Ask. And then I will decide."

He spoke instantly. "Do you believe Niall Kier is in Oslo?"

"I was right there next to him when the invitation was made. And the gentleman who extended it also included a very generous offer, I might add."

"That's not an answer to my question."

Which had been exactly the point. She sighed. "I only know what I was told." Which was to tell anyone who asked that Niall was in Oslo. "Of course, I cannot offer proof for what I believe." She leaned forward. "But if you are going to ask me to be strictly specific, then of course I must answer that I don't really know where Niall Kier is, but neither do I know just where my butler is at the moment. Or my friend, Gyda Winther. Or the queen, for that matter."

He only gave her an assessing look.

"Have you asked his other acquaintances?"

"Everyone I've asked believes him to be in Oslo."

She lifted a shoulder. "Well, then."

He sighed. "Very well. Now, tell me what you know."

She explained. He listened to her story all the way through before he began to ask questions.

"How can you be sure the maid gave the viscountess the knife?"

"Well, first, I believe the girl, Beth, is telling the truth. However, I suspected you might not, so I questioned the staff. All of Beth's tales were confirmed. A maid, bringing fresh glasses for the sideboard, saw the exchange of the knife in the parlor."

"She saw the viscountess take it, with her own eyes?"

"She did. And, beyond that, the housekeeper noticed the knife in the viscountess's possession days later."

"What of the club members who were purportedly with Beth during the ceremony? Did you speak with them?"

"I did. Both confirmed that Beth stayed with the group the entire evening."

Detective Caden crossed his arms. "I admit, I'm impressed, Miss Levett. You've done some good work."

"Thank you." Kara eyed him closely. She'd been complimented before on her investigative accomplishments. Inspector Wooten had been puzzled, slightly scandalized, and ultimately, though reluctantly, impressed with her. Enough to request her help with a sticky interview, when he needed a woman's touch. She'd worked a little with Constable John Norland several weeks ago, and he'd seemed surprised but accepting of her talent. But

Detective Caden? She sensed an undercurrent beneath his words. Was it annoyance?

"Of course," he continued, "I would have preferred if you had come to me earlier with your suspicions."

"Well, I would have preferred not to be insulted and questioned as a murder suspect in my own home, but here we are."

"Yes. Here we are." He pushed back from the table. "But let us go, then, and question the viscountess."

She straightened. "Without another argument? You surprise me, Detective."

His look grew serious. "You'll find I am a man of my word, Miss Levett."

"I'm glad to hear it. But do finish your turnover before we go. They are too good to waste, and you might need your strength before this is over."

⫸⫷

KARA AND THE detective were ushered into a small parlor in the late Viscount Marston's lovely home in Knightsbridge. As Kara had predicted to herself, the room was done up in scarlet with touches of gold. It seemed to be the viscountess's signature color scheme. Kara had only seen the woman up close a few times, but each time, she'd worn a variation of the theme. Knowing this, and knowing that not even Malina could breach the etiquette of mourning, Kara had prepared for this encounter. She hoped to annoy the woman silently and thoroughly, without saying a word.

She had dressed accordingly, in a lovely day gown several shades darker than ivory. The bodice fit low across her shoulders and pointed in a vee toward her waist. A lush décolletage was embroidered with entwining green vines dotted with scarlet flowers and the occasional gold-threaded bud. The decoration continued on the sleeves and upon the tulip edges of the front of the gown and around the hem. She'd even fashioned a scarlet and gold sling for her arm. In short, Kara looked like she'd bloomed specifically to sit in this parlor. A fact that was not lost on the viscountess when she swept in, wearing a mourning gown of black matte crepe.

A quick glance at the woman's tiny waist showed no indication of her rumored condition, Kara noted.

Malina looked between the two of them. She gave no word of welcome, introduction, or invitation to sit. "What are *you* doing here?" she demanded haughtily of Kara.

Detective Caden took a step forward and introduced himself. "Good morning, my lady. I've brought Miss Levett along because she has some information about the weapon that was used to kill your former maid."

"What weapon?" Malina asked, bored.

"A knife," Kara said clearly. "A knife that Sally forcibly stole from another girl at the club. A knife that she was seen passing to you, as a gift. A knife that was last seen in your possession."

"What knife?" Malina said, uncooperative again.

"A small one with a thin, curved blade and a handle stained blue," Kara said. "There were symbols carved on the hilt and etched on the blade."

"Yes. I know it," Malina said sharply. "What of it? You cannot possibly know that the girl was killed with that specific blade."

"Actually, we can, my lady," the detective said respectfully. "Do you still have the blade? May we see it?"

"No, no." Malina waved a hand. "That shoddy thing was stolen weeks ago, along with several of my jewels."

Caden took out his notebook. "Stolen? Did you report the theft, madam?"

She seemed annoyed by the question. "No. What use would that be? None of it had any real value. And I'm fairly certain that it was Sally herself who stole the things. They disappeared around the time she came here, begging for her position back. I sent her off, still without a reference, and I assumed she snuck back in and took what she could get her hands on, in revenge."

"Convenient," Kara murmured.

"You don't believe me?" Malina snapped. "Ask my maid, if you must. She'll tell you."

Detective Caden started to demur, but Kara straightened. "Perhaps we should. It's best to be thorough."

Malina glared at her before crossing to a corner and giving a tug on a bellpull. When a footman entered, she snapped an order at him. "Find Betty and send her in. The detective wishes to speak with her."

The footman bowed and departed.

Malina shot Kara a superior look. "Did you drag the detective here with the thought of accusing me of killing the girl? How was I to manage that, when I was taking part in the ceremony myself?"

"I don't know. But you managed to lay suspicion on me when I was not even present, so call us even," Kara answered calmly.

The door opened, and a young, pretty girl stepped in. She kept her head down and her hands folded in front of her.

"Good afternoon, Betty," Detective Caden said kindly. "Don't be nervous. We've just a few questions for you."

The girl looked up and sent a glance toward her mistress. "It's Bridget, sir."

"Oh, I beg your pardon. Bridget. We'd like to ask you about a certain knife your mistress owns." He described it.

The girl looked startled. "That blade?" She looked to her mistress. "My lady told us that it was stolen."

"You can confirm that it was taken from the house?"

"Well, sir, it must have been. It's not in my lady's possession now."

"Thank you, Bridget. That will be all, then."

The girl left, and the detective turned back to Malina. "Do you have any idea where Sally Doughty went after you turned her away?"

"None," Malina answered flatly.

"Did she ever mention any family? Friends? Where she grew up?"

Malina sneered. "She was my maid, Detective. Not my bosom friend."

"Well, then." The detective shut his notebook with an audible snap. "I believe we are finished here. Thank you for your time, my lady." He gave a curt nod and strode out.

Kara rose slowly. She met Malina's steely gaze with a direct one of her own and followed him without saying a word.

Caden had asked the hackney coach to wait for them. They set off back toward the city in silence. Kara's mind was focused on the problem of discovering where Sally had gone after she was let go. Perhaps someone she knew could shed light on why she had gone to the ceremony at Lake Nemi, or on any other enemies she might have had.

"I can speak with the staff at the club," she mused out loud. "Perhaps Sally mentioned friends or family to someone there."

"No," Detective Caden interrupted.

She frowned. "No?"

"No, Miss Levett. No. That is enough. I hate, on principle, to agree with anything Frye says, but in this case, I have to do it. I tell you now, do not involve yourself in this case any further. It's clear that you do not care for the viscountess. It's also clear that women do not have any place in these sorts of enquiries, or I would not have been plunked down in the middle of your rivalry with Lady Marston."

Kara reared back. "I remind you, sir, that *I* brought *you* valuable information on the weapon that killed that poor maid. The fact that it happened to involve a woman I do not care for is irrelevant."

"It is relevant when I have to wade through your sniping at each other to get to the facts," he said in disgust. "Police work is serious business. A detective must reason with higher logic and thinking. He cannot use the circumstances of a case to get one up on his nemesis."

"That is not what I did!"

"Didn't you? Would you have pushed your way into seeing the maid's body if it hadn't been the viscountess who pointed us in your direction for an interview?"

She hesitated, considering his point. "Yes. I would have," she said at last. "That murder occurred on my land and has unsettled and worried a group of women that I am part of and care for. I would have wished to understand the details of the enquiry, even had the viscountess not been involved."

"I don't believe you," he said baldly.

She stared at him, shocked.

Caden knocked on the ceiling of the coach. "Stop here!" he called.

He practically jumped out before they had rolled to a stop. "Take the lady where she wishes to go," he said, handing the driver a fistful of coins. He shot a dark look at Kara. "Good day, Miss Levett. I don't want to see your name associated with this matter again."

He stalked off, and Kara was left staring after him, wondering where it had all gone so wrong.

Chapter Seven

NIALL WAS TIRED of being on the streets. He'd picked up a tail on his return from Knightsbridge. Whoever had stepped in to save him in that fernery had shown no inclination to show themselves, but apparently they had an interest in knowing what Niall would do next.

He was fairly sure the boy following him was not the one who had fired those shots. Youngish, lean and hungry-looking, the lad was, nonetheless, as stubborn as a bur. The early hour made it difficult, but Niall thought he'd lost him when he headed into White Hall, circled the Admiralty, and ducked into Scotland Yard, but as he left and headed for the Strand, he felt a prickling between his shoulders. Looking back, he realized the boy had picked him up again.

Exasperated, Niall hopped on the back of a town coach that had left the footman's platform empty. He held on all the way to St. Paul's. When the carriage slowed, he jumped down.

Making his way around the church, he evaluated his options. He couldn't go anywhere he might normally be associated with. Kara's offer had been kind, but he couldn't take her up on it. He felt a twinge low in his gut at the thought of her, but he kept on, racking his brain. It was just as he was approaching Watling that he looked up and saw his raw-boned shadow grinning at him.

How the hell—? The boy must have ridden on the back of his own carriage, or several, perhaps. Damn. He was like a bur in a bear's tail, nearly impossible to remove—and not only that, the boy must have passed him on his ride, then jumped down to await him. Niall suffered a moment's fleeting respect for the cursed brat, before ducking into a lane and taking off running, headed for the river.

It took nearly an hour of weaving in and out amongst the fishmongers, taverns, run-down shops, and warehouses before he finally lost the boy again. Exhausted from the chase and his sleepless night, he took stock of his locale and headed east to the St. Katharine Docks.

Off one of the warehouses along the west dock stood a narrow, dirty, covered yard with a two-room shack at the back. A weathered, soot-stained man looked up as Niall slipped through the gate and closed it quickly. Seeing Niall, he grinned a welcome. Niall smiled back at Pounder Bissett and held a finger to his lips.

Pounder, like many men of the dockyards, went by his given nickname, using it in every area of his life as a point of pride. He made his living in this yard cramped with his forge, jigs, and varying massive molds. Here he forged and molded dock hooks, beam clamps, metal bitts for securing loads, and any other sort of tool that could be used in the loading and unloading of the ships that fueled London's trade. He also, on his occasional day off, isolated himself in his workshop—the smallest room in the shack—where he crafted fine metal clasps, jewelry mounts, and delicate wire fittings.

They'd met in the backroom of a famous jeweler's shop in Ludgate Hill. Niall had been filling an order for his compass rose pendants and jeweled thistle broaches. Pounder had been delivering a set of finely woven gothic crosses, made into dangling earrings, pendants, and stickpins. They had struck up a conversation, continued it over a pint—and a friendship had been born.

Pounder's brow rose as Niall nodded toward the workshop

and mimicked sleeping, but he nodded permission. With a grateful look, Niall crossed to the small room, collapsed into the single chair, propped his feet on an overturned bucket, and dropped instantly into sleep.

He awoke hours later with a crick in his neck. In the next room, he could hear Pounder's woman humming as she readied the evening meal. Standing, Niall stretched to loosen the kinks, then paused, his eye on the tools and bits of precious metals on the worktable. The idea struck him then. And he cursed himself for a fool, for not thinking of it earlier. Opening the door, he peered out into the yard.

His friend was at a scrolling jig, using his bulk to force a thick piece of metal to bend. He nodded at Niall, finished up, tossed the metal back into the forge, and headed over.

"Thank you," Niall said quietly, clasping his friend's arm. "I needed that."

"What is it?" Pounder asked. "Trouble?"

"Of some sort. I need to keep out of sight until I figure it out."

"You are welcome to stay here. You know that."

"I appreciate it, but I've work to do. There is one thing I realized you could help with, though. It's a commission. I'd pay you well."

"Anything you need, Kier. You know that."

"Two small items. Fine goldwork. Are you willing?"

"Of course. Especially if you pay well." Pounder grinned.

"I'll draft it out for you. May I borrow a bit of paper and a pencil?"

"In the desk." Pounder nodded toward the workshop. "Help yourself. I've got to shift that piece in the fire."

"I'll get it all down and leave it on your table before I head out." Niall hesitated. "Thank you, Pounder. This is important. I'll come back in a few days to pay you and fetch the pieces."

"I'll work on it in the evenings."

"Give Alice my best, but not tonight, eh? It's better if she doesn't know I was here."

Pounder nodded and clapped him on the back.

Niall went back inside and drafted images of two pieces, with only slight variations. He left some folded bank notes, just in case Pounder needed cash to get materials.

Drawing out another sheet of paper, he wrote out an accounting of yesterday's encounters. He tucked it in a pocket until he could find a suitable messenger to deliver it to Stayme. He crossed the yard and eased out of the gate while Pounder was occupied with the point of his hook.

The workday was coming to an end out in the docks. Stevedores were securing last loads and anticipating the pints awaiting them. Fog was rising on the river, and the smell of the Thames was rolling in with it. Unfortunately, Niall could smell himself, even over the river's stink. Pond water, sweat, and soot did not make a sweet combination. But if his plans for tonight were to have any chance of success, he needed to be sure his aroma did not announce his presence.

Heading west, he caught an omnibus and headed for Marylebone.

KARA DIRECTED THE driver to take her to the train station, then sat back, succumbing to a dark mood. Detective Caden's words kept swirling about her head. Perhaps there was some truth to them. She had to admit it—she'd enjoyed getting a little of her own back from Malina.

She leaned back against the squabs. To be turned away in such a way was both embarrassing and irritating. Worse, the detective's harsh words and critical manner opened a door that allowed all of her own doubts to rush in.

It was not pleasant. She was tempted to slam the door closed on them all again. Forge ahead. But she hesitated. He was right about one thing—she was barging in, uninvited. In her previous involvements with the law, she'd first been working to clear her own name. After that, she'd been asked to help clear a friend's. But now? Was this just vanity on her part? Unwarranted confidence?

She tried to push away the uncertainties Caden had dredged up, damn him. Sitting forward abruptly, she lowered the window and called to the driver, changing her destination. If she was going to head home, she could at least return bearing gifts. Turner deserved a special token of appreciation after all the extra work he'd done, acting as her third arm these last weeks. And Gyda had been unsettled, knowing her knife had been used in such a terrible way. It might lighten Kara's own mood to lift theirs.

When the carriage slowed, she descended into Cranburn Street, near Leicester Square, and entered Eliassen's Patisserie.

The crusty old man who ran the place greeted her with a grunt. "Back for the braided almond paste pastries, Miss Levett?"

"I am indeed, Mr. Dahl. You know Turner's fondness for them. I thought I'd take him back a box."

Another grunt and a wave of his hand sent the baker's journeyman back to box up the baked goods. "I don't see Miss Winther with you? I have those little donuts she likes so well."

"I was hoping you would." Gyda had discovered this place, with its selection of pastries from the regions of her childhood. After much pleasant experimentation, they had all found some new favorites. Kara, knowing Gyda's preference, called back to the journeyman, "And a dozen of those little donuts as well, please?" They might stand a chance of making Gyda smile again.

The bell above the door rang as another customer came in. Kara moved aside, examining the crispy cardamom biscuits and the lingonberry cakes as Dahl moved to greet the newcomer.

"Do you have a recommendation?" the customer asked.

Kara wondered what Dahl would advise a newcomer to try. "Miss?"

She looked up, surprised. "Oh! I'm sorry, I didn't realize you were speaking to me."

The woman gave a faint smile. "You seemed as if you are familiar with the place. I thought you might be able to recommend something."

"Oh, of course." Kara eyed Dahl, who slanted a glance toward the apple and cream pastries. "These are lovely," she said, pointing in that direction. "Or the butter biscuits just melt in your mouth."

The woman gave a nod.

"Happy to give you a sample, as a friend of Miss Levett," Dahl told the woman.

"Oh, I'm afraid I don't know ..." Kara paused. "Wait." She frowned and then remembered, in a flash. "I have seen you, haven't I? Though we were not introduced." She looked over the woman's dark hair and eyes and the simple cut to her gray gown. "You were in the park with Miss Wilkes when I met her, were you not?"

The woman smiled. "You have a good eye, Miss Levett."

Kara smiled expectantly.

"I am Miss Scot. I've been hoping to make your acquaintance."

"Indeed? Are you interested in chemistry, as Miss Wilkes is?"

Miss Scot chuckled. "No one is as interested in chemistry as Clémence. I do enjoy science, but not to the exclusion of art and music, history and politics, and all the other fascinating aspects of our world."

"An admirable goal, to aim to become well rounded in your interests," Kara remarked.

"You have some admirable traits yourself, I think. I have heard of your work at the women's club. Lake Nemi, isn't it?"

"It is, but I cannot lay claim to its success. Miss Narrone is the founder and guide of the club. I am but a member, and contribute as all the others do."

Dahl made a noise as if to remind them he was still waiting. Miss Scot turned to him with a smile. "I should rather like to try the butter biscuits, please."

The baker handed over a biscuit and a napkin as his journeyman came running back with Kara's second box.

"Mmm. Delicious," Miss Scot announced. "You are right—they melt in the mouth." She eyed the two boxes the journeyman was tying up for Kara. "You are taking treats for your friends? How lovely. It is one of life's blessings, to have friends one can give these little attentions to, is it not? Someone to do things for?"

"It is," agreed Kara.

"The luckiest among us also have friends who we will do *anything* for," Miss Scot remarked, her tone suddenly intense.

Kara nodded.

"The trick is to know the difference."

Kara searched the other woman's face. "I don't think there's a trick to it. Surely your heart tells you the difference?"

"The heart can be mistaken. Fooled. Led astray." Miss Scot took a step closer. "It's shocking when it happens. Hurtful. Heartbreaking. And dangerous."

"Dangerous?" Kara thought a moment. "Do you mean, when friends become enemies?"

"I knew you would understand. You have seen darkness in your life."

It always gave her a little jolt when she was reminded that some of the worst parts of her life were well known and open to public comment. "Not that sort, thank goodness," she said lightly.

"You have been very fortunate, then. When those who are meant to care for you do not, things can grow very dark, indeed." Miss Scot looked Kara over once more. "Take guard against such a betrayal, but more importantly, take care not to perpetrate such damage."

Kara's back stiffened. "It appears you know a little about me, Miss Scot, but clearly not enough, if you think I would ever do such a thing to anyone, let alone a friend."

"I am glad to hear it," the woman said solemnly.

This entire episode had been bizarre, but Kara could not help but feel as if she'd been given a warning. "I must be going. Now, if you will excuse me ..."

"Of course." Miss Scot turned to Dahl. "I shall take two dozen of those." She smiled at Kara. "I shall emulate your very good idea, Miss Levett. Good day to you."

"Good day."

Kara gathered up her boxes, shook off the odd encounter, and took the train back to Bluefield. To her disappointment, neither Turner nor Gyda were available. She turned over the treats to the footman, Tom. "Place them in their rooms, please?" she asked. "I don't wish to upset Cook. You know how she gets when we admire someone else's efforts."

Alone in her rooms, Kara found her earlier doubts edging back in, eroding her usual determined attitude. Damn Detective Caden. He'd derailed her focus. The insecurities she usually held at bay reared their ugly heads, and worries about Niall rushed back.

Were there other reasons Niall refused to let her work with him to find his pursuers? He'd been intent on leaving her and their friendship behind, not so long ago. Was this an elaborate way to make his exit without giving her a chance to fuss?

For she had fussed when she'd sensed his withdrawal. She'd forced him to face their attraction, to acknowledge what he was giving up. He'd changed his mind when she was injured. Had he changed it again, now that she was healing?

She slumped back on her favorite chaise as dark reflections and worry overran her. She stared out the window, unseeing, and wallowed in her fears.

But she couldn't let this go on. It wasn't in her nature. Rallying her determination, she examined her worries one by one. Faced her fears and concerns. And gradually, she fought back. Defeated each one.

Caden was wrong. This was not a vendetta. Goading the viscountess was not her main motivation. Just an added benefit, she thought with a wry smile. She would have been interested in the investigation into the maid's death regardless of Malina's involvement. And she would have been willing to help in any way.

And her doubts regarding Niall were nonsense, as well. He had let her in, as far as he could while still protecting her. She'd felt his true affection, his longing, the care he felt for her. She believed in him. In what they had together. In what they might be.

Pushing off the chaise, she straightened her skirts and headed for her laboratory. She needed to think about everything they'd learned. Plan for where to step next. She would do her best thinking while her hands were busy.

Kara let herself in and went to the sea turtle, flung the cover off the nearly finished piece—and gasped.

Around the mechanical creature's neck hung a pendant on a chain. Tears threatened as she touched it with shaking hands. It was a compass rose. Niall's talisman. But it was not his usual, finely wrought piece. It shone, the compass fashioned delicately of silver and mounted on concentric circles engraved with nautical elements.

With a happy sob, she lifted it off and clutched it to her breast. She was incredibly glad she'd reaffirmed her own beliefs before she found this. Now it served as reward and confirmation.

Tears did flow, though, when she found the engraving on the back.

K—

We navigate together now.

—N

She donned the necklace and let the pendant rest next to her heart. For long moments, she sat there, clutching it tight, relishing the return of her joy and confidence. At last, she threw an apron around her neck, resolved to think while she worked.

She'd already crafted a few swaying pieces of seaweed to add to the base of the piece. The clockwork was already set up. It wouldn't take long to insert the new elements. Carefully, she began while she mulled it all over. Did she truly believe Malina might have murdered Sally Doughty?

After struggling with the angle of her injured arm for a few moments, she looked down at her sling, then removed it. This would be a good test, something simple. She went back to work, still thinking. All went smoothly. No pain. And all the while, her mind was as busy as her fingers.

No, she decided as she attached the last gear. She didn't think Malina had killed Sally herself. But she absolutely believed the woman would have hired or convinced someone else to do it for her. The question was … why?

"Miss? Miss Kara?"

She snapped out of her reverie, startled to find Turner beside her. From the worried look on his face, it hadn't been the first time he'd called her name.

"Are you all right?" he asked.

"Yes. Of course. I'm sorry. I was lost inside my head."

"Cook has set out a late luncheon. Will you come to the house? Or shall I bring a tray out here?"

She wiped her hands on the apron. "I'll come in, thank you. I think we are finally finished with this one," she said, nodding toward the turtle. "Would you mind contacting Mr. Vestry? Ask if he would care to inspect it here before we call it finished?"

"Of course."

She slid down from her stool. "Turner?"

"Yes?"

"It seems certain to me that the viscountess is somehow connected to this girl's death. Is it only me? Am I allowing my own prejudices against her to sway my judgment?"

"The girl was summarily dismissed after arguing with her mistress, you said?"

"Yes. Without a reference. And there has been an intimation that their relationship was closer than most."

"So, they argued, then the girl gave her mistress the knife in an attempt to appease her. She was let go, then was found days later, murdered with the same blade?" Turner made a face. "It would seem miraculous if the lady didn't know something about the maid's death."

"It's a relief to hear you think so, too," Kara said. "But why? Might it be connected with her husband's death? Or with the looking into Niall's past? Could Sally have seen or heard something she shouldn't?"

"It would make sense. Mr. Kier did believe there was something suspicious about the viscount's death."

"I just cannot shake the certainty that Malina knows something about all of it." She slid out of the apron and folded it over the chair.

"But what can you do about it?"

"Perhaps nothing at all. But I do believe I will go to Lake Nemi and ask some more questions."

"And what of the detectives?" He held up her sling in silent reminder.

She gave a little shrug as she took it from him. "They are free to pursue whichever wrong avenues they like, of course."

Chapter Eight

DONNELLY HOUSE WAS a small-fronted, unassuming place. It catered to a small clientele, the sort of men who knew that true privacy commanded—and was worth—a hefty price. Any new member had to be nominated and vetted and willing to pay. Niall had been offered up to the place by Stayme, of course, and had never regretted a moment or a sou spent on it.

He entered through the back, via an alley that was as dirty and odiferous as any other in London. But stepping inside, he entered another world. A porter at a tall, elegant desk greeted him in a room done up in shining tile floors and blue flocked wallpaper.

"Good evening, sir." The porter took his coat and hat without remarking on the smell or his generally disreputable state.

"Good evening, Jones." All of the porters were called Jones. "I'll have a private bath, if you please. My clothes will need the full treatment. Coat and boots too, I'm afraid."

"Very good, sir. Would you care for a companion this evening?"

"No, thank you." For an extra sum, a member could ask for a woman's company. She was guaranteed to be pretty, clean, and refined enough to pass for a lady. He could hire her as a bathing assistant, as a friendly ear to converse with for the evening, or as a temporary mistress willing to perform any service he could dream up. Niall considered himself too much of a gentleman to ever partake of such an offer, but he was damned if he could resist the Turkish baths. "I would like some bath salts, though, Jones. Something to soften the water, but nothing to scent it."

"Of course. If you will follow me."

A hidden door led to wide stone steps that descended below street level and opened to a spacious hall below. Gas lamps shed warm light over the stone walls. Classical statues stood in arched niches. Art hung on the walls, and several doors branched off the space. Niall knew the frosted door straight ahead led to the public baths and saunas. More than a few lucrative business contracts and political agreements had been successfully brokered in there, but Niall was happy to follow Jones down a different corridor to a gorgeous, carved wooden door that opened to a private bathing room.

The porter strode around to turn a few knobs and start the hot water streaming into the sunken tub. From a wooden cupboard he brought out a jar of bath salts. "Enjoy your bath, sir."

"Thank you." Niall stripped and piled his clothes and boots near the door. He kept his wallet, watch, and boot knife close by the edge of the tub. Once it was full, he sank down into the steaming tub, closing his eyes in bliss.

He sat and soaked for a while, then sat up to rummage through the small, inset shelf offering soap and lotions. He scrubbed himself from head to foot twice and lathered his hair up, too, then he drained the tub and ran fresh water in again. This time, he tossed in the salts, sank in up to his chin, and sighed. He might have fallen asleep.

When he roused, the water was cool and his clothes had been folded neatly and placed just inside the door, smelling sweet and looking fresh. He had no idea how they accomplished such miracles. He hadn't even heard the door open.

Niall dressed slowly, loath to leave the warmth and luxury,

but at last he opened the door to set out—and nearly ran into Watts, Lord Stayme's enigmatic butler.

"This way, sir," the servant said quietly.

Niall sighed and followed on his heels as Watts left the way Niall had come in. The butler never said a word. He picked his way down the alley and emerged onto the street, crossing to a carriage that waited in the evening's growing shadows. He held open the door.

As soon as Niall stepped in, the coach moved forward.

"Blood and blazes, but sometimes I forget how much you look like her." Stayme sighed. "And then I see you in a certain light and ..."

Niall did not have to ask which *her* Stayme referred to.

But Stayme moved on, as if he hadn't spoken. He looked Niall over. "A waste of time, I should think, cleaning up before you head into that mare's nest in Seven Dials."

It was exactly where he was headed. "I was rank. Enough so that my stink might have given advance warning of my presence." He paused. And how do you know what I'm planning, in any case?"

"Because it makes sense. You can't go back to that shrew, Malina's. They are onto you there. They'll be waiting." The old man took out his vesta case, struck up a match, and lit a cigarillo. Niall shook his head when Stayme offered him one, and was grateful when the old man turned his head to blow the smoke out the carriage window.

"I read your note. She said she held them in her hand. We know what she's speaking of, Niall. You told me she saw them."

"A glimpse only, I thought." Fury raged in Niall's chest again, as it did every time he thought of her perfidy. "She should never have found them. I don't even know how she knew to look for them."

Stayme waved his cigarillo. "She was likely only looking for valuables to steal. She's kept quiet so long, the most obvious explanation is that she didn't know what she'd seen. But somehow that has changed. Someone has opened her eyes."

"How? Who could have mentioned anything to her?"

"We can't know how it happened. But she has an inkling what those miniatures mean now. Alone, they would be bad enough, but if she's seen the papers, too?" The old man shook his head. "Your note said that her visitor spoke of a plan. There's a conspiracy afoot. Someone means to stir up trouble, and they mean to use you to do it."

"I know you think it's linked to those supplies Kara and I found in Seven Dials. I'm not convinced. But I mean to find out."

"Guns. Powder. Bullets. Maps. Angry men in debate." He pointed a finger at Niall. "I know all the groups, all the plotters. I hear all the whispers. It's late in the year. The cold is moving in. All the casual troublemakers will draw in and hibernate for the winter. Fair-weather rabble rousers, they are. There is nothing controversial in Parliament at the moment. No one but a few Irish grousing in pubs. Except for the mystery of what's going on in Boyd's Yard. I *still* don't know who accumulated that stash."

"Even if you are right and those people are somehow connected to these probes into my past, what they can they hope to accomplish, truly? I have kept quiet, as was demanded of me. I've stayed away, kept to myself and my business. If I am not making demands or threatening to go public, why should it profit them to know the truth?"

"Don't be naïve, boy." Stayme snorted. "Guns. Powder. Bullets. Maps." He pointed again at Niall. "You. You are the flash, the spark."

"It might be a scandal, but it's not the start of a revolution."

"It doesn't have to start out as a full revolution. Riots. Restlessness. That's enough at the beginning and can easily grow into more. They'll start there." The old man sighed. "Don't you see? It all balances on the eye of a needle. At any given point in time, it doesn't take much to stir up a scandal, erode confidence and loyalty. It's easy to stir up discontent. People carry grievances. They harbor ambition, jealousy, and greed. There is always a low level of flammable discontent. You are a good match to set to it."

"I don't see it. It's old news."

"It's potent stuff, boy. Religious controversy. Marital strife. Doomed lovers. Secret babes. It's the sort of story people like to get worked up about. These people will use you to stir up that soup of discontent, then they'll ladle in a stash of weapons and gunpowder—and just like that, they could change the world."

"But who is it? Who wants to change the world?"

"Who doesn't? Britain is at the top of the world's power structure, and there are any number of governments, trade alliances, companies, or individuals that would love to topple it off. The important question is—who is spearheading this 'plan'? That's the head of the snake we must see about cutting off. And that could be anyone. Someone who feels like they were passed over for something. Who feels entitled to more of … whatever it is they value. Someone who has an axe to grind against someone in the government or royal family. I don't know who they are, but I know some things about them."

"They are organized," Niall commented. "And well connected in the underbelly of London."

"Worse, they are ruthless, efficient, and dangerous. I've already lost people to them." Stayme shook his head. "I don't like you going in alone."

"There is no one to take in with me." Kara Levett's image flashed in Niall's mind's eye. He'd never met anyone he'd rather have at his side. But as intrepid, multi-talented, and useful as she might be in such a situation, he wouldn't put her in danger for his sake.

"I'm sorry, Niall." The old man sounded humbler than Niall had ever heard him. "I have people everywhere, but they are eyes and ears, not fists and teeth. Perhaps I should have—"

"You've done what you promised her," Niall interrupted. "You told me the truth. You've watched over me. Now I must do my part."

"I can call in a few favors," Stayme said. "It would take a little while, but I can find someone to back you up—"

"And what would we tell them? What will they see and hear? And in any case, I've been watching and listening, too. I've seen the activity, heard the rumbles in the streets surrounding that spot. I know as well as you do that something is starting to stir. I have to go in, if only to find out what it is, if it could possibly be connected to whatever Malina has begun. Once we know, we'll have a better idea of what sort of favors are needed."

Stayme sat silent a moment. "You have her spirit as well, boy."

"Good. I'll put it to use. Now, you should drop me off a good way away from Seven Dials. You shouldn't be seen there, and it will be better if I go in on foot."

Stayme nudged a portmanteau resting at his feet in Niall's direction. "If you've truly been paying attention, you will know what to do with these." He smirked. "Impress me, boy."

Niall took it up and peered inside. Two bottles of gin, a dingy overcoat, and a green felt hat that had seen better days. He grinned. "The sot who's set to watch Dun Alley?"

There were a number of street people posted at various spots around the rookery. They were meant to keep watch, deter visitors or repel intruders, depending on their post and their condition. This particular man was posted close to Boyd's Yard, and he was in poor shape. Emaciated and often drunk, he harassed anyone who approached the alley that led into the Yard from Queen Street. Niall had passed him several times in the past few days. He might have suspected the drunkenness was a ruse, but the man held a different bottle near every day.

"Very good," Stayme said with satisfaction.

"Just put me down in the right spot," Niall said. "I'll put these to good use, too."

EVENING WAS APPROACHING by the time she'd finished dinner, so Kara took the carriage into the city. She had no idea how long she would be, and she didn't want to leave herself at the mercy of the train schedules. She instructed her coachman to drop her off and head for the nearest livery, but when they arrived in New Street, in front of Lake Nemi, her footman opened the door onto chaos.

Shrieking sounded from above. Some sort of spat was going on, for as she looked up, a petticoat came sailing out of an open window. It joined a jumble of clothing, books, and trinkets scattered over the steps and pavement. A young woman was scrambling about, trying to gather everything up. With Beth's help she was stacking, shaking, and folding, but items were still raining down.

The footman gave Kara a questioning look. "Are you sure you wish to stay, Miss Levett?"

Eyes wide, she took in the scene. "I'm not entirely sure, Tom. Wait here a moment, will you?" She approached Beth. The girl looked troubled, so Kara gave her a quick squeeze. "What is it? What's happening?"

"The viscountess," Beth whispered.

"Malina? Here?"

The girl nodded. "She showed up a little while ago. Emelia told her to get out and never darken our door again. They are having a great row. Emelia ran upstairs and is tossing out everything that belongs to the viscountess, along with every token she gave her during their friendship."

"Good heavens," Kara breathed. "Why is Bridget not out here helping to gather all this up? I didn't think Malina went anywhere without her maid."

Beth lowered her voice. "Bridget's gone. Walked out. That's Mary. She's a parlor maid in the viscount's house, but her ladyship pulled her up to act as her lady's maid, until a new one can be found."

"Bridget left? Since this morning?" Kara's heartbeat quickened. What could have happened? "Come, Beth. Introduce me. I wish to ask Mary a few questions."

Beth took her over. Mary bobbed a curtsy, but her hands were shaking as she tried to fold a beautifully trimmed capelet.

"Here, let me help." Kara took the garment and guided the girl to the stairs. "Why don't you sit a moment?"

The girl glanced up to the open window, where shouting could still be heard. "Thank you, miss. You are very kind." She looked down. "I'm sorry. This is not what I'm used to."

"So Beth said. I hope you don't mind if I ask after Bridget? Is she unwell? It's only that I saw her in the viscountess's parlor just this morning."

"She's fine, as far as I know," Mary said quietly. "But she was worked up and that angry, wasn't she?"

"Do you know why?"

"She was already unhappy in her position. We could all see it. The mistress can be ..." She glanced upward again.

"Yes, I see," Kara said encouragingly.

"But Bridget slammed right downstairs this morning, her bags all packed. She said it was the last straw, it was."

"What was?

"Being asked to lie to a police officer," Mary whispered. "She said she weren't brought up to lie to the law. She'd rather go back to serving the taproom at her uncle's tavern than be mixed up in such."

"Her uncle's tavern? Do you know the name of it? Where it's located?"

Mary nodded. "Aye, miss. We all heard enough about it. He's at the Owl and Moon, in Cheapside."

"Thank you, Mary." Kara looked up. "Here now, watch yourself." A ladies' magazine came fluttering down from the window. Kara caught it, smoothed it out, and set it on a stack of books. She gave Mary a coin. "You've been very helpful. Thank you."

The girl heaved to her feet. "Thank you, miss."

Kara turned to Beth. "Is Gyda inside?"

"No, she had business to tend to."

"Would you mind coming with me, then, Beth?"

"Where to, miss?"

Kara motioned to her footman and guided the girl toward the carriage. "We're going to talk to Bridget."

Chapter Nine

THE OWL AND Moon was a tavern tucked into a courtyard off Milk Street, not far from the City of London School. The sun was setting when Kara and Beth left the carriage near the school and set out to walk the rest of the way. They were both quiet. Beth by nature, and Kara because she was rehearsing arguments in her head, trying to come up with a way to convince Bridget Carter to cooperate with them. She suspected it was not going to be an easy job.

They'd nearly reached the turn into the courtyard when she heard her name called. She looked up and found Miss Wilkes, Eleanor's friend, walking toward them. A servant followed behind, carrying several boxes.

"Miss Levett! Good evening to you." The woman stopped, smiling broadly. "What are you doing in this part of town?" Her arched eyebrows rose higher. "Have you also discovered the chemist's shop on the next street over? I swear, he can find almost anything for me. Not to mention, he keeps me in tubes, vials and other glassware." She gestured back to the box her servant held.

"Oh, no. We are just visiting a friend in the area."

"Well, what a happy coincidence to run into you. I was speaking of you not long ago."

"Were you?" For some reason, her statement made Kara feel

uneasy.

"Yes. I spoke with Mrs. Lindsay about inviting you to her salon. The next one is just a few days away. She's convinced Mr. Frederick Archer to come and present to us his new wet plate collodion process for developing photographs. I hear it's quite an advancement. I admit, I am fascinated with the idea of photographs and what use we might put them to." Miss Wilkes grinned. "Not to mention the science of the chemistry behind the development."

"How kind," Kara said. "Thank you for thinking of me. I will watch for the invitation."

"I meant what I said about having you give the salon a demonstration of your work." Miss Wilkes tilted her head. "Why don't we meet to discuss it?"

"That would be lovely," Kara said. "If you send a note to Bluefield Park, I would love to work it into my schedule. But alas, it's growing late, and we must be going."

"Oh, let's just do away with schedules and plan to meet tomorrow? We could breakfast together if you have a busy day planned. I know the perfect place."

Kara gave her a smile and tried to sound wistful. "I am sorry. I am right in the middle of an important project, but once it is finished, I hope to have a bit more freedom. I will get your address from Eleanor and we'll set up an appointment."

Miss Wilkes made a moue of disappointment. "Very well. I admit, I am busy with a few projects of my own." She waved and set off. "Good evening to you!"

Kara sighed in relief and pulled Beth along to the courtyard. The sign outside the tavern was nicely carved and freshly painted. The yard was swept clean and lit with torches. They were needed, as it was significantly darker here behind four walls. Kara was grateful for the light as they pushed through the lingerers near the door and made their way inside. The taproom was buzzing with talk, laughter, and calls for more ale.

Beth cringed at the noise and the crowd, but Kara tucked the girl's hand in her arm and pulled her along to the end of the bar. She ordered them both cider and set about watching for Bridget.

A single serving girl was working in the busy taproom. She was quick and agile, but clearly overwhelmed. Kara watched her increasingly agitated glances toward the kitchens. She waited—and was rewarded when the girl pressed past her and cracked open the door to the back.

"I don't care what ye're afraid of, Bridget Carter—get out here with that food before someone starts a kick-up!" Turning back to the bar, the serving girl loaded her tray with pints and set off again.

After a moment, the door swung out and the maid, Bridget, emerged with a tray laden with food. She paused, her face going pale when she caught sight of them. Pushing on past, she aimed a dark look in Kara's direction.

Sighing, Kara waited.

When Bridget came back her tray was empty, but her expression was fierce. "You cannot be here!" she whispered at Kara. "There's already been someone about, asking questions. If you are seen here, my goose will be cooked!"

Startled, Kara straightened. "Who has been asking questions? About what?"

"No one I want to meet in the alley out back," Bridget retorted. "Go on with you, now! You need to leave!"

Her mind working furiously, Kara placed a hand on the girl's arm. "Bridget, that is not good news. We must speak. We should likely get you out of here. Is there a private parlor? A place we might talk?"

The girl hesitated.

"Here now, Bridget!" A slack-jawed man had wobbled up to press in next to Beth. "Lemme buy yer friend a drink!"

Beth shrank away, and Bridget thrust her tray between her and the drunkard. "Back away, Jem! You leave this one alone!" She glared at Kara. "Take the passage to the left, behind the table with the guest book. Private parlor is first on the right. I'll be there as soon as there is a lull."

Kara took Beth and followed the directions. Soon after they had found the parlor, a maid came in and started the fire in the hearth. She left and returned with a tray of bread and butter and half a pear tart.

Beth tucked into the food. "I didn't know you could hire a quiet room in a place like this," she marveled. "I much prefer it in here, don't you?"

Kara was moving about the room, peering out the window toward the stables out back and cracking the door to check the passage. "I'd prefer it if Bridget came quickly," she said, worried.

But it was another twenty minutes before the girl showed up. Sweeping in, Bridget dropped into a chair and propped her feet on the hearth. "Well, that's one thing I will miss, working for that daft woman. My feet were never barking at the end of the day."

Kara approached and sat down next to her. "Bridget, I must apologize. When I brought the detective to the viscountess's home, I never meant for you to lose your position."

Heaving a sigh, the girl straightened. "It's not your fault. Ask anyone in that house—I already had a foot out the door." She shook her head. "Such goings-on! Not what I expected, when I left here to go into service."

"What did you expect?" Beth sounded genuinely curious.

Bridget shrugged. "Quiet, for the most part. I knew I'd be sewing, ironing, keeping the lady's wardrobe neat and ready. Doing her hair, caring for her jewelry. I longed for a peaceful night's rest in a bed that would never be rented out from beneath me. Calm camaraderie in the servants' hall." She waved a hand toward the ruckus that could still be heard coming from the taproom. "None of the endless noise, drunken laughter, bad jokes, tweaks at my skirts, and pats on my bottom. Serving one lady all day sounded almost easy, compared to forty louts in the taproom every night."

"But you didn't find peace as the Viscountess Marston's maid, did you?" asked Kara.

Bridget snorted. "I should say not. Not in that house!" She shook her head. "It's the lot of a lady's maid to keep her mistress's secrets, but surely there are limits! Messages and men in the house at all times. And what they say of poor, dead Sally!"

Beth's eyes widened. "What do they say?"

Bridget lowered her voice. "The servants say Sally lay with the viscount for a span of months. Once her ladyship found out, did she let the girl go? Turn a blind eye? No! She seduced the girl right away from him. Won her over completely and bound her with a strange, intense sort of loyalty. Partners in mischief and skullduggery, they were."

Kara understood then. "The viscountess expected the same sort of loyalty from you?"

"Demanded it, I should say," Bridget said. "And how should I feel loyal to a woman who asks such odd things of me?"

"Odd things?" Beth seemed quite caught up in Bridget's story.

"Messages and assignations are one thing. But dressing in her clothes? Switching roles? Accompanying her into the deepest bowels of the rookeries? Sending me in there, quite alone? That woman showed not the meanest ounce of concern for my safety, and that was enough for me. I was ready to pack my bag, but this morning? Lying to Scotland Yard? That was the final straw." She looked at Kara. "I did see that blade you described."

"My knife?" Beth asked breathlessly.

Bridget lifted a shoulder. "'Twas the one you described, miss. I saw it only the once, soon after I took the position. One of those late-night callers arrived. A man in the study. She bade me bring her the knife, and she took it down with her when she went to meet him. But she didn't bring it back up."

Kara breathed deeply, absorbing all of this. "Did you see this man? Men, you said. Different men? Coming in the night?"

"I never saw much more than a glimpse, but they were not always the same. They pulled their collars high and their hats low when I let them in the kitchen door. Different men at different times. And some of them sounded foreign!" She sounded indignant.

"Foreign?" Kara frowned. "Could you tell where they came from? By their accents or clothes or anything of that sort?"

Bridget shook her head. "I'm sorry. I don't know one foreigner from another, but some of them were definitely not English. But one who came the most often—he was English. He had a slight twang to his words. Irish, maybe? He always stayed the longest. And it was him she gave the knife to."

"You have no clue as to his identity?"

"No. He was the most careful. Always hid his face. A big man, he was, but I never got a good look at him. The closest I ever came, I came upon him in the parlor, when I didn't know he was there. Standing by the fire, he was, and he turned right away from me, to keep me from getting a good look at him. Something to hide, that one had. That's what I always thought to myself. The only thing I could see, beyond his size, was a bit of a red shine to his hair, where the firelight hit it."

Kara filed away the slight description. "And you think those men are connected to your forays into London's slums?" Her mind was racing, recalling when she and Niall accidentally discovered a cache of weapons and supplies not so long ago. Remembering the shock and horror Lord Stayme had displayed when he found they'd seen it, and been seen there.

Bridget gave a slow, reluctant nod.

Kara leaned in. "Was it in Seven Dials? Is that where the viscountess took you?"

Bridget drew in a sharp breath. "You know of it?"

"I know something is going on in those buildings surrounding Boyd's Yard. Something dangerous." Kara stopped. "Men have come *here* asking questions, you said? Already? You just left the viscountess's house this morning."

"I know," Bridget whispered. The fear that lay behind her bravado showed in her eyes.

A sudden thought occurred to Kara. "Bridget, you said *men* came today, asking questions. Were they just men? No women with them?"

"I don't think so. I didn't stay to find out. I went and hid upstairs while my uncle tried to convince them he hadn't seen me."

Kara nodded. "Either way, it's dangerous. You should not stay here," Kara declared. She went to the window and looked out again at the yard that led to the stables. "You should leave with us. Tonight." She turned back to look at the white-faced girl. "You went in, you said. How far? How much did you see?"

"All the way," the girl whispered. "Her ladyship—she's mixed up in it. In the trouble they are planning. They do different sorts of business from there, but there's more to it. They have plans. Organized ranks. A leader. There's a place, deep in there. It's different. Clean. Rich. Someone *lives* there. Someone important."

Kara stilled. "Could you find it again?"

Bridget shook her head, clearly frightened. "No. I cannot go back in there. Nor should you. I was protected, before. Still, the men, they lurked. Muttered. They tried to frighten me. It was only fear of the higher ranks that held them back. If I went in now …" She shivered. "I'm sorry. No."

Kara did not let her disappointment show. "Could you write it down for me? Directions?"

Bridget hesitated.

"Listen. I have a friend. A woman of wealth and breeding. She's not exactly conventional, but she's good and kind and honest. Her household is respectable. I could take you there. Have her maid train you up. Show you what service is like in a truly aristocratic household." Kara sat down next to Bridget and took her hand. "I'm sorry, but I think you need to disappear. Tonight. At least for a while. It's not safe for you to stay here."

"It's what I was afraid of," Bridget admitted. "I've seen too much."

"That's it exactly, I'm afraid," Kara confirmed. "You must write a note to your uncle. Tell him you are going to the country to visit a friend. I'll take you to my friend's home in Mayfair. No one will think to look for you there. You should likely use a different name. But I ask, in exchange, that you write out the directions for me. Tell me how to get in there. To the inner sanctum. Safely, if possible."

"I ..." Bridget looked alarmed. "You cannot! If you know even the smallest bit of what they are plotting ... they'll come for you, too."

"I am already their enemy," Kara said grimly. "I sealed it, showing my hand over that knife. I must fight back. For myself and for others. But you, Bridget? You have a chance. And you deserve to find the peace you were looking for." She eyed the girl frankly. "Shall we help each other?"

The girl bit her lip, thinking. A shout of laughter echoed down the passage, and hearing it, she straightened her shoulders. "Yes. I'll go and fetch paper and pen."

"No, let me." Beth stood. "No one knows me. I'll just ask one of the maids." She slipped out of the room and was quickly back, supplies in hand.

Kara gestured for her to set them down in front of Bridget. "Write it all down. Every detail you can remember."

"It's tricky," Bridget warned. "There are traps. And hidden doorways—"

"I know," Kara interrupted. "I would prefer your guidance, but I'll take what I can get. Write down everything you can recall. My carriage is outside. We'll get you safely to my friend's as soon as you're finished."

She crossed to the window and watched, worrying, as they waited.

IT WASN'T AN act. The watchman on the corner of Queen Street and Dun Alley was indeed drunk. Slumped so that his feet extended across the alley, the drunkard was alert enough to discharge his duty. As Niall approached, he roused himself enough to lurch toward him on his knees, his hand outstretched.

"Here now, guv! Give us tuppence, eh? Help out a poor soul who ain't had a meal in days?"

Niall supposed that the slurred words, the smell, and the grime-covered, skeletal hand reached out in supplication would have been deterrent enough for a casual passerby. But he also doubted any casual strollers frequented this spot, this late at night.

He paused near the watchman. "I've got better than tuppence for you, should you agree to be cooperative," he said. Reaching into the portmanteau, he pulled out a bottle of gin. Shaking it to reveal the full contents, he stepped over the man into the shadows of the alley. "Interested?"

"I ..." The drunkard was tempted. He eyed the bottle with longing, but shook his head, at last. "Ain't worth the trouble, guv. Just ye go along now, and save yerself the trouble, too."

"How about two bottles?" Niall set the portmanteau at his feet and pulled out the second. He swung them both. "Would that be worth the trouble?"

The watcher swallowed audibly. "What do ye want?" he whispered.

"Only your silence. You stay here, in your spot. Sample the first. You never saw or heard a thing. When I come out—"

"If ye make it out," the drunkard wheezed. "And that ain't no sure thing."

"You should hope I do, for that's when you get the second bottle. But if I find you have raised the alarm ..." Niall lowered his tone. "Then my friends will know. And I'll make sure *your* friends know you cooperated."

The watcher ran a hand across his chin. "Don't matter. Either way, they'll want to see the end o' me."

Niall sighed. "I am sorry for it, but I must go in." Crouching down, he looked the man in the eye. Impossible to tell his age. Drink and exposure and all the hardships of life in London's streets had rendered him wizened and weak. "Listen. I'll give you the bottles, if that's what you want. But I'd like to see you away from here, away from the threat of harm—from them, but maybe from yourself, too."

"Oh, I want the bottles," the drunkard said, eyeing them eagerly. "But I got me a brother, what keeps a farm near Dartmoor. Runs sheep." The drunkard waggled his brows. "Wouldn't mind a visit."

"Dartmoor sounds eminently safer than London," Niall agreed, standing again. "When I come out, I'll hand over the second bottle and the blunt for a train ticket, heading west."

"And the bag?" The watcher indicated the portmanteau.

Niall snorted. "And the bag."

The drunkard held out a hand. "Agreed. Give it over."

"You saw nothing. You heard nothing."

"Naught but me and the rats out here tonight." He snatched the bottle.

"How are you meant to give the alarm?"

The watcher sighed. "You know the doorway from the Yard? The one with the stone steps and the pillars?"

"Yes." Niall recalled it from his first time at this benighted place, when he'd been chasing a man he needed to question about a woman's murder.

"There's a bell tucked into the corner against the wall, on the left side of the stairs. A good-sized one. I'm to step inside the door and ring it good—the noise of it carries a good way in those buildings."

"Where is the next watcher stationed?"

The drunkard shook his head. "Not so many of us needed, not on the inside during the dark hours. They are in there themselves. The League. And it's that lot ye need to watch out fer."

"The League?" Niall's heart quickened upon his hearing a name for his enemy for the first time.

"No, no. Better that you don't know," the watcher told him.

"Thanks for the warning." Niall reached into the portmanteau and drew out the overcoat and the hat—nearly twin garments to the ones the watcher wore.

The wizened man gasped in dismay when he saw how closely Niall resembled him once they were on. "Never mind," he wheezed. "Just give me the blunt fer the ticket now." He shook his head. "I'll be heading fer the train, straight off."

"You're sure?" asked Niall.

"Ye're goin' to get yerself killed, man. No need to be takin' me along with ye."

"Very well." Niall pulled folded notes from a pocket and tossed them in the bag. "Safe travels," he said, handing it over.

The drunkard struggled to his feet. He started to turn away, then stopped. "Oh, hell's bells. It ran clear out o' my brainbox." He turned back. "Listen. Don't go in. Not just yet. They're expecting someone tonight. If I'm not here when he goes through—if ye're not here—they'll kick up a fuss."

"Whom are they expecting?"

"I don't know, do I?" The man's exasperation was clear. "Do ye think they invite me to tea and fill me in on their plans?" He sighed. "Just sit here till he comes along and let him pass when he flashes the sign."

Now Niall was intrigued. "What is the sign?"

"It's like this." The watcher splayed both hands wide and placed one atop the other, fingers pointing in opposite directions. "Keep watch," he warned. "It will only be for a moment."

"Let him through if he flashes that sign?"

"Aye. And chase off any that don't. But he'll be through here soon, so I'll be going."

"You were only expecting the one visitor?"

"Only one that I know of." The drunkard set off. "Good luck to ye," he said as he ambled away.

Niall considered. If he went in now, he might not have enough time to discover anything before the expected visitor came and sounded the alarm. And he had to admit to a certain curiosity about who might be entangled with the plotters. He beat back his impatience and settled against the corner.

The stone was cold against his back. Queen Street lay mostly quiet at this hour. A couple of men hurried by, keeping to the other side of the street and making sure their faces were turned away. A prostitute sauntered by, but Niall clutched his bottle and feigned sleep and she let him be.

After that, he passed the time exploring the pockets of the overcoat. Stayme had possessed the foresight to stuff it with a few potentially useful tools, as well as a folding blade. Another half-hour and the cold had begun to seep into his bones. At last, though, a man came marching confidently from the direction of Seven Dials. Tall and thin, he was dressed in a tidy, dark-colored suit. He carried a satchel over a shoulder and resembled nothing so much as a clerk from a counting house or warehouse. Approaching without hesitation, he flashed the sign.

Niall gave him a barely perceptible nod and noticed movement in the shadows behind him. The clerk didn't seem to be aware of it. The man stepped over Niall and went on down the alley. Niall pretended to slumber on and waited.

Out of the dark emerged another form. A larger shadow, moving in the first man's footsteps without making a sound.

Niall feigned sleep once more, watching the figure through slitted eyes. He was a large man, broad through the shoulder. Wearing a dark peacoat with a scarf wrapped high and a woolen cap pulled low, he stepped quietly, and though he glanced at Niall's slumped form, he never made the sign.

Was there something familiar in the way he moved? It niggled at Niall's brain as he let the man pass without a challenge. Might this be the same man he'd seen in Malina's study?

This could prove interesting.

Chapter Ten

B RIDGET CARTER HELD up well until Kara was ready to leave her at Eleanor Braddock's house. The four of them were in Eleanor's parlor when Kara stood to take her leave. "Don't forget to choose a new name," she reminded Bridget. "The servants will be in a tizzy of gossip about you and your arrival even before breakfast is served. You'll wish to have your name and your story ready."

Bridget abruptly burst into tears.

"Oh dear," said Kara.

Beth rushed over to sit next to the sobbing girl and clutch her hand.

"I ... I ... I was so *angry* when I saw you in that taproom tonight!" Bridget wailed. "But ... but I should have been grateful, instead." She let out another sob. "I am! I am grateful. If I had stayed, they would have come, wouldn't they? And it would have been tonight. I would have been dead before breakfast."

Eleanor's brows rose, but Kara sat on the girl's other side and patted her hand. She gave a nod to her friend's questioning gaze. "We cannot know for sure, I suppose, but I suspect you are right, my dear. Which is why we must see you safely settled here. Pick your story and never stray from it. Do not tell a soul anything different."

The girl started to cry again.

"If the situation is so serious, perhaps a slight change in your plan is warranted, Kara." Eleanor tilted her head upward. "I can have Bridget placed in a guest room instead of the servants' quarters. I shall put it about that she is the daughter of an old friend, who has lost her family and fallen on hard times." Clearly thinking as she went on, Eleanor continued. "Perhaps we can say she is staying with me until she travels abroad with the church? Only my own maid need know why she is truly here. Mason knows how to keep a secret, mind you. If we keep Bridget to her rooms and mine, then no one will know that Mason is polishing her skills."

Beside Kara, Bridget had straightened. "Oh, Mrs. Braddock," she whispered. "Would you do such a thing?"

"Of course. Once you are judged ready, we can find you a position and put it about that my young friend has departed, going on to save souls in the Orient."

"They could never see through such a scheme, could they, Miss Levett?"

"I can scarcely imagine they could." Kara smiled. "Thank you, Eleanor."

"Not at all." Eleanor looked to Bridget. "Now, it is only for you to pick a name, my dear, and I will have you shown upstairs."

"Imagine," Beth marveled. "Picking your own name!"

Bridget frowned. "But how shall I choose?"

"Make it something removed from your regular life, I should say," Kara said. "Perhaps someone who inspires you? Someone you admire?"

Bridget brightened. "I do have an interest in the paintings of Mr. John Everett Millais."

"You do?" Kara asked, surprised.

"Indeed. Anyone can attend the Royal Academy exhibition, you know," Bridget said primly.

"We do know," Eleanor said with a grin at Kara. The pair of them had met, argued, and bonded over works at the Royal

Exhibition years ago.

"My uncle was scandalized last year by Mr. Millais's image of Our Lord as a boy in the carpenter's shop, but I quite liked it."

"She truly is an art fan!" Eleanor exclaimed. "We shall get on famously."

"Oh, have you seen Mr. Millais's *Mariana*? It's my favorite. I feel like she might just step right out of that painting." Bridget looked bashfully at Kara. "I should quite like to take the name Mariana."

"I have seen it, and it is lovely," Kara agreed. "But if you mean to be called Mariana, I recommend a duller surname to go with it. Something common. Smith, perhaps."

"Mariana Smith. Yes," Bridget breathed.

"Excellent." Eleanor stood and pulled a bell cord. "Now, you should settle in and rest, my dear."

"I'll go with you," Beth offered.

"Thank you," Bridget said. "Thank you all, so very much."

The girls were led away, Bridget's tears forgotten for the moment.

"Honestly, I too thank you so very much, Eleanor," Kara said. "I'm sorry to come asking for such a favor with no warning—"

"Nonsense! You did just as you should. The girl is in real danger, then?"

"I believe so. And we cannot allow another maid to be killed because of Malina's self-absorption."

"You believe the first maid knew too much about Malina's entanglements?"

"I do. I may not think much of Malina, but I don't think she would do away with the girl over a spat. And based on what Janet said tonight ... I think Sally must have known something of the men Malina has become involved with." Kara paused. "I also think I know where they can be found."

Kara told Eleanor of her and Niall's first accidental encroachment on Boyle's Yard and what Bridget had said tonight.

"Oh, no!" Eleanor straightened. "I can see it in your face. You are not to go in there again, Kara Levett!"

"Well, I cannot go alone," Kara admitted reluctantly. "And I don't know where Niall is or how to contact him. Rachel said he hasn't shown up at the building near the park." She gave her friend an anguished look. "I cannot help but worry that they might have found him."

"You cannot go in there looking for him," Eleanor insisted. "I doubt these men would hesitate to dispatch you for your knowledge. You'd be no different from Sally or Bridget to them."

"I need someone to go in with me, but who? I cannot risk Turner."

"The poor old dear is slowing, isn't he?"

Kara pushed away the pain that came with that truth. "Inspector Wooten is out of town. I certainly cannot ask the odious Detective Caden."

"What about that nice constable that worked with you when you were looking into Janet Ott's murder? He seemed amiable, you said."

"I already owe him a favor," Kara mused. "I hesitate to ask for another. And in any case, I really shouldn't involve anyone from Scotland Yard. They are all meant to believe Niall is in Oslo."

"Oh, yes. I'd forgot. It's all quite complicated, isn't it?"

"I need to mull it over. But thank you for your help tonight."

"Of course, my dear. And before the girls return, I wanted to tell you that Miss Wilkes asked me to pass along her regards."

"Oh, how nice. And how odd. I ran into her earlier this evening."

Eleanor looked surprised. "She asked more than a few questions about you. She seems quite interested in you."

"I admit, she makes me feel uncomfortable. But I cannot quite pin down why."

"She did ask the strangest thing," Eleanor said.

Kara raised a brow.

"She was quizzing me about our friendship. How we met. How long we'd been friends. The sorts of things we do together.

It was strangely intense. And then she asked me if I am ever *afraid* of you!"

"What?" Kara blinked. "Afraid of me? Did she intimate that *she* was afraid of me?"

"No. That didn't seem to be what she was getting at." Eleanor shook her head. "I rather wondered if she wasn't afraid of someone, though. I found the whole conversation unsettling." She tilted her head. "In any case, I hear the girls returning. I shall be sure to send you a note to tell you how Mariana is getting along."

"Thank you. I'll get Beth home, and then I'll have a long think about how to get into that maze of buildings."

CLIMBING QUIETLY TO his feet, Niall followed both men as they moved into Boyd's Yard. He stepped carefully in the alley and paused in the shadows when it opened up into the courtyard. He was just in time to see the second man slip into the building on the left, the one with the stone steps and the pillars. Head hanging, shuffling, he made his way across the yard. All the buildings here were an interconnected labyrinth, pitted with traps and secret doors and set up to confound any men of law who might come looking for cracksmen or other criminals. Anyone could be watching, from any direction.

Niall paused at the corner of the steps long enough to find the bell and yank the clapper out. He tucked it into his pocket, then followed the men into the building.

He stood just inside and waited for his eyes to adjust. Nothing stirred, though he could hear a few domestic noises from the upper floors—murmurings and the clink of dishes. The entry hall was only dimly lit and smelled just as bad as it had the last time. A tiny lamp burned at the top of the stairs, several stories up. It shed just enough light for Niall to see that the mold still grew rampant on the walls, but the thick, sticky coating on the floor had been disturbed and worn away, pushed to the corners by a great many passing feet.

There. The creak of a board, off to the side of the staircase. Niall knew that route. He'd raced that way before, hot on the trail of a suspect. Stepping carefully, he moved as quickly as he could and came around just in time to see the second man glance into the alcove on the left.

Niall was familiar with the spot, with the trap in the middle and the cleverly disguised passage that led out of it. But the man he followed moved straight on, further into the darkened corridor.

What a sight they might have been to anyone watching. The clerk striding with calm confidence through the maze of passages, the large man moving in the shadows behind him, and Niall bringing up the rear. He did have to duck into a doorway once, as the clerk went through a heavily braced archway that had been opened between buildings, and the man in front of him ducked to the side of it. Ahead, Niall could hear the clerk speaking to someone and see the light of a half-darkened lantern. Words were exchanged, then the light moved on and the clerk went the opposite way down the intersecting corridor. His shadow followed. Niall followed the shadow. At a corner, the follower paused again and stood, peering around. They stayed, still and silent, where they were for several long minutes.

When the follower moved on, Niall paused in the spot where he'd stood watching. He saw the big man hesitate in front of a set of double doors, then move on. When Niall carried on after him, he heard the murmur of male voices behind the doors. Several of them. He heard someone call out something in German, followed quickly by the throaty laugh of a female. Shaking his head, he moved on.

At the next turn, Niall found himself following the pair through a familiar area of squared corridors and office-like rooms. He'd been here before. He hesitated long enough to open a door, and then another. Both stood empty, where, before, many of these rooms had been stacked with gunpowder casks and other supplies. Trepidation grew in his heart as he followed the men into the section he knew came next—an odd warehouse space that had been formed at the intersection of several buildings.

Someone must have known what they were doing when they removed walls to create this large, empty space in the middle of the slums. But Niall took grim notice that the stacks of narrow boxes, casks, and other supplies that had been stacked in here last time were all gone as well. To where had they been moved? And for what use?

The men he trailed were there, though. Niall watched the clerk's booted feet disappear from the top of one of the two staircases that had been left to access the space—the less elegant, more industrial one on the far side of the room.

His follower lightly ran up, passing the spot where Niall's prey had once slammed a hinged, spiked board from above, trying to skewer him. The follower disappeared up and through the portal at the top. Niall neatly avoided the trapdoor he vividly recalled at the base of the stairs and climbed after him.

When he reached the top, he stopped to listen before poking his head through the portal. Quiet footsteps moved away. He peeked over the edge, just enough to see what lay above.

It looked like the counting room of a prosperous business. A high desk and stool sat facing him. A large calendar hung on the wall next to a mass of papers caught on a clip. Books and ledgers were everywhere, lining the walls and stacked in piles on the floor. A tallow candle burned in a dish on a table next to the desk. In short, it looked like the sort of place a clerk belonged, yet it stood empty.

A door stood open to another room. From that direction he heard the quiet creak of a door.

He lifted himself up and glanced back darkly at the hinged board that sat ready to slam down to close the portal. The spikes looked deadly and out of place in this business-oriented room.

An open, glass-paned door led to the next space. It appeared to have a similar function, but was more richly appointed. Here the desk was low and massive. A carpet stretched across the floor. The books and ledgers were still many, but they were covered in leather, and many were embossed with a strange design of jagged lines, like you might see in cracked glass. Another dim light burned, this one a small glass oil lamp.

What *was* this place?

A doorway lay beyond the desk. It was cracked open. The soft carpet hid any sound Niall might have made approaching it. Standing to one side, he leaned over and peered in.

Inside, the second man stood alone. In a parlor. There was no other word for it. The lower section of the walls had been covered in carved wood wainscotting. One wall had been stripped down to stone and boasted a massive hearth that reached to the floor and stood large enough to roast an ox. A small table sat near a window and held a lamp with a fringed shade. A settee sat along one wall, and a stuffed armchair waited before the hearth.

The man he'd been following ducked to look under the settee. He glanced out the window, then bent over the far wall, running his fingers over the wainscotting and pushing against it.

With a start, Niall realized the man was looking for a hidden door. Had the clerk come in here? And gone … where?

Heaving a sigh, the follower straightened. Pulling off his woolen cap, he spun about and headed back in Niall's direction.

Niall started to duck away from the door—and stopped, his jaw dropping in shock.

The follower—he wasn't the man who had snuck into Malina's house in the dead of night. He was—

"Rob!" Niall gasped. He threw open the door. "Rob McRae!"

"Niall!" His closest friend, his oldest confidant, stopped and gaped in surprise.

"What in seven hells are you doing here?" In London. In the midst of this wicked place.

Pleasure suffused Rob's countenance. "Looking for ye, ye great looby, what else?" He kept his voice to a whisper, but closed the distance between them and wrapped Niall in a great, pounding embrace. "By the Great Bruce's balls, but it's good to see ye, lad! We've been that worried for ye!"

Niall stared at him, utterly befuddled. "Worried?"

"Aye! Such things we've heard! Me da wrote me about the rumors goin' 'round." Rob glanced uneasily over his shoulder. "He said these gomerals found their way to Jedburgh. And as far as Hartrigge, they went, askin' questions about ye." His expression darkened. "They even came to me at Eyemouth. They knew you'd turned over the forge to me. Wanted to know why and they had any number of other nosy questions, too." He lowered his voice. "And they were askin' about your mam, as well. I knew it meant trouble, so I had to come and find ye, didn't I?"

Niall grasped his arm. "You are a better friend than I deserve, Rob."

"How very touching."

Both men started violently. Niall looked past Rob and found the clerk standing there, in the parlor that had been empty but a moment before. The tall, thin man had a grin on his face and a pistol in his hand.

"Damn me, but it must be my lucky night!" He raised the pistol as Rob swung around. "Stay there." He looked over at Niall. "By God, but you've raised us a merry chase, haven't you, Mr. Kier? But now, here you are, right where you are most wanted." He laughed. "I couldn't have calculated the chances of this, not in a thousand years. You might as well have tied a bow in that long hair of yours, such a pretty present I shall make of you!" The clerk's expression darkened as he glanced again at Rob. "And you. I knew you were lying when you said you hadn't seen him in years and had no notion where he might be."

"Was no lie," Rob said wryly. "I hadn't. Nor would I have found him so easily, had I not followed ye."

The clerk blinked. "You've been following me since Eyemouth?"

Rob shrugged.

"You know, I don't even give a damn, so thrilled am I to have Mr. Kier here at last. And at the point of *my* gun! How pleased she shall be!"

"She?" Niall asked sharply.

"Indeed. Though she is not here at present." The clerk sighed. "No matter. We shall keep you safely stored until she returns."

Niall had barely registered the man's use of *we* when he felt the cold press of a metal barrel against his neck. Beside him, Rob stiffened. Glancing over, he saw a rifle barrel resting against his friend's nape.

"Come along, the both of you." The clerk gestured with his gun. "You can carry on with your reunion while you wait."

⟫⟫⟫⟪⟪⟪

BETH CAME DOWN from seeing Bridget settled, and she and Kara set out for Lake Nemi. The hour had grown late, and silence lay thick in the carriage. Her mind whirling with possible ways forward, Kara had asked Beth if she minded a detour through Mayfair. The girl had agreed, but when they'd driven into Berkeley Square, and she sent Tom to knock at Lord Stayme's door, he was told that the viscount was not at home.

They'd driven on then. Kara thought Beth must have fallen asleep. They'd been traveling for a little while, and Kara was again deep in thought when Beth spoke up.

"It's the viscountess, isn't it?" the girl asked. "She's got herself mixed up with some bad men. They are the ones who killed Sally?"

"It's starting to look that way. At least, it's a strong possibility."

Beth heaved a sigh. "Why are there so many of them?" she asked despairingly. "Men and women alike? People who are hard and selfish and uncaring? People who think nothing of hurting others?"

"I don't know," Kara whispered.

"I want to help," the girl declared. "I will help."

"That's very admirable," Kara said, knowing how hard it was for the girl to step outside of the safe bubble she'd manufactured at Lake Nemi. "I do appreciate your offer. And you've already been a tremendous help."

"I can do more," Beth insisted. "I'm quiet. People like to talk to me. Tell me things. I'm no one. Just a girl of no importance. They don't get suspicious when I ask questions."

"You are right. That would be useful. Thank you, Beth. If we need someone for such a role, I will come to you."

"Good." The girl sounded satisfied. "I won't let you down."

"I know." Kara reached over and took her hand. "I'll try not to let you down, either."

The carriage was making the turn onto New Street, but it slowed down almost before the turn was complete. Far too early for them to have reached the club. The coachman gave a shout. Kara sat up and peered out the window, just in time to see several dark forms streaking past.

Her coachman yelled again. And once more. She felt the carriage rock as Tom jumped off his stand at the back and ran ahead. She put down the window. "Tom? What is it?"

After a moment, she heard the footman call her name from ahead. "Miss! Miss Levett! You'd better come quickly! It's Miss Winther!"

Kara gasped. Opening the door herself, she leapt down without the step. Tom was crouched over a familiar figure, kneeling partly on the pavement, partly in the road.

"Gyda!" she cried, rushing forward. Blood streamed over her friend's face.

"Kara," Gyda said faintly. "Damned cowards jumped me. Four to one. Didn't find me such an easy mark, though," she said with a rusty laugh.

"Gyda, we've got to get you back to the club. Beth!" Kara called. "Run ahead and have them fetch the doctor!"

"No, no," Gyda protested. "No time for that."

"That's a nasty wound." Kara bent down to examine the cut at her hairline. "It needs cleaning. And stitching, likely."

"Just stick a plaster on it. We've no time for more." Gyda gripped her arm. "The bastards have got Niall!"

Chapter Eleven

"WHERE DID YOU think to put them?" The man behind Niall had moved the tip of the rifle barrel from his nape to a spot between his shoulder blades. "You know she won't be back until after first light. Or perhaps not even until midday."

"You can't leave them up here," the other armed man said. "She won't like that."

"Do not presume to know any such thing or to speak for the lady," the clerk said coldly.

Niall was nearly trembling with the tension of not knowing whom they spoke of. Not Malina, surely? But who else?

"You know how she is," Rob's captor said slyly. "She'll want to—"

"I do know," the clerk interrupted. "And you should know you'll end up in the river as easily as those government informers we caught, if you speak out of turn again." The clerk suddenly straightened and snapped his fingers. "That's it. Where did she keep those uninvited visitors, before she was finished with them?"

"Cellar room, beneath the tavern," the man behind Niall answered.

"Those blokes are long gone now. Put these two there until she's ready for him." The clerk grinned at Niall.

"Ye're not coming?" Niall's captor asked.

"No. I've a report to write." The clerk grinned. "And a bank to research."

Niall's stomach dropped.

"Why bother with both of them, though?" Rob's captor sounded eager. "This one's extra. Why not give 'im to me? I'll take care o' 'im for you."

"Because, clearly, you are a fool," the clerk said dismissively. "This one is leverage."

Rob's incautious captor scoffed. "I 'eard the plans for tonight. By this time, they'll have that woman wrapped up, safe and sound. That's real leverage, eh?"

Alarm struck again, an arrow to Niall's gut. He felt sick. That woman? Leverage? Were they talking of Kara? Had they gone after her?

The man behind Rob continued. "This one here's naught but extra. Nothing but trouble. I know how to make trouble disappear."

The clerk glanced coldly at the man behind Niall. "What's his name?" He tilted his head toward Rob's captor.

"Clancy," the man said flatly.

"Listen closely, Clancy." The clerk's expression had gone dark. "This is the League, not some fly-as-you-might street gang. You will no longer torture, maim, or kill for sport or in your free time. You have no free time or time for sport. You have no opinions. You have only duty. And that is to do what you're told. *Only* what you are told. You might be asked to maim, torture, or kill, but only then will you do so, and you will keep your opinions about it to yourself. Is that understood?"

Sullen silence filled the air. But the sound of that word filled Niall's brain. The League? The bum outside had used it, too. That was how these men labeled themselves. He'd known they were organized. Well supplied. But a league? A league of what? It implied size, structure, and worse—ideals. He suddenly worried that this was a much larger problem than they had anticipated.

The clerk stepped closer. "I *asked* if you *understood*?"

"Understood," Clancy ground out.

"Good. Go on, then. Get them secured." The clerk turned away. "And take them around, so you don't have to cover them while you climb down the hatch."

Niall's mind was racing as he was prodded to turn around and go back the way he'd come in. These men were serious. If they were interfering with Kara ... Rage flared in his chest. He could not let himself—or Rob—be locked away.

He glanced back to his captor's flat expression—and noticed the room they'd just left was empty. The clerk had disappeared again.

They moved into the counting room, and Niall's captor nodded toward the spiked, hinged board. "Behind there." He pointed with his chin. "There's a door. Open it."

Niall couldn't make it out in the shadows. He glanced briefly at the spikes. If he could knock the man behind down ... But no. Two men. Two guns. It would have to be something else. Depending on what lay behind the door—

Behind him he heard a gasp, then an odd clunk. He whirled to find Rob in possession of one of the rifles and Clancy tumbling down the narrow steps beneath the portal.

Rob pointed the gun at Niall's captor. "Drop the rifle."

The man hesitated.

"*Now!*" Rob insisted.

The man heard the intent in his tone. Sneering, he tossed the rifle aside, toward the open portal.

Niall reached out and snatched it up by the barrel, just in time. He stared down at Clancy, who was still tumbling. "Oh, hell," he said. "He's going to hit—"

He did. Clancy landed heavily at the bottom of the stairs, and the trap that Niall knew lay hidden there was sprung. The floor dropped away, and the man hurtled ten feet down into the pit that had been designed to capture and incapacitate the unwary.

"Holy Mother of—" Rob glanced over at Niall. "I didn't expect ... He aimed the gun away from me for a moment to look down there. I grabbed it and used it to push him over the opening. I didn't know ..."

"If the stairs didn't break his neck, the pit likely did," the other man spat out.

Niall raised the rescued weapon a little higher and pointed it at the man's head. "Make another sound and I'll be forced to send you after him, with a bullet in your head." Without looking away or moving an inch, Niall said to Rob, "There's a length of rope in the outer pocket of my coat. Get him tied up."

The man opened his mouth, and Niall stepped forward until the barrel hovered inches from his chest. "If noise is going to give us away, it might as well rid us of you." He raised a brow and cocked the rifle. "Are you willing to die for your *League*?"

Niall waited. The man's answer might tell him something about this mysterious group.

The man shut his mouth and didn't resist as Rob shoved him in a corner and tied him hand and foot—and fastened them close together with the leftover rope, as well.

"Gag him," Niall added. "Use his neckcloth."

Rob finished. "I know you'll be tempted to try to get out of this," he said to the glaring man. "I don't recommend it. Hard enough to balance with your hands and feet together, but with spikes and an open portal nearby?" He grinned. "Don't risk it, lad." He took up his weapon and started for the stairs beneath the portal.

"No," Niall said quietly. "This way." He shoved the man's feet aside and opened the door in the shadows beyond. Rob slipped through, and Niall followed, only to stop on the other side, surprised.

"What is this place?" Rob whispered as Niall closed the door behind them.

The room was vast, nearly as large as the makeshift warehouse space below, he realized. "I don't know. It's not what I thought we'd find." They gazed up, where the center of the roof had been replaced with a great glass dome, reminiscent of the

Crystal Palace. The cloudy night sky was clearly visible. Light must flood the place during the day, which made sense of the large number of lush plants and potted trees sitting about. There was an alcove fitted out as a lavish bar, a few tables scattered throughout, but no other furniture.

"It's a reception room, I think," Niall breathed. "I've seen similar spaces in embassies."

"Who the hell are they receiving?" Rob asked. "The Emperor of Russia?"

"Damned if I know." Niall had turned back to examine the door. It was a simple Suffolk latch. He fished around in his pockets again and found one of the nails he'd discovered in his earlier inventory. Bless Stayme for a stash of useful oddities. He shoved the nail in the groove beneath the thumb latch. "That should stop them from coming through there." He cursed as a regular thumping started on the other side. "Hurry, before they come and investigate that noise." He started across the space. "I chased a man through here once. I think the other stairs that lead down into the warehouse are behind that short wall. There should be a corridor with outlets on the other side."

He and Rob raced through, passed the stairs, and reached the corridor just as shouting started from the rooms they'd just left.

Rob tried the first door they encountered and they peered in. "Is that a *schoolroom*?"

Niall stared. It did look like a schoolroom. A flag had been pinned to the wall next to a slate board. It featured the same odd design he'd seen on the ledgers, but the cracked lines were laid out over a map of Europe. It would seem that the League had an official emblem.

Rob had opened the next door. He whistled low, and Niall moved to look over his shoulder. It was a large room, so large that it looked to take up all the rest of the corridor. Dim light came from a bank of windows and shone on tables and counters filled with glass beakers, vials, and burners. It was an impressive chemist's laboratory.

Niall paused to inhale. The sweet aroma that lingered over the place reminded him of … something.

"Here!" Rob had moved to open a door at the end of the passage, on the other side. "A corridor. Where's it go?"

"No idea, but we'd best find out." They scooted in and went single file through the narrow passage. "It's connecting to another building," Niall whispered as he noted the change in the walls as they went.

It let them out into a dusty storeroom.

"Listen," ordered Niall. Raucous laughter and loud voices drifted from below. He eyed the huge, cracked cask that stood in a corner, nearly reaching the ceiling. *Old Tom* was printed on one side. "A gin shop," he guessed.

Rob was looking over a wall lined with smaller casks. These ones sported the jagged lines of the emblem he'd seen earlier. Rob rubbed a finger along the top of one and held it up, covered in black. "What sort of gin shop stores gunpowder?"

"One we don't want to linger in," Niall answered. "Let's go down. We can't go out the front, not with a crowd of witnesses, but maybe there will be another way."

The ruckus grew louder as they reached the street level. Rob pointed down the corridor where a half wall of windows showed a kitchen. "Kitchen door. Out the back."

They moved quickly past a great oaken table and a large stove, banked for the night. Past the larder and on to a short passage with a wooden door at the end. Niall yanked it open— and encountered a locked, barred door.

In disbelief, he shook the unyielding bars.

"Are they keeping people out or in?" asked Rob.

"They are not keeping us in," Niall said with determination. "But if we go out the front, surely someone will give chase." He headed back toward the kitchen and paused on the way past the larder again. "Another door in the back, there," he said. "Cellar?" He paused. "Sometimes these shops share cellar space."

"Let's find out."

They descended.

"More gunpowder," Rob said. "By all that's holy, no one better dare strike a match in this place. Between the powder and the gin, it would all go up in a fireball."

"There's a door." Niall moved toward it, noting the even stone surface of the cellar floor. He cracked the door, peered out—and then opened it wide, staring.

Rob stopped just beside him, gaping. "I don't know who ye are up against, lad, but they have *quite* an operation."

An understatement. They eased out, gazing at the huge, vaulted cellar stretching out before them. The walls and floor were of stone. Above ran a long gallery with more linked offices. And on this level, below ground? It was a space three times as large as the warehouse they'd left behind, and it had been stuffed with a treasure trove of goods. Stacked wool and animal skins. Huge rolls of bleached linen. Wine, brandy, and gin. Hogsheads of tobacco and crates of boxed cigars.

"Weapons," Rob said, indicating a stack of long boxes.

"Let's get out of here," Niall said urgently. "There must be other exits."

"There must be guards, too," Rob whispered. "Keep low."

"No need." A large form stepped out from behind a stack of crates. Several more melted out of the shadows around them. "We've been hoping for something to liven up a long night's watch."

"He's the one, ain't he? Look at him," another of the men said, his voice raised in excitement. "He's the one she's had us all searching for!"

Niall and Rob both raised their weapons.

"Go ahead," the apparent leader of the men said. "You've two bullets between you, and I've a dozen men. You cannot—"

He dropped as Rob fired his weapon, hitting him square in the chest.

"Stay back!" Niall turned in a circle, his own gun raised and ready. "The next man who moves will go next!"

Rob set his back to Niall's and took up his rifle by the barrel, ready to swing it like a club. Another man stepped out of the shadows, holding his own cudgel. He had his eyes fixed on Rob as he pushed his way through, closer than the others had ventured.

"Stop there," Niall ordered him.

The man kept coming. He raised his cudgel—and Niall fired and dropped him.

"It's been a while since we've been in this much trouble," Rob said, crouching into a fighting stance. "But the only way out—"

"Is through," Niall said grimly. "Let's just get through."

"Hold this tight." Kara placed Gyda's hand on the bandage she'd placed onto the cut near her hairline. "Are you sure you don't want to have a doctor in to look at it? It might scar."

"I quite fancy a scar or two," Gyda retorted. "And this one is out of the way. Makes for a good story, but it's not enough to mar my good looks."

Kara gave a helpless laugh. "Fine, then." She went to rummage in Gyda's drawers. "But if I have to tie something around your head to hold the bandage in place, it might as well be decorative. Here we go." She lifted out a blue brocaded ribbon. After she'd tied it and pinned it ruthlessly, she stepped back to survey her handiwork. "Shall I arrange your hair to hide it?"

"No. Don't bother. I just want it all tucked out of the way." Gyda took up a hand mirror. "I look like a savage, do I not?" She shot Kara a look. "Fitting, as we are going into battle, not to a tea party."

"Are we, then?" Kara sank down onto a chair. "Let's go over this from the beginning. We'll be quick, but I want to thoroughly understand as much as we can before we decide our course of action."

"There's only one course of action," Gyda began, but at Kara's look, she sighed. "Very well." She settled back onto her bed. "But if I am to truly start at the beginning, then I must go back a week or so."

"Even before Sally was killed?" Kara asked.

Gyda nodded. "That's when I began to suspect I was being watched. I know you are familiar with that feeling."

"Yes," Kara agreed wryly. "Multiple kidnapping attempts do lend themselves to an interesting array of experiences."

"And abilities." Gyda toasted her with the cup of heavily sugared tea Kara had insisted she drink while they worked on her injury. "In any case, I was right. I had picked up a shadow. Skilled lad, too, although I did manage to shake him. What I couldn't work out was—why? I have scarcely been in trouble in London at all," she said with a grin. "Then, when you and Emelia came to me, I wondered if it might be something to do with Malina. Now I know that it must." She raised a brow. "And I must also presume that Niall is not in Oslo?"

"No."

Gyda's mouth thinned. "Kara, I—"

"You finish first, then I will take a turn."

"Very well. Several times I found myself having to work to lose that young fellow. Tonight, though? They lay in wait for me, just up the street. I never knew they were there until I was surrounded."

Kara's hands clenched in her lap.

"They thought they had it easy." Gyda grinned. "I soon disabused them of that notion. You recall that collapsible baton that Inspector Wooten showed us? I've been carrying one since they started following me. It's not as effective as one of my Viking axes, but I jammed the bollocks of two of them and dislocated the jaw of another, almost before they were done with their crude threats and nasty banter. They set into me, then, and it was fierce fighting, I tell you!"

Kara shook her head at the blaze of excitement in her friend's eyes. "Those men had no idea they had taken on a Viking shield maiden," she said in admiration.

Gyda snorted. "Those ignorant fools have no idea a shield maiden has ever existed. They expected to find yet another weak, vaporous English female. All screams and fainting." She grew serious. "But Kara, they did know of my connection to Niall. Once I'd knocked them all down but two, one of the remaining was ready to give in and let me be. I was hurt and bleeding, but still on my feet. But a downed man snarled at him. He said I was needed to bring Kier to heel. To force him to surrender."

"But you said they had Niall?"

"Another came running in right then. He skidded to a stop, staring at the mess we'd all made, and he said that word had come. Kier had been taken. They had him at the labyrinth."

The labyrinth. Kara could guess well enough what that meant.

Gyda was watching her closely. "You know it?" When Kara nodded, her friend gave a small, determined smile. "Good. The hesitant man said they didn't need me. But the other one still standing said he didn't fancy going back without me. They all went silent, then, as if acknowledging his point."

"What happened then?"

"I threw my baton at him and struck him in the bridge of his nose. It knocked him back. He went down—and right then, your carriage turned onto the street. Your coachman started shouting. The last man turned and ran, and the others dragged themselves up to follow." Gyda sat up straight. "But if you know where they've gone to ground, then we must go after them. We cannot leave Niall in their hands."

"It's all I've been thinking of all night—how to get in there." As promised, Kara filled her in on everything they'd discovered. "So we know these men killed Sally. They nearly got Bridget. They have Malina mixed up in their scheming. I don't know what they want with Niall, but it cannot be good."

"All the more reason to—"

"I know!" Kara exclaimed in frustration. "Thanks to Bridget, I know how to find my way in, but there are a great many of them, by all accounts, and we know they are well armed and supplied. I cannot go to Scotland Yard for help. Even Emelia is unavailable, passed out upstairs. Beth says she dosed herself to sleep after her argument with Malina." She frowned, considering. "I can perhaps recruit a few of Bluefield Park's footmen." She straightened. "Perhaps we can wait for Lord Stayme—"

"No," Gyda interrupted. "We've no chance of raising any army of our own, and that means our best chance is to sneak in, unseen. The two of us."

Kara stilled, her heart racing.

"I know you can fight," Gyda said. "Between the two of us, we can do this. We must."

Kara did not remind her of her injured arm. That one wasn't her striking or knife-wielding arm, after all. But if they got caught in a situation where she would need to climb, or hang ... She pushed the thought away. There were other troubling reflections to rush in to fill the void.

"Gyda, you know about the *studies* my father arranged for me, in an effort to keep me safe."

The other woman nodded.

"All of my training, all of my unorthodox lessons—they were all focused on helping me to escape. To run from trouble. This is the exact opposite. We are running into danger this time." She drew a deep breath and looked Gyda in the eye. "I won't lie. It terrifies me. But I would do a great deal more, and worse, for Niall."

"Good." Gyda stood. "We must prepare. Give ourselves the best chance of success."

"I believe I know the best way for us to go in, but we'll need a distraction." Kara cast about in her head, searching for an idea. "Perhaps young Harold and Davey Dobbs can provide one? Start a fight? Attract attention."

Gyda grabbed a sheet of paper, her mouth twisted into a grin.

"Street brawls amongst boys are nothing new in these parts, Kara dear. If we need a distraction, we want one that no one will look away from. I know just the person to provide a good one. I'll arrange it." She started scribbling, then glanced up again. "You have a pair of trousers, do you not? There's no use us going in there with belled skirts swinging. Not if we are going to fight."

"I sent Beth on to my rooms near the park before I started cleaning you up. She'll fetch the right clothes and a few other useful items. She should be back shortly." Kara paused. "I'll be ready quickly when she returns. Perhaps you should rest a little." She glanced at Gyda's wound.

"I'm fine, but I'll get ready and then lie down for a few moments, until Beth is back. But then we should set out straightaway." Gyda gave Kara a look. "In another situation, I might suggest waiting until just before dawn. Those are the quiet hours, when exhaustion sets in and focus wavers. But something tells me ..."

"I know," Kara said as her friend's words trailed away. "I have a bad feeling about this too."

Chapter Twelve

S HADOWS GATHERED IN the side street where Kara and Gyda waited. Mists moved sinuously at their feet, winding about their ankles like cats. Kara felt as twitchy as a cat—one whose fur had been rubbed the wrong way.

"What sort of apothecary shop is open at this hour?" she muttered, peering around the corner at their target.

"The sort that hides an entrance into the connected network of buildings run by a bunch of criminals," Gyda answered, pulling Kara back. She seemed totally unperturbed.

"How long shall we wait for your friend before we go in on our own?" Kara asked.

"There she is." Gyda pushed away from the wall as a woman turned the corner. She strode toward her and grasped her shoulders. "Josie, dear. You are a darling for doing this."

"For you, dear Gyda, I will cast the pearls of my dramatic skills before these swine. And I shall have to do a great deal more before I consider my debt to you repaid." The woman kissed Gyda on both cheeks. "Do not fear," she reassured her. "I shall capture every eye."

"I have no doubt."

Gyda stood quite a bit taller than the other woman. Kara doubted her friend had rested before they left Lake Nemi. She must have spent the time fashioning the intricately braided crown piled high on her head, which she'd covered with a fashionable beaver hat. It fell low enough on her brow to cover her bandage, thank goodness. She looked every inch a gentleman, in fact, turned out gorgeously in a dark wool suit and a richly embroidered waistcoat. Next to her, Kara felt like she would pass as a servant or a groom, in her dark trousers and an old-fashioned frock coat she'd confiscated from Turner long ago.

"Kara, meet Miss Josie Lowe. Josie is an understudy for a major role at the Adelphi Theatre." Gyda smiled at her friend. "But she won't languish as an understudy for long, and you shall soon see why."

Kara gave the woman a nod. "Thank you for your help, Miss Lowe, but please, do not allow yourself to be placed in any danger. We will move as quickly as we can so that you may get in and out."

"No worries," Miss Lowe said briskly. "I know how to read a room. I'll go in and hit them hard and sweep out again once you are through." She rolled her eyes. "What sort of apothecary is open at this hour?"

"Precisely," Kara agreed.

"It would be one thing if the shop truly meant to service the sick or even offer comfort or safe haven to the women forced to walk these streets at these late hours, but I eyed it as I passed and it seems there are naught but a gaggle of men hanging about. Bully boys, if I had my guess."

"Which is why we need you, my dear," Gyda said.

"Exactly so." Miss Lowe abruptly shook her shoulders and took several deep breaths. "Right, then. Prepare yourselves. I'm going in." Without further preamble, she turned and swept around the corner.

Kara and Gyda hesitated a moment, then followed at a slower pace.

"Here's a spot, then," Gyda groused out loud in a low, masculine tone of frustration. "We'll stop in and see if they have a pack of vespas, and I'll dock the cost from your pay, for dropping mine in the sewage."

Ahead, they watched Josie push through the crowd of men hanging about the apothecary shop. She pulled the door open wide and entered with dramatic dignity.

It was lost on the men. They were huddled together, muttering.

"What's so special about this bloke, I want to know." An older man spat into the street. "A lot of trouble we've been about to find 'im, and 'e walks in, all by 'isself?"

Kara slowed. Were they speaking of Niall?

"Only two things worth so much fuss," another said wisely. "Either money or blood."

"Might be sommat else," a younger thug said, crudely grabbing the front of his trousers.

"Nah." The first man was the only one who didn't laugh. "You know she's not that sort." His tone held a warning. "And you'd be wise not to forget it. Make a crack like that, where she or one of the officers can overhear ... It'll be the last one you make."

"I has me own theories," the confident one said.

Kara wanted to stay to hear them, but Gyda was moving steadily forward with all the confidence of a young buck about Town, and Kara was forced to hurry to catch up. They followed in Josie's footsteps and entered to find her at the counter, speaking with the apothecary.

"A larger bottle, if you please, good sir." She cast sad eyes at the man. "It would take a goodly dose, would it not, to cast off this cruel world once and for all?"

The apothecary paused, pulling back a bottle of laudanum he'd been about to hand over. "Well, and no one likes to hear such a thing from a pretty lady, do they? Perhaps you should take a pause, young lady. A bit of reflection might do you good. Come back in a day or two? See if you feel so strongly then."

"No. I've waited. Suffered. And I am through with it all, sir."

Josie drew herself up straight. Great, fat tears began to run down her cheeks. "Marriage is akin to slavery in some instances," she said on a hitched breath. "I don't want to live through another day where he is free to touch me, hurt me, hit me in hidden places, as often and as horribly as he wishes."

"Oh, my dear." A sturdy older woman stepped out from the back, her face full of sympathy as she gazed at Josie.

The actress began to sob. "I cannot bear it!"

Two customers—prostitutes, by the look of them—moved closer to her, eyes wide. Two men in the far corner—guards?— watched in fascination, too. Kara nudged Gyda, and together they edged toward the opposite corner of the room, past the counter, where a curtain hung and, according to Bridget, hid the entrance to the cellar where they could find the connection with the next building in the labyrinth.

"No longer will I suffer his horrible attentions," Josie proclaimed. "I am ruined by them. Polluted by his touch." She threw her reticule down on the counter. "Take it all! My skin crawls at the thought of the clothes he paid for touching my skin!" She yanked the ties of her cape and tore it off, tossing it toward one of the prostitutes. "Have it, with my blessing!" Without hesitation, she started unbuttoning her bodice.

"Here, now! Ma'am! This is not the place for this!" The apothecary sounded slightly panicked. Josie paid no attention and wrenched the bodice wide. "You cannot disrobe in my shop, madam!"

"Now!" Kara gave Gyda a little shove, and they both ducked behind the curtain. She immediately turned to grab the fabric and make sure there was no betraying motion to give them away.

"Madam!" The apothecary's tone was rising. "I must insist! Please, cover yourself."

"Do not berate her!" the older woman scolded him. "Look at the bruises on her arm!"

"Perhaps you are right," Josie said slowly. "Yes. Yes, of course. I am sorry. I will go. Perhaps all I need is a bath and cup of tea ..."

It was the last thing they heard as Kara and Gyda eased further down the stairs to the cellar.

"There should be a lantern hung on the wall at the bottom," Kara whispered. It was there. She lit it and held it high.

"Good heavens, he's got more brandy down here than a Cornwall smuggler," Gyda breathed.

"And so much bleached linen," Kara added. "For bandages, perhaps?"

"Where to now?"

"There's meant to be an opening behind a set of shelves. There. Help me to shift them?"

But the shelves moved easily on oiled hinges, and together they slipped into the next cellar. It was filled with long crates. One had the top pried off. Gyda peered in. "Pikes and pitchforks? It's meant to be a secondhand shop above. What do they want with these?"

They stared at each other. "Do they mean to start a riot?" asked Kara. "Arm the crowd?"

"Well, I doubt they mean to plant potatoes." Gyda looked about. "That's a lot of weapons. That means money. Planning. Goals." She looked suddenly sober. "These men are not amateurs. We need to get Niall out of here."

"Through here." This door was not hidden. It stood tall and wide and boasted a lock added to the latch. Kara stopped in front of it. "Hold the lantern, will you?" She reached to the specially designed belt she sometimes wore while she worked. It was meant to hold tools and different-sized pouches. She took out her lockpicks and had the door free in a few moments.

Gyda raised a brow.

"I've been practicing," Kara muttered.

Easing the door open, they peered through.

"Odin's *arse*," Gyda swore.

The familiar oath reminded Kara of Niall and had her swallowing a sudden lump in her throat. "Put out the lantern," she whispered. "We'll leave it here."

It wasn't a cellar that came next, but a huge, cavernous ware-house, arched and lined in stone. Torches lit the place in intervals. Above, offices and a gallery were more brightly illuminated.

They gaped at each other in surprise.

"Look at all of this!" Gyda breathed.

"Listen!"

"I hear it. Fighting?"

Thuds. Grunts. Cursing. The crash of something large falling and hitting the stone floor.

"Over there," Gyda said.

They started moving, keeping close to the stacked goods. The fight was a good distance away. Kara stalled as they drew closer, sucking in a breath. "It's Niall!"

Gyda cursed under her breath. "There must be at least ten of them."

"Nine," Kara corrected her. "Look. One of them is fighting with him, not against him."

"Who is that?"

"I don't know, but we don't want to hit him by accident."

They moved forward again until they reached a stack of crates that stood taller than either of them. Gyda took out her baton and her short Viking axe. Kara pulled out a pair of gloves and donned them before she opened a flat pouch at her waist. She pulled out a handful of small, jagged discs.

"Those are so tiny," Gyda whispered.

"Just watch. And don't move in until I am finished with them." Creeping closer, Kara moved from crate to cask, seeking cover until she was close enough. Ducking behind a hogshead of tobacco, she breathed deep and took one of the discs in her right hand. Then she slid around the curve of the hogshead and carefully took aim.

She hit the first man in the back of his neck. He stopped and slapped at the spot like he was swatting a bee.

Gyda slipped in behind her. "What good is that?"

Kara didn't answer. She threw another four metal discs in succession, hitting two men in the shoulder, one in the back of the thigh, and another square in the back.

Before she'd finished, the first man had dropped out of the fight. He was crying out in alarm, slapping at his neck and cursing. "What the ... What is it?"

One by one, the others followed suit, the fight forgotten as they writhed in pain from the sting and burn that continued to spread.

"Get it off me!"

"What in blazes?"

"Water! Wash it off!"

"*Damnation*, it burns!"

"The cell room! There's a keg tapped in there." The man she'd hit in the midst of his back was tearing off his coat and pulling at his shirt. "The ale. Try the ale!"

Still cursing and slapping at their wounds, all of them stumbled off toward a row of rooms beneath the gallery.

"What in ...? Never mind. I take it back." Gyda definitely sounded impressed. "I can see you've been practicing other things, as well. Five down in the blink of an eye."

Kara was well satisfied. She hadn't even had to move her recovering arm at all.

"Get ready," Gyda warned. "Four left. They are coming this way."

The fight was moving toward them as Niall and his ally took advantage of the suddenly depleted numbers of their enemy. Gyda squeezed Kara's arm, then jumped up on a crate, climbing higher to gain the advantage, waiting as the fight advanced their way. When they were in the right position, she jumped off, swinging out at one of the men facing off against Niall.

Kara took the opposite route. Pulling out a blade, she sprinted toward the two men fighting Niall's ally. She went into a crouch and lashed out, slicing the tendon at the back of an assailant's ankle as she raced past. She might have hit both ankles if she'd been able to use her other arm. She straightened and ducked behind a stack of wool before turning to see the man curse and stumble. His ankle gave way, and he fell.

There were only two men remaining to fight on, but Kara had eyes only for Niall. He was facing off with a bull of a man, and he was armed only with a spent rifle. As she watched, he swung it hard at his opponent's head. The assailant ducked and charged forward, grabbing Niall by the waist, lifting him up, and slamming him against the crate Gyda had leapt from.

Niall struggled wildly, but the bull began to squeeze. Kara could see it as Niall struggled to breathe. He reached out, dug into his pocket, and pulled out something metal and bulbous. He began to hammer at the bull's head, but with no apparent effect.

Kara stepped in close behind the big man. Reaching up, she cupped her hands and boxed his ears, hard.

Cursing, she stepped back. She'd felt that in her shoulder.

The bull stiffened and roared in surprise, shaking his head. Kara took advantage of his distraction to press her blade against his side. "Drop him," she said. "Or I'll carve out your kidney."

The bull froze.

"*Now!*"

He dropped Niall, who fell to the floor. But in the same motion, the bull turned and knocked the blade out of her hand. He grinned evilly and took a step toward her—then sank like a rock as Gyda came from behind and knocked him in the head with the blunt end of her axe.

Breathing heavily, Kara nodded her thanks. Gyda gave her a blazing smile in return. Together, they turned to Niall.

He sat where he'd been dropped, chest heaving. "Kara! Gyda! You ... I ... What ...?"

Kara stepped forward and offered him a hand, helping him to stand. She stared up into his dark eyes. A loud hammering echoed in her head. It wasn't more fighting. It wasn't the footsteps of more adversaries. It was the pounding of her heart.

He returned her stare while a hundred conflicting emotions

crossed his face. She couldn't look away. She wanted to see them all. Feel them all. Because the same surprise and swift fear, the embarrassment and pride, they ran through her veins, too. Her muscles tightened and a hum of recognition vibrated through her, from head to toe.

"It was my turn," she said simply, in answer to his stammering.

He looked fierce, and she thought she'd made a mistake.

But he heaved a great sigh and wrapped her in his arms.

She stilled. Mind and body. She felt like she'd been under assault from frantic emotions since the day he'd left her laboratory and the detectives entered her parlor. Finally, the frenzy that had beaten in her chest for days faded. She pressed against him. Stood cradled in strength that was made of tenderness. All those opposing emotions melted into a steady beat of pleasure. Surrender. Blessed relief. And the shuddering, awestruck joy of coming home.

"There's no time to *linger*," Gyda said irritably.

They broke apart. Niall blinked at Gyda, and Kara realized that her friend had lost her hat. She stood, proud and fierce in her gentleman's getup, with her glorious blonde hair braided high and a trickle of blood coming from beneath the ribbon holding the bandage Kara had applied.

"You look like you've been rampaging through the halls of Valhalla," Niall told her. "What happened?"

Gyda looked thoroughly pleased with the compliment. "Ambushed. By your friends here." She looked down at the giant at her feet. "We should get out of here before they recover or more of them come along."

"Let's go," Niall said.

The other man—his ally—staggered up.

"Introductions later," Gyda said, striding back the way they'd come. "We're going."

Kara followed. Niall positioned himself behind her as they hurried back to the unlocked door, but a strange feeling still swept over her. All the hairs stood up on the back of her neck. She glanced about as they went, peering around stacks and into the long spaces before and behind them, but saw no one. As they reached the door and Gyda paused long enough to crack it and make sure the cellar beyond was clear, Kara looked again.

The stone floor was empty, save for the men lying where they'd left them. A few were groaning and hobbling to their feet, but they were absorbed in their own misery.

The uneasy feeling persisted, though.

She glanced up—and started violently. A lone silhouette stood up there in the gallery. It was far enough behind them that she looked small from this vantage, but Kara could see it was a woman. Her hands were braced on the railing as she watched them go.

And Kara swore the woman's gaze remained fixed on her as they went through the door and made their escape.

Chapter Thirteen

NIALL HELD HIS silence as the ladies led the way out. Rob limped a little, he noticed as they moved. Niall was sore in several places himself, but it was his mind that was busy, trying to imagine what had been going on while he had been in hiding. What in hell had happened that these two had known where to find him? And that they had come in after him, alone?

"We need to go up and out here," Kara was telling Gyda. "Through this shop. The men outside the apothecary were speaking of Niall. They might well recognize him."

Gyda clambered up the stairs to try the door at the top. "Hold a moment. This bloke was smart enough to lock up and block access to his shop." She held her axe poised over the door latch. "Get ready to run, in case someone comes to investigate the noise."

A couple of well-executed blows had them through.

"Out the back," Kara whispered.

They made their way through the back rooms. Rob groaned as they found this back door was also blocked with an iron gate. But Kara had her lockpicks out and quickly had the way clear. Rob shot him an amused look as they spilled out into an alley. At the end, they found a nondescript carriage waiting.

"Take the circuitous route we discussed," Kara ordered the

coachman. "Be sure we are not followed before you head for our destination."

There was a definite air of relief as they all settled in against the squabs. The sky had begun to lighten at dawn's approach. Farmers' carts began to fill the streets, heading toward the markets.

"Keep your eyes peeled," Gyda ordered them. "We need a safe place to bed down in, and we cannot risk leading those goons to it."

They all watched the windows, but Niall sat, staring straight ahead as all the pieces of the puzzle began to click into place inside his head. The League. They were significantly more informed than he had suspected. They were significantly more determined to get a hold of him, too. And the miniatures. Whoever was at the head of this League—they knew. They were looking for proof. They'd known where to ask questions, too, damn it. And that clerk, he'd mentioned researching a particular bank.

Damn it all to hell. Niall was behind, and now he had no choice but to catch up.

After an interminable ride about the city, the coach stopped in a deserted mews. Kara reached beneath her bench and drew out a carved and painted crest. She passed it out to the coachman, who affixed it to the side of the vehicle before driving on. Niall had to admit, it was clever. Anyone who might have spotted their plain coach earlier would look right past this one, with its coat of arms.

The next time they stopped, Gyda told them all to disembark. Niall looked out the window and thought they must be some-where in the warren of streets outside Covent Garden. It was still early, but there were somberly clad men on the pavements, making their way to work. Here and there, a shopkeeper swept in front of his store or wiped his windows and doors to a shine. None of them looked the least surprised to see a fancy coach heading home at the break of day.

They had pulled up outside a large, comfortable-looking rooming house. Gyda climbed out and strode in like she owned the place, with Kara trotting at her heels. Niall and Rob followed to the top floor, which appeared to serve as a large, single dwelling. The door opened, and they were ushered in by a young, pretty woman, fashionably dressed and looking as if she were on her way out.

"You weren't followed?" she asked.

"No." Gyda squeezed her hands. "Thank you, Josie. You were magnificent last night, and your help now is greatly appreciated."

"Of course, my dear. Come in, come in. I have laid in plenty of supplies. But it would be wisest if I followed my regular schedule. I have a voice lesson today and a breakfast appointment beforehand."

A sudden thought jolted Niall out of his exhausted fog. "Breakfast? We are near to Dobbs' Pie Shop, are we not?"

The woman paused in the act of pinning on her hat. "We are. I know the place."

He exchanged a quick glance with Kara. "If you would be so good, might you take a message there for me? I'll write out a quick note. There's a boy there, Harold. If you give it to him and tell him it's from me, he'll know what to do."

"Yes, I've seen the lad." She nodded. "You'll find pen and paper at the desk, over there."

Niall scratched out a few sentences and turned the note over to the young woman. "Thank you. It will keep one of us from delivering it."

"You are welcome, and yes, from what Gyda has said, it would be best if you all stay tucked in here. No one will come by today." Josie let her glance roll over all four of them. "You all look like you could use a good rest. I won't be home until after tonight's performance. All will be well as long as you keep quiet up here."

"Thank you, again, Josie." Gyda followed the young woman to the door and locked it behind her. Turning, she leaned back and looked to Niall. Glancing around, he realized they were all staring at him.

He stared back while his heart swelled with gratitude.

"Introductions might be in order now," Gyda remarked. She waited. "Niall?"

"I cannot," he said roughly. "I am too overcome. I don't know how it happened. I'm sure I'll be horrified to find out. But I am incredibly grateful that you all came after me."

Rob cleared his throat. "Well. Let us allow Niall his sentimental moment, eh? I'll start. I am Rob McRae. Niall's childhood mate, co-conspirator in mischief, and fellow blacksmith." He raised a brow at Gyda. "Judging by the fine workmanship on that axe at your belt, I surmise you are Miss Gyda Winther." He bowed as Gyda grinned.

Rob turned. "And you?" He allowed his gaze to travel up and down Kara's form. "You cannot be anyone other than Miss Kara Levett."

She smiled and inclined her head. Together, they all turned to look at Niall again.

He wanted to wrap each of them in a great bear of a hug. He wanted to sit with them and laugh and tell stories and share memories. He wanted to rejoice as they all got to know each other—and he prayed there would be time for all of that. But first … "I need to hear how you all ended up in there tonight," he said urgently. "All the details."

"I think there are a few details we need from you, too," Kara said gently.

He nodded, his heart thumping. "It's time, I know. But let me hear all of your news first, please? And don't leave anything out. All of your adventures and anyone or anything out of place or odd. It might end up being a piece of this puzzle."

"And let's eat while we talk," Gyda said. "I'm as hungry as I am tired." She pointed at Kara. "And the first thing I want to know is what you did to those little discs that removed those men from the fight so easily."

Kara grinned. "Turner and I developed a coating for them, based on the juices released by the stinging nettle plant. The more they touch the area, the deeper and wider they spread the sting and the burn. It's really quite uncomfortable."

"Diabolical, the pair of you." Gyda shook her head and headed for the kitchen. They all sat and spoke over a joint of ham and plenty of bread, fruit, and cheese. Niall chuckled a few times as Gyda talked, but mostly he winced and cringed and grew angrier as their tales went on. When it was his turn, he drew a deep breath ... and faltered.

"I ... Since I was old enough to know the truth, I've been told that I *must* keep this secret." He snorted. "It's not even my secret. Not truly. But I've done as I was asked. I've kept quiet. I've been careful. But it's out of my hands now. It's clear that this League, whoever they are, know the truth and hope to make use of it. Somehow. The proof of it does exist. Based on what you've all said and what I heard in there tonight, they are after it."

"They are after *you*," Kara said.

"Proof of what, Niall?" asked Gyda.

"There is no one on Earth I would rather share all of this with. The three of you. It is time you knew." Niall paused. "I'm going to share it all. I promise. But I feel honor-bound to speak with someone first."

"Stayme," Kara said quietly.

He nodded. "He's the keeper of this secret. He always has been. He's the one who told me the truth. He's nurtured and guided and protected me since I was in swaddling clothes. I've promised him any multitude of times that I would not reveal it. Now, I feel I must explain, catch him up, and tell him I'm going to share the burden."

Gyda yawned. "Fine, then, but you should sleep first. Now, while we are safe and undiscovered. You don't look like you could string two sentences together, in any case."

"Stayme was out last night," Kara said. "It was already late when I stopped by to ask for his help, but he wasn't there. He'll probably still be abed now."

As if speaking of it had given it weight, the ache of exhaustion in his chest settled further. "His people will probably not wake him for Harold's message. He'll get it when he rises." He yawned as well, and nodded in reluctant agreement. "Very well. A couple of hours of sleep, then. And then I'll go and meet him."

⟫⟫⟩⟨⟨⟨

SOMETHING PULLED AT Kara, tugging her from sleep. She resisted. She and Gyda were sharing Josie Lowe's comfortable bed, and she was wrapped in a warm cocoon of deep, dreamless slumber.

"Kara." Another tug at her hand where it rested outside the soft blankets. "Kara. Wake up."

Her eyes snapped open. "Niall."

Silently, he beckoned her as he backed toward the door. She lay still a moment, fighting off the drag of sleep before she carefully eased her way out of the bed. She'd slept in her trousers and shirt. Grabbing up her belt and coat, she trailed Niall out to the sitting room.

He raised a finger to his lips and indicated Rob, asleep on a settee. Leaning in, he spoke close to her ear. "I'm sorry to wake you. I wished ... I wanted to ask ..."

She waited.

"Would you come with me?"

"Now? To see Stayme?"

He nodded.

"But I—" She swept a hand before her. "I don't have any other clothes."

He snorted under his breath. "His lordship has seen far more scandalous sights, trust me." He grew serious. "In any case, I want him to see. To understand."

Understand what? That there were others who cared for Niall? Others who would risk everything for him?

"I need ..." Niall shook his head. "I would like to speak with you. Alone. If you would care to listen."

Kara's heart started to pound. "Yes, of course." Was this it? Was he going to share the burden he'd been carrying alone for so long? "Give me a minute to get ready."

"Tuck your hair up securely," he urged. "And wear your belt. You never know when we might need it."

They started down the stairs, but at the first landing, Niall beckoned her to the side. Puzzled, she followed him into a corridor and past several closed apartment doors. He glanced back and forth to be sure they were alone, then he grabbed her and pushed her against the wall.

She gasped.

"You frightened me to death," he whispered. "Such a reckless, foolish thing to do." He pressed his forehead against hers. "But thank you for coming for me."

He wrapped his hands around her ribcage, and she reveled in the warmth of his touch. Yes. It was right. His hands belonged on her.

Ducking down, he kissed her. She answered without restraint. Since Gyda first told her he was in danger, she'd been carrying an icy knot of dread in her chest. The last of it melted away now, giving way before the warmth of pleasure and relief.

Safe. Together. And wanting to be here.

He pulled away. "We have to go. But I had to kiss you or go mad."

They set out, and Kara soon realized they were heading for the Covent Garden Market. The sun shone bright, though the air was cold. It didn't bother her. Nothing bothered her. Not the lack of sleep, not the fact that they were likely being hunted right now, nor the bulk of questions that needed answered. At this moment, all that mattered was that she and Niall were side by side once more. Working together. Facing their problems together. Her heart lifted. Her step grew light. This. This was what mattered. What she needed.

Though it was late morning now, she saw as they approached that the place still bustled with activity. Late-coming maids, mothers with children, and housekeepers with baskets bartered with determination, talking loudly to be heard over the constant cries of the sellers hawking their wares. Kara reminded herself to quell her high spirits and keep to her role. She ducked her head as they moved through the crowd, watching the colorful pageantry of it all in the corners of her eyes.

Niall led them to the south corner of the market, where the sellers of potatoes, carrots, turnips, and other rudimentary vegetables held sway.

"You couldn't have chosen a spot near the flower sellers?" She drew her coat tight against the chill.

"No, I could not." He approached a table set up with a shining, elaborate urn with copper moldings, kept warm by a charcoal fire in a specially crafted foot at the bottom of the piece. "Largely for one reason. Because over there, there is no hot elder wine." He smiled at the gentleman behind the table. "Two, please."

The seller nodded and handed over two glasses, each with a piece of toasted bread resting on the side. "I've cured figs, as well, sir, if you've a mind." He gestured to a cart not far away, laden with baskets of baked goods. "Or my wife has some lovely, fresh pastries."

Niall handed a glass to Kara, who sniffed at the spicy aroma in appreciation. "We'll take two Coventrys, if they are filled with her blackberry jam," he told the man, reaching for his purse.

"That they are, sir, but you'll have to pay my wife for her goods. She keeps her own business separate."

Nodding, Niall grinned. He handed Kara the second cup and jerked his chin toward a nearby bench. "Grab the bench. I'll bring over the pastries."

Kara sat, enjoying the direct sun and balancing the drinks. She regarded the couple thoughtfully. Complementary, but separate. An interesting arrangement.

Niall came over, and they juggled positions until they were

both settled with a drink and a three-cornered, jam-filled puff.

"This hot elder wine is one of Stayme's favorites. Timb only sells it in the cold weather."

"We'll be hard-pressed to squeeze the viscount onto this bench."

"We'll have to walk on when he comes. We don't want to stay too long, in any case. But for now, I want nothing more than to sit in the sun with you."

She nodded and took a sip, letting the spicy flavor roll over her tongue. He was right. It did pair well with the sweet pastry. She savored every bite, feeling her heart lighten. She just wanted to tilt her head back and absorb the sun and revel in the warmth of Niall's form pressed to her side.

But he finished his Coventry, then leaned forward to cradle his cup in his hands while his arms rested on his thighs. "This isn't how I thought this would play out," he said quietly.

"What?" Kara asked, aware of all the possibilities. But then she realized. "Telling your secrets? Sharing your burdens?"

He let out a long breath. "I never thought I would tell anyone. Ever. I couldn't imagine wishing to tell anyone." He turned his head to look at her. "But then I met you, Kara. I want you to understand."

"I'm listening."

"I wanted to tell you first. Tell you everything. More, perhaps, than I can share with the others."

She pressed her lips together.

"Do you not wish to hear?" he asked, drawing up straight.

"I do! You know I do. But I hate to think of you hiding anything from Gyda. Or even from your friend, Rob. He clearly cares for you."

"I'm afraid what they learn will change the way they see me. Treat me."

"I cannot imagine that would be so."

"It's different with you. Of everyone, I trust you to look hard and see *me*. No matter what you hear."

"Of course."

He gave a laugh, but there was a note of despair in it. "You say it so lightly, but it's a rare thing. You are rare." He shifted on the bench. "I told you once, that night—"

"The night you left," she said softly. The night they'd kissed and he tried to leave her, but she refused to let him go.

"Yes. I told you then. How much I admire you for going your own way. Seeing with your own vision. It strikes a chord with me, Kara. I want to see the full spectrum of life. I've seen you do it, look at the world and marvel at the beauty and the light, but you also recognize the dark and the despair. You don't let either one overrule the other. You look with a balanced eye, and you are the same with people. So many look and see only status, rank, wealth, or varying degrees of their lack. But I've seen you look and recognize spirit and effort, accomplishment, belief, and heart. You are endlessly kind because you see the humanity in others. The good, the bad, and the potential. You encourage everyone around you to become their best, just by being the best version of yourself—even when it's not the expected version."

He sat back and watched her closely, his gaze full of everything he was feeling. "You are a wonder, Kara. You've been given so much, but you do not let it define you. You've lost much, but you haven't let it break you. You go your own way, and you don't give up on anyone. You refused to give me up, and it filled a hole in my heart I didn't even realize was there. And now I have to hold you to that promise. I have to ask you to stay, even once you know the truth. For I've found I need your clear vision of me. I need you to see me only for who I am."

Tears threatened, but she fought them. She couldn't cry here, on a bench near the potato sellers of Covent Garden. "Tell me, Niall."

"I will. I am. Just remember how much your faith and steadfastness have meant to me." He shook his head. "The women in my life, they've largely been inconstant. You know how Malina treated me. I was a steppingstone to get her from the Scottish countryside to a bigger world. And my mother ... Well, she was flighty. She was spoiled. I thought it was because she was a late-in-life child, born long after the others. Or perhaps because my father died when I was very young. Everyone coddled her and catered to her airs. I did it, too. It just seemed the way of things."

"Unbalanced?" she asked.

"Exactly. One day she was in another uncertain temper, and I saw everyone in the household scrambling to turn her up sweet—and I stopped in my tracks. Why? My mother was often vague, occasionally kind, but mostly absorbed with her own thoughts and needs. What about such a temperament earned respect? Or deserved such singular treatment? I took myself off to chop wood and think. I decided that day to look at the people around me and to try to emulate the ones whom I honestly appreciated. I never wanted anyone to wonder why I was treated with respect. I wanted to earn it." He looked over at her. "I did love my mother. I want you to know that." He grinned, and it was full of fond reminiscence. "She called me *mon chou*."

She laughed. "My cabbage."

"Always. She loved me, in her fashion, and I loved her. But I needed to look elsewhere to find someone to emulate. To find the kind of man I wanted to be. Luckily, I didn't have to look far to find a great man to learn from."

"Who was it?"

"Greig McRae," he answered at once. "The local blacksmith. A massive man. Incredibly strong, but with the gentlest soul. Hardworking and demanding, but also patient and kind."

"Rob's father?"

"Yes. Rob and I were already best mates. He was starting to teach Rob his way around the forge. I asked if he would teach me as well."

"Obviously, he did. And look what you've done with your skills," she said warmly.

"I learned so much from him. But eventually, I had a need to go out on my own. When my apprenticeship was done, I wandered through Scotland a while, before settling in a small fishing village on the coast. I opened a smithy. I made hooks, net weights, and boat parts, whatever was needed. But I wanted to *create* something new. I fooled around a bit, then started to fashion small amulets for the fishermen and sailors of the port."

"Your compass rose charms?" she asked with delight. "That's where they began?"

He laughed. "Yes. Sailors are a superstitious lot. They decided they were good luck, and the demand grew."

She placed a hand over her chest, where the pendant he'd given her hung concealed beneath her boy's clothes. "Thank you for mine," she whispered. "I haven't taken it off since I found it hanging about my turtle's neck."

His gaze softened. "I meant it. That inscription." He lowered his voice. "I confess, I've missed you. I've become used to having you beside me as the world tilts sideways." He grinned. "We navigate better together."

Her mouth twitched. "I feel the same. And now that we've reunited, I've absolutely no desire to strike out alone again. I'm afraid you are stuck with me."

His hand moved, as if he wanted to reach for her—but then remembered where they were. He nodded instead as his gaze locked with hers.

"Tell me the rest," she reminded him.

"Very well." He let out a long breath. "The compass rose talismans became a small but steady income, and I started to design other things as well. I was twenty years old. Full of myself. Full of plans. That's when I went back to Jedburgh for a visit—and everything changed."

"What changed it?"

"I wasn't the only visitor in Jedburgh that summer. Nor was Greig McRae the only male influence in my life. My mother had a friend. A man who adored her, who had been a regular visitor for as long as I could remember, as long as anyone could recall."

She frowned. "Stayme?"

"Yes." He closed his eyes. "You have to understand how different he was. He was almost ... otherworldly. I was surrounded by gruff, steady Scotsmen. Kindhearted but rough men. Stayme was so different. He was smooth, educated, fashionable, and urbane. He came a couple of times each year, at least, bringing gifts and telling the most amusing tales. He'd done so my whole life. He'd done so the whole of my mother's life. I didn't understand until that summer that he was part of the reason why my mother was catered to. What people whispered about her."

Kara frowned, thinking of what he'd said about his mother. "They gossiped about her? Assumed that she was ... fostered out to your family?"

He nodded.

"They said she was likely Stayme's natural child?"

"That summer was the first time I understood what the whispers implied."

"Was she? His daughter?"

"No. He was not her father. But he was a great friend to the man who had sired her, and a great admirer of her mother."

Her lips pursed. "He was asked to watch over her, then?"

"I think he rather wished to."

"Her parents were important, then. She was the illegitimate child of ... whom?"

"Stayme took me out alone one day that summer. He told me the truth of it all. And showed me the proof. He had documents." He shook his head. "We'll speak of them later. But he had something else, too."

Breathless, she waited.

"Stayme showed me a miniature, encased in a portrait locket."

"A portrait of one of her parents?"

"Her father. It was done in gold, with twenty-four rose-cut diamonds framing it."

"Good heavens."

"Even more impressive, the cover of the miniature was a large, transparent diamond. A portrait diamond, it was called. The well-known London jewelers, Rundell and Bridge, had fashioned the locket."

"Oh, yes. I've heard of a portrait diamond, although I've never seen one." She thought back. "The most famous one must have been the one King George IV was buried with. It covered a depiction of his rumored first wife. The woman he supposedly married when he was young. Mrs. Fitzherbert."

"Yes. It was said Mara Fitzherbert had a matching locket with his portrait in it."

"I remember hearing that. But who was in the portrait that Stayme brought you?"

He said nothing, but she looked into his face and saw the truth.

"Wait! Are you saying …?"

"The Prince of Wales married the Catholic widow, Maria Fitzherbert, in 1785. It was a secret ceremony, performed by a chaplain whom the prince freed from debtor's prison."

"But it wasn't a valid marriage, was it? Because neither the king nor the Privy Council had approved it beforehand."

"Technically, they broke the law, contracting the marriage. It couldn't be recognized. The law said no Catholic or the spouse of a Catholic could become monarch of England. But the pope declared the union sacramentally valid."

"What a disaster."

"The Prince of Wales was not going to give up his claim to the throne. I've been told he truly did love her. You know what he was, though. He had other interests and massive debts. He was finally persuaded to separate from Maria Fitzherbert in 1794. Marriage to the German princess, Caroline of Brunswick, was arranged. His enormous debts were paid once they married in 1795."

"And they had a daughter, Princess Charlotte, soon after," Kara recalled.

"Yes. But Prinny and Caroline despised each other. Their marriage was a misery. They moved to separate residences soon after the princess's birth. The prince was free once more, and eventually, he went sniffing around again, after Maria Fitzherbert. They reconciled in 1800. The year my mother was born. The same year that those miniature portraits were painted by Richard Cosway."

"And that was the portrait locket that Stayme showed you? A miniature of the *Prince of Wales*?"

He nodded. "And there was a third portrait. In another locket. One I've never heard even a whisper about. Done at the same time, by the same artist. A portrait of Maria, holding Anne. Their daughter. My mother."

"But that means ..." She clapped her hand over her mouth. "You are the grandson of King George!" she whispered.

"Yes. The son of his illegitimate daughter. *Not* in line to rule," he said firmly.

"Well, that hardly matters, does it? The Catholics in England would recognize the first marriage as valid. No wonder they hid her away. What a political mess it might have caused." Her eyes widened. "And beyond the Catholics, think of Queen Caroline's family and supporters. They would have called it another form of abuse and neglect. Your mother's existence would have caused upheaval on all sides."

"It's why Stayme has been the only one to know of the truth."

"Until now," she said slowly. "The League. They know? They want to use you to start a scandal?"

"That's what Stayme and I believe."

"But why? And who are they?"

"Those are the things we need to discover. Stayme—" He stopped. Pulled out his watch. "Stayme is late." He looked at her in alarm. "He is very rarely late."

The disturbing possibilities bloomed in both of their heads at the same time.

"Harold must have delivered the message. He's never let me down. Stayme would absolutely know what it meant, that we should meet here."

"We don't know that anything is wrong," Kara said. "Perhaps he slept late. He might not even have seen your note yet."

"I must go and be sure."

"Even if they haven't interfered with him, they might be watching."

"We'll be careful. Let's go."

She hopped up, but he grabbed her collar and spun her around. To the world it must have looked like he was reprimanding a servant boy, but she saw the emotion in his eyes and the lightness that hadn't been there before.

"We have trouble and danger ahead of us, still," he whispered. "But no matter what happens, I want you to know ... I'm glad you know my secret. I can't tell you how *free* I feel, knowing I can talk to you about it. I've been longing to tell you, to have you know who I am."

She smiled at him. "I have long known who you are, Niall."

Unspoken words and promises flew between them while they stood there a moment longer. Until he sighed and let her go. And they turned to business again. Together.

Chapter Fourteen

THEY LEFT THEIR glasses with Mr. Timb, and Niall headed south. "A hack will be fastest, don't you think? We'll be likeliest to find one on the Strand."

To his relief, they found a cab quickly. "Curzon Street," he told the driver. "Just get us to the corner near Berkeley Square."

Kara kept silent as they headed west, her gaze focused straight ahead. He wasn't surprised. He'd given her a lot of information to absorb. Holding his own silence, he sat back and let her run through it all in her head.

Suddenly, she sat straight up in her seat. "Malina!" she gasped. "That's how the League knows who you are?"

"It does appear so. I knew she was tangled up with someone, but it's your interview with her maid that proves her connection with this League." He blew out an exasperated breath. "*The League.* League of what? What are they hoping to accomplish?" There were so many things he didn't know. "And who knew what first? It feels like it might be important. Did Malina work out the truth for herself? Or did the League discover it and approach her?"

"You didn't tell her yourself? While you were handfasted?"

"No!" He made a face. "I told you I never wanted anyone to know the truth. I meant it. I was so confused and ashamed and bitter. I dreaded the thought of anyone knowing, ever. I didn't tell Malina. I met her that same summer. It was perhaps not the best time to begin to court a young woman. But truthfully, she pursued me. I was surprised, but it was a balm to my embittered spirit. Here was a girl, beautiful and full of life. She knew nothing of my secrets, and honestly, I thought I should take her quickly, before anything came to light."

Kara cleared her throat. "Niall, I do not doubt the appeal you must have presented, even so young. I'm sure there wasn't a girl within miles of your home who didn't dream of you."

He laughed. "I like to hear you say so, but I was as green as grass back then."

The corner of her mouth tilted up. "Having been a foolish, eager young girl myself, I think I can judge better how they think. But honestly, knowing what we know about Malina now, and having heard what you said about the whispers surrounding your mother, I wouldn't be surprised if they were not exactly why she chased after you. She likely thought your connection with Stayme might get her, or both of you, somewhere beyond your little village."

"I realized as much, but it wasn't until later. The longer we were together, though, the more I knew I'd made the right decision not to tell her anything."

Her expression softened. "I wish I could say I was sorry, but I'm not."

Here, at least, he could take her hand. And because they were both dressed roughly, neither wore gloves. He cradled her hand between his own, relishing the warmth of her skin, noting with approval each callous, solder burn, and rough patch. It was a small, sturdy hand, capable of so much. He moved his gaze over her in her boy's clothes and couldn't help but smile.

He'd never met a woman like her. Hell, he was pretty sure there had never *been* a woman like her. What other beautiful woman would hide her charms beneath a boy's cap, a smudged face, and a worn coat? She was almost too pretty to pull it off, but too loyal and fierce and utterly trustworthy to leave him stuck in the clutches of his enemies. His heart swelled at the thought of it. He bent to press a kiss upon that accomplished hand and pushed away the thought of feeling those tiny callouses touch him. Someday ...

She leaned in to him a little, and he closed his eyes.

"Niall," she said softly. "When you and Rob were telling us what happened in there last night, you said the man who resembled a clerk repeatedly mentioned a woman. The woman who was looking for you. The woman who would be so happy to see you." She glanced up. "I don't think he was talking about Malina."

Surprised, he nodded. "I don't either, actually. I don't have anything to base it on, except that I don't think Malina possesses the skills to create or run such a complex organization, nor the ability to inspire such loyalty."

"I saw a woman. In the labyrinth, as they call it. When we were fleeing that underground warehouse. She was far behind us, up in the gallery. She was watching us go. It was really too far to tell, but it wasn't Malina. I know it wasn't. She was watching us with malice, though. I could feel it in my bones."

He sighed. "I have no idea who she could be, and that is what bothers me the most."

"Has Malina seen the portrait lockets?" Kara asked.

Sitting back, he kept a hold of her hand. "She has." He frowned at the memory. "I didn't show her, but I cannot say that it wasn't my fault that she saw them. We both bear the weight of our failed handfasting." He sighed. "I knew she was bored and unhappy. She encouraged me to turn my smithy over to Rob. I did it, but then realized it was because she wanted to move to the city. I wasn't ready, though. Instead, I built a forge in the barn at home and set about practicing my craft, learning new skills, developing my sense of design."

"You were absorbed in it." She spoke with the voice of experience, which was one of the similarities that he loved sharing with her. "Alone with the ideas in your head and the fire in your belly."

He smiled as he recalled they'd also been in a carriage the first time he said those words to her. "Yes. You know what I mean. Anyone who's ever been caught in the grip of a creative project would. But still, it likely wasn't fair of me to indulge it."

"Likely it was impossible not to."

"Perhaps. But Malina couldn't adapt to life in a cottage on the cliffs, with nothing near but the expanse of the sea. She wasn't suited to such a quiet existence. She grew pouty and shrewish. I thought it might help if I took her with me while I consulted with a potential client near Edinburgh."

"It didn't?"

"No," he said flatly. "Quite the opposite. In fact, that day put all of this in motion." He waved a hand. "My client was congenial and eager to hire me. He also had a friend visiting him at the time. The Viscount Marston."

"Oh dear."

"Indeed. He was young, handsome, rich, and titled. Irresistible, I suppose. Certainly, Malina could not resist. She flirted shamelessly. I was mortified. I took her home and vowed never to take her back."

Kara grimaced. "I'm sure that didn't go over well."

"It did not. But after a few days, she found a distraction. Her sister was having a difficult confinement. Malina started to visit her for a few days at a time, to help out. Or so I thought."

Kara gasped. "She didn't!"

"I didn't find out the truth of it until later, but those days were spent with Marston. I don't know what she told him. Some tale of neglect, I'm sure. It held a kernel of truth in it, to my shame. But I was so tired of being berated and harangued and accused of misleading her. I spent more time in the forge, and she became vague and distracted, even on the days she spent at home. She gave up all pretense of keeping house or tending to chores, laundry, or even the animals. She was so touchy, her temper easily riled. Then things began to go missing."

He paused a moment, remembering the sick misery of those days. "Small things," he said quietly. "Books from my little collection. The vase I gave her for her birthday. One day I came in and noticed the silver candlesticks I'd bartered for a ship's repairs were gone from the mantel. There was no sign of Malina. I don't know how I knew, but all my hackles rose and I tore through the house, looking for her."

"What happened?"

"She had somehow discovered the space hidden beneath the floorboards, under the bed. When I came in, she'd just managed to get the box out and open. She couldn't have seen the miniatures for more than a second or two before I burst in and snatched the box away."

"I suppose it was long enough." Her voice sounded far away, and he knew she must be imagining the scene.

"No. I don't think she understood at all, then, what she'd seen. We had another row, and I took the box with me, back to the forge. After a while, she came out to the barn. She was wearing a dress I'd never seen before. She held up the length of fabric we'd used at our handfasting, the one that had been looped around our hands, linking us. She tossed it into the forge fire, spun on her heel, and left."

"What did you do?"

"I watched it burn. And then I went back to work. But not for long. Because after a while, I realized it wasn't just the forge smoke I was smelling. I stepped outside and saw the cottage blazing. I watched it burn, too. And then I went back to work again."

They sat in silence for a few moments.

"Every time I think I could not despise her more, I find a new reason to do so," Kara said fiercely.

"She would have used it against me then, had she understood what those portraits were. And now you know why she's tormenting me now. Somehow she realized what it was that she'd glimpsed. All of this started a couple of months ago, when Stayme discovered her husband was searching every corner of London, looking for a pair of miniatures."

"And here we are," she said.

"And here we are—at Curzon Street, that is."

They climbed out. Niall peered about them, but saw no one who looked familiar and no one who looked as if they cared about what the pair of them were up to. He led the way quickly, ducking into the narrow, curving entrance to the South Bruton Mews. He hurried along the back of this row of houses facing Berkeley Square, until he came to Stayme's home. With practiced ease, he manipulated the sticky gate latch and let them into the yard. "Straight through and to the right. You'll find the door to the servants' entrance."

"You've come this way before."

"Many times. We've been careful not to be seen together too often over the years. A number of our meetings have had to be in secret."

He didn't bother knocking. The servants all knew him. Except ... there were no servants bustling about the passages, as there should have been. The chairs around the great table in the servants' hall were pushed out every which way, as if they'd been quickly abandoned. The kitchen stood empty, though a pot boiled on the stove and a brace of guinea fowl lay, half plucked, on the table.

Moving quickly, Niall went to the stairs. At the top, a couple of scullery maids stood at the open green baize door, wringing their hands in their aprons and staring out over a crowd in the corridor.

"Excuse me. Let me pass, please." Niall pushed through, with Kara right behind him. The servants looked relieved to see him. Several of the maids were crying. A footman sat near the door, his face gone pale, while the housekeeper tied a tourniquet above a slash on his arm.

"Odin's arse! What's happened? Where is Stayme?" he demanded. He looked around for the butler. "Watts?" he bellowed. "Where are you?"

"Here, sir."

Niall whirled about and looked upward. Watts, Stayme's unflappable butler, lay on the landing, battered and bruised. One of his eyes had begun to swell shut. Niall raced up and began to assess him for worse injuries. "Where is his lordship?" Dread was growing in his gut.

"Gone," Watts said flatly. "Taken. They came in the upstairs windows. They must have climbed the drainage pipes."

"Who was it?" Niall growled.

"I have no idea. There were quite a few of them, though."

"Was a woman with them?" asked Kara, who had climbed the stairs behind him.

Watts frowned. "No. I don't believe so."

Dread was rapidly turning to fury. "Was Stayme harmed?" Niall asked.

"He resisted. They roughed him up a little, until they got him trussed up. I tried to stop them, and so did Young Charles, but we didn't stand a chance against them. They just swept us out of the way and took him out. It was just minutes ago." The butler nodded down toward the entry hall. "They left a note. Cook says it is addressed to you, sir."

Kara was already running back down. She took up the note and brought it back up to him.

Niall turned it over. It was affixed with a seal, marked with the same symbol he'd seen in the buildings in Seven Dials. Cracks laid over a map of the European Continent, reaching from England, all the way to the Russian Empire. He broke it open.

Mr. Kier,

How kind of you to come to call. And how disappointed I was to have missed you. It's been amusing, playing cat and mouse with you, but I find myself tiring of the game. It's time we moved on to more serious play.

As you see, I have the old man, your friend and mentor. I will not harm him. Not straight away.

To be blunt, Mr. Kier, I want those miniatures. Bring them to me before sundown tomorrow and Lord Stayme will be returned, unharmed.

I'm sorry to say, the time of your anonymity is past. All of England must know who you are. It's a shame I have to disrupt your life in this way, but it must be done. In truth, although we share no blood, our experiences have been so similar, I almost feel a family connection with you.

Nevertheless, I will have my demands met, or you and the viscount will pay the price.

Yours,
PHS
League of Dissolution

"Dissolution?" Kara was reading over his shoulder. "Dissolution of what?"

Niall helped Watts to his feet. Once the butler stood steady on his own, he turned to face Kara. "It doesn't matter. We are going to put a stop to them." He started down the stairs. "We need to call a council of war."

⋙✦⋘

KARA HAD TO stop Niall from charging out the front door of Lord Stayme's townhouse. "They knew you would come. They left the note. Surely they have someone watching. We cannot charge out of here and go straight back. We don't want to lead them to the others."

"They don't need the others. They have Stayme!"

Kara grabbed his arm when he would have pushed past her. "No, Niall! Think! These are the sort of people who will use every advantage against us. I do not intend to give them any more than they already have." She let him go. "We might actually have an advantage here, in fact. I don't think anyone saw us come in the back, do you?"

"I saw no sign of it."

"Then they likely don't yet know we've seen the note. Let's keep it that way. Keep at least part of their attention focused here."

"Out the back again, then."

"After we send someone out to see if it is still clear." She looked around at the gathering of servants. "But we need it to look natural."

The cook began to make her way back toward the servants' stairs. "Send Molly out to dump the vegetables I had on the stove. They are scorched. I can smell them from here."

Kara and Niall followed her to the kitchen. The housekeeper came in a moment later. "Watts and Charles have been settled into bed. We need to send for the doctor."

"Wait a moment?" asked Kara. She was looking to the kitchen maid, Molly, who was coming back inside with the empty pan.

"There's someone loitering about beyond the back gate," the maid reported.

"We didn't see him on the way in," Kara said. She looked to Niall.

"So, either he wasn't in position yet, or he's reported us and they will be returning to grab us, if they can. Either way, we need to go."

"We need to go in disguise," Kara said. "Do you have any livery that would fit Mr. Kier?" she asked the housekeeper.

The woman eyed him, assessing. "It might be a bit snug."

"Put it on," Kara told Niall. "You can go and fetch the doctor. If they follow, that should allay their suspicions."

"And what of you?" He stepped closer. "Didn't we just say we were going to stick together?"

She breathed deeply, trying to inhale calm along with his scent. "It won't be for long, and it will get us safely out of here. This is my bailiwick, remember? Avoiding and escaping capture?"

She thought a moment. "If they saw us, then they saw a man and a boy enter. You go out as the footman, and I'll take a maid's outfit and a basket and act as if I'm going to the market." Her mouth twisted as she nodded toward the empty pan. "Those vegetables will need replacing."

"Where is the nearest apothecary?" Niall asked.

The housekeeper mentioned a place a few streets over.

"I'll head there after I send the doctor," he told Kara. "Meet me there."

She shook her head. "Wait. It's Thursday, is it not? What time is it?" She looked to the cook, who indicated a clock at the other end of the kitchen. Kara nodded. "Good. I have a better idea. Do you have a scrap of paper and a pencil?"

"Of course." The woman tore off half a sheet from a notebook and searched through a drawer.

Kara scribbled an address and handed the folded paper to Niall. "Meet me here. Make sure you've lost any followers before you head that way."

Niall glanced at it, put the note in his pocket, and nodded. Moments later, Kara and several of the viscount's servants watched as Niall, clad in the navy, double-breasted coat of the viscount's livery, trotted out the front door and headed out of the square.

"Oh dear." It was Molly, the kitchen maid, who pointed as a man peeled away from the garden fence in the middle of the square and set off after Niall.

"Mr. Kier knows how to handle himself," Kara reassured her. "Now, if those men come back, don't resist them. They'll likely be looking for us. Just swear you've seen no sign of us." She held up the note that had been left for Niall. "Who here knows how to heat this seal and affix it so it looks like the note was never opened?"

No one said a word.

Kara rolled her eyes. "Come, now. You all work for Lord Stayme. I know what that means."

After a moment, a footman raised his hand. "Mr. Watts has been teaching me," he said sheepishly.

A moment later, Molly raised hers.

Kara handed the note to the footman. "Make it look perfect and set it back where they left it." She took the maid by the arm. "Molly, I suspect you will be just the person to help me. I need you to walk me out into the yard in the back." She explained as they made their way back to the kitchen, where she took up the basket the cook had for her.

"If you don't work for his lordship, miss, you should." Molly's tone was admiring. "You think of everything."

Kara took that as the compliment it was meant to be. She drew in a deep breath as they stepped outside. In the mews, a shadow detached from the wall and perked up in attention as they approached the gate.

"You're the lucky one, aren't you?" Molly grumbled. "I wish I got to go out to the market. All the downstairs rooms smell like scorched onions."

"What?" Kara demanded in feigned surprise. "What if there is more excitement? I'll miss it!" She sighed. "Oh well. Someone has to go, or we'll have no dinner."

"Stew again," Molly sighed.

"Better than going hungry."

"Well, don't dawdle," Molly urged. "Or the stew won't have time to *stew*."

Laughing, Kara went through the gate. She eyed the man as he went past, but he never moved from the wall. Giving Molly a wave, she headed for the street.

Chapter Fifteen

T HE MAN WHO had followed Niall from Berkeley Square was there, still loitering down the street a little, when he emerged from the doctor's house.

Niall cursed under his breath. It was harder by a degree of difficulty to lose someone while wearing livery. Damned shiny buttons and distinctive tails. Thinking quickly, he headed back in the direction of Stayme's home, but ducked onto a side street and into a tavern that he knew catered to servants from the grand Mayfair homes.

He was in luck. There was a groom in the taproom, nearly his size. For a pint and the trade of the livery jacket, the man handed over his long, worn coat. Niall donned it, bought a left-behind, slouchy hat from the innkeeper, and went out the back.

He took a few odd turnings to be sure he'd lost his shadow, then set out for the address Kara had given him. When he found it, he stopped a distance away to double-check the address. Yes. It was right. But he was staring at a milliner's shop in a lane just off Bond Street.

What in ...?

Shrugging, he went on. As he approached the door, he realized someone else was reaching for it from the other direction. "Turner!" he gasped.

The butler looked as startled as him. "Mr. Kier!"

"Have you seen Kara?" demanded Niall.

"Have you seen Miss Levett?" Turner asked at the very same moment.

"She ordered me meet her here," Niall answered.

"When did you last hear from her?"

"I saw her an hour past. We split up to shake off some ... interested parties."

Turner was visibly relieved. "Oh, thank goodness."

"How did you know to come here?" Niall looked up at the sign over the milliner's door.

The butler hesitated, then glanced around. "Perhaps we should go in and find a private place to talk."

Niall followed him in, then stopped, gazing about the frilly, feminine showroom.

"Good morning, gentlemen!" A pretty redhead, tiny, trim, and neat as a pin, glanced over at them from where she stood, assisting a customer. "Oh, Mr. Turner! Have you come to pick up the young miss's lovely new bonnet? I swear, she's outdone herself with the colors on this one."

"Indeed, Miss Burke. Thank you."

"It's nearly finished and ready to go. If you can wait a moment, I'll finish up with Mrs. Bradford, then I'll pack it up for you." She arched a brow. "Unless you gentlemen are in a hurry?"

"No. Not at all." Turner glanced toward the back room. "Perhaps we should go in the back? We've no wish to frighten your customers away, and I confess, I wouldn't mind sitting at your worktable. I don't have the stamina I used to, I'm afraid."

"Never say so, sir! You look as spry as the first day I met you. But of course, you must make yourself at home. I won't be but a few minutes."

They made their way back to the workroom, which was far more functional than frilly, with a table, desk, and shelves full of ribbons, feathers, fruit, and many other millinery supplies. Niall took a seat next to Turner, but felt slightly unnerved by the stuffed bird sitting on a shelf next to his temple and seemingly glaring at him. He switched seats. As he sat again, Turner held a finger to his lips and nodded toward the door.

After a minute or so, the buzz of regular conversation began again in the showroom.

Niall gave the butler a questioning look.

Turner let out a long breath. "Miss Levett left Bluefield Park last evening. She was expected back last night. She didn't come home. And she didn't send word."

Niall understood at once how that must have worried Turner, and likely the rest of the staff, too. Kara had been abducted and held for ransom when she was a girl. Scotland Yard had been largely ineffectual in finding her. It had been Turner who solved the mystery—and rescued her. There had been several other attempts to snatch her in later years, as well. It was one of the main reasons why Kara had developed so many unusual skills, and it was why she was careful to keep Turner apprised of her whereabouts.

"We have an arrangement," Turner continued. "If she's been out of communication, then we have set up a plan. Specific spots for different days. Near this time in the afternoon. If she has been out of contact, but is able to move freely, then she will meet me there. Or she might send word. Today is Thursday. Miss Burke has kindly agreed to be our arranged Thursday meeting spot."

"A good plan."

"It is nerve-racking to have to make use of it. If Miss Levett doesn't turn up, then I must really begin to worry. But if you've just seen her, then I'm sure all will be well."

"I would have thought she'd be here by now, though," Niall fretted. "She must have picked up a tail as well."

"I am reassured, knowing that is all that might delay her. Don't worry, sir. That girl knows how to throw someone off her scent."

Niall nodded.

"While we wait, though, perhaps we could talk? I am caught

up on Miss Levett's adventures, at least through last evening." The butler gave him an expectant look. "Perhaps it is time you tell me what in blazes is going on with you, sir."

The door opened and Miss Burke popped her head in. "Everything all right, Mr. Turner?"

"I believe so, thank you. We are expecting Miss Levett at any moment."

"Oh, good! I was nervous there for a moment. I'll leave you then, as I've a pair of ladies just come in."

"Thank you, Miss Burke. We should be out of your hair before long."

The milliner shut the door again, and Niall gave the older man a long look. He could scarcely believe he was considering answering his question. Fully. It went against every instinct. Yet Niall knew that Turner was nothing if not trustworthy. And experienced. And if Niall couldn't put a stop to the League of Dissolution's plans, then everyone was going to know his secrets soon enough.

So, he told Turner. Everything. The butler listened without interrupting, then he asked several thoughtful questions. Niall answered them all. After a moment's silence, the older man said, "Thank you for confiding in me. I know that could not have been easy."

"I'd sooner you pulled my fingernails out," Niall admitted. "But worse is knowing Stayme is in peril because of me."

"Believe me, I understand the frantic churn of guilt in your gut," Turner said quietly. "But Stayme chose his own course, and it sounds to me as if he did it out of love—for your mother and for you. None of this can be laid at your door, Mr. Kier. But that won't stop us from doing everything we can to free the viscount and to get you out from under the thumb of this League of Dissolution." The corner of his mouth turned up. "Pretentious name."

"Serious organization," Niall countered. "We've got to think. Come up with a plan."

"I have thoughts." Turner paused, gauging his reaction.

"Let's hear them." Niall gestured. "Your experience with this sort of thing outweighs mine."

Before the butler could answer, voices sounded outside the door. It abruptly opened. "Ah, good, you are both here," Kara said, breezing in.

"What happened? You were delayed?" Niall asked.

"Apologies. They had a man posted outside the square. He saw me leave the mews and decided to follow. It *was* a bit late in the day to send a maid to market, I suppose. The crowds there were thin, too, which made it harder to lose him." She shot her butler a look. "Turner, are you all right? Is everything as usual at Bluefield?"

He raised his brow. "Everything save for the fact that you went out of contact."

She flushed. "I am sorry. It couldn't be helped."

"Oh, and that Detective Caden has been to the house twice, looking for you. Once last night and again this morning. He says he has further questions for you."

She waved him off. "Detective Caden can go hang." She looked between them. "Is that why you two look so serious?"

"Mr. Kier has been catching me up on developments," Turner told her.

She shot Niall a questioning look, and he nodded. "Yes. All of it."

"Good. That saves time." Grinning, she looked to Turner. "Did Niall tell you I used the discs?"

"No." The butler brightened. "How did they work?"

"Like a charm! Just like we intended. The burn was utterly distracting. They dropped like flies."

Turner looked pleased. "Good. We'll need to concoct more of that coating." He raised his brow at her maid's outfit. "I did bring a selection of clothing and an assortment of other tools and gadgets I thought might be useful, were you mixed up in something ... adventurous again."

Niall cleared his throat. "As a matter of fact, she is."

"Apologies again," Kara said. Reaching under her skirts, she pulled down the legs of her trousers, then wiggled out of the maid's dress. Her boy's clothes were underneath. Taking her coat and hat out of the basket, she put the dress in. "I'll have Miss Burke send this back to Stayme's." She grinned at her butler. "And we can get to work. We'll let Turner's logistical mind get busy. He'll be a huge help."

"Thank you." Turner inclined his head and then turned to Niall. "You said that the man who looked like a clerk mentioned a bank?"

"He did. My friend Rob told us that the men who were nosing about in Scotland asked all sorts of questions about my mother, her friends, relatives, relationships, and even where she did her banking. She used a local bank, but Stayme also kept an account for her here in London. No one was supposed to know about it, but I have to assume someone did, and let it slip to those men from the League. Perhaps someone from the village bank itself, as they were seen in there." He rubbed his temple. "And yes, those lockets and their miniatures are indeed locked away there. I'll need to get them out of there and somewhere safe, now that they have discovered it. And I'll have to get them out without them knowing."

"*We* will," Kara corrected him. "You are not alone in this anymore."

Turner spoke up. "And if I may make a suggestion, a couple of faux lockets might not come amiss."

"Already on it," Niall said. "But I like the way you think. There are still steps to take, though, before we have everything ready. Let's get back to the others. We have a lot to accomplish in a short amount of time, if we are to see Stayme safe."

Turner stood. "Actually, why don't you give me the address and I'll meet you there later? I think I should head to the bank now. Your League is unlikely to recognize me, and I can pose as a client looking for a place to store valuables. I will get the lay of the place and search for circumstances we can exploit."

Niall slowly nodded in approval as Kara grinned at him.

"I told you he was good," she said gleefully.

>>>><<<<

FOR THE THIRD time in one day, Niall found himself telling his secrets and baring his soul. He might have thought it would get easier. It didn't. He was exhausted. Not surprisingly, Rob and Gyda did not take the news as calmly as Kara and Turner.

Rob sat straight up in his seat as Niall spoke, his eyes growing wider. By the time Niall finished, Rob was on his feet, pacing. He put his hands atop his head and moved back and forth in the sitting room. "I can scarcely believe it. I ... You ... I thought it was Stayme! We all thought it was Stayme. But it wasn't."

"It wasn't."

"Your grandsire is ... was ..."

"He was a randy old prick of a wastrel who had multiple women before, during and after both times he engaged in a relationship with my mother's mother," Niall said sharply.

"Well, yes, by Great Bruce's balls, he was. But he did it all with a crown on his head!"

Niall bit his lip. "No. I think the crown was only for state occasions."

"You know what I mean!" Rob circled his hands above his head. "Figuratively!"

Gyda, who had been sitting quietly, suddenly cursed. "Odin's arse! Now I owe Emelia five pounds!"

Everyone watched and waited.

She shrugged. "I wagered your forebears were French aristocrats." She shot him a defensive look. "Well, your accent is delicious. No one can deny it."

Niall laughed and sank down in his chair. "Perhaps I should have told you both long ago. Neither of you will let me wallow in doom and gloom, or even take myself seriously."

Kara left the window, where she'd been watching the street. "Nothing about your bloodline should send you wallowing in gloom, but the situation is serious."

Gyda took her hand. "We know, Kara dear, but Niall did look in need of some lightening up. We'll all work better if we are balanced." She stood up and began to count off her fingers. "We are approaching a dire state of things, though. Sally Doughty is dead. Stayme is abducted. Your secret past is about to be trumpeted to the masses. And we can lay it all at the door of these same men."

"The League of Dissolution," Kara said disparagingly. "Who are they and what do they want? The dissolution of *what*, I want to know." She pursed her lips, thinking. "Those marks you described, Niall. The cracks over the map of Europe. Can that truly be their aim? They want to destabilize all of it? But why?"

"They do have an international element," Rob said. "You said the maid you spoke to mentioned foreigners. And Niall and I both heard German being spoken in that great maze of a place."

Gyda slammed her hand upon the table before the settee. "It doesn't matter who they are. We can figure out what they want, and why, later. Right now, only three things matter. We find a way to free Stayme. We find a way for Niall to keep his miniatures. And we try like hell to keep his secrets from being spread everywhere."

"We'll never be able to spring Stayme," Niall said. "Not now. They are onto us. We'd need a hundred men or more. I'm going to have to give over the lockets and trade them for his lordship." Gyda started to object, but Niall raised his hand. "Counterfeit, if we can possibly make it happen. I've already started someone on the lockets. We'll need portraits to go inside." He eyed Gyda. "You know Ansel Wells. Can you sneak out of here and get to his place without being seen?"

She snorted in answer.

"Good. Get him started on those two miniatures. I have

sketches he can use, but he has to get them done quickly. Tell him I'll pay him a premium price."

"Nothing lights a fire under that lad like money. I'll find him, pump him full of coffee. Or whisky. Or whatever combination of the two works. I'll make sure they are done by morning."

"Thank you. Hopefully, we'll be able to make the trade quickly and get Stayme out without anyone being the wiser."

"That still leaves us the problem of getting the real miniatures out of the bank." Kara stopped suddenly. "Wait. If they already know which bank they are in, won't they just break in and take them for themselves? They clearly have recruited thieves and cracksmen to their ranks."

"I don't think they will," Niall answered slowly. "We've seen plenty of evidence that they don't want attention focused their way."

"At least, not yet," Rob said.

"I think that's exactly it. They want to operate underground and unseen. At least until they are ready to make their big splash."

"With your story." Kara sniffed.

"A break-in like that will draw all the wrong sort of attention. The bank would not want to leave something like that unsolved. They would bring in Scotland Yard, their insurance men, and likely a few private enquiry agents. Too much scrutiny, fast and hard. Before they are ready."

At his words, Kara made a sound. Niall saw the color drain from her face. "Before they are ready? Niall, they need all the pieces of the puzzle. And the final piece is you."

He frowned.

"You and the miniatures. They'll need you both."

"They know the facts. The miniatures are all they need to back them up."

"No. They will need you," she insisted. "You are tall and handsome and charming. Talented. A man who has worked hard and succeeded in making a name for himself through his own skills. You are a man the common people of England can admire. Cheer. Support."

"You are a direct descendant of old King George," Gyda said. "The queen is only his niece."

"It doesn't matter," Niall said. "The Royal Marriages Act—"

"Doesn't apply here," Kara interrupted. "If dissolution and destabilization are truly their goals, then the League doesn't need you to take the throne. They will just want people to dissent. They will rile them up with you and your story. A misbegotten government in charge. Catholic rites denied. A hidden marriage. A strong, young man, wronged by those who should have protected him. That will stir up the people. And you saw all those weapons the League has stored. Pikes and staffs and pitchforks. They will rile them up and send them out. They want shouting. Discontent. Riots. People in the streets. They want the government fearful and the police preoccupied. Why? There could be any number of reasons. But they need you and the miniatures both." She frowned. "Perhaps we shouldn't give them any miniatures at all."

"We must," Niall insisted. "I won't risk Stayme. I'll give them the real ones, if I must, but I'd much prefer to give them counterfeits and keep the one piece of my past that my mother left me."

"Giving them the counterfeits might shove a stick in the wheel of their plans, in any case," Gyda mused. "You know the art world. They'll know the difference between the master who painted for the king and the work of Ansel Wells."

"And the jewelers," Kara added. "They are world famous. Surely they will be consulted. They'll be able to tell if the pieces are their work or not."

Niall sighed. "If ruining their prospects were the only goal, I would not hesitate to refuse their demands. But I will *never* allow them to harm Stayme. And I think we all know by now that they will do it. So I need fakes that are good enough to fool the League. They won't stand up to scrutiny by the experts later, I'm sure. But by then the damage will have been done. The story will be out."

"It might dampen enthusiasm for their cause, if they are revealed as fakes eventually."

"It might. But all that will come after the initial scandal and uproar, so I will think about that later. Right now I want to get Stayme and keep my property, if possible. They know where the lockets are. That means they must see the real miniatures removed from the bank. But they must not apprehend me leaving with them, which is surely what they will try."

"You cannot go anywhere near that bank," Kara insisted.

"She's right." Everyone looked around as Turner came in. "You need to lock that door, by the way," he said.

Kara went behind him and locked it, then came to take his arm. "I'm so glad you made it here. Did you discover anything useful?"

"A good bit. And you are right. You cannot be the one to go to the bank, Niall. They are already there, waiting for you. I picked out at least six of them. They'll have the lockets from you before you've taken two steps out of there."

Niall shook his head. "I cannot allow any of you to take the risk in my place."

"We cannot allow *you* to take the risk," Kara argued. "It's dangerous to you and to countless others."

"There's a password needed to retrieve the lockets. And a key to the strongbox."

"Give them both to me." Kara eyed him closely. "You trust me, do you not?"

He shot her an exasperated look. "You know I do."

"You'll need to trust us all," Turner told him. "I believe we can safely get your miniatures. We can actually use their need of you to lessen the risk. I spent a fruitful afternoon at the bank. I've got the information we need and even more, thanks to the obliging charwoman who cleans the place after hours."

"Come and take some tea, Turner." Kara beckoned them all.

"Come, everyone. Let's sit at the table and hear what he has to say. And then we can start making plans."

"We'll use our wits and all of our assets," Turner said. "If we work together, we can get those lockets out and leave the League chasing their tails."

Chapter Sixteen

K ARA SHIFTED NERVOUSLY while she waited at the print shop across the street and down a bit from Darrow's Bank. It was a solid, anchoring building on the Strand, and people flowed past as she pretended great interest in a series of prints poking affectionate fun at Lord Palmerston. She kept track of everyone around her while she watched for the signal.

There. Turner, a good deal further down the street, gave the sign that everyone was in place. Sending up fervent prayers that this would work, Kara watched closely.

Here he came. Niall strolled down the other side of the street clad in a long brown coat and a hat that slouched forward and shadowed his face. He strode at an easy pace toward the bank. Traffic was heavy, and she lost sight of him a time or two as larger carriages or wagons passed—but she saw the moment the first watcher noticed him.

The man had been lingering in a doorway, savoring a cheroot. He straightened when he caught sight of Niall and held his hand up, circling his finger. Niall stopped ten feet away and looked him in the eye. Abruptly, he turned and stepped into the street, hopping a step forward and back, dodging traffic as he crossed. When he hit the pavement several doors further down the street from her, he set out away from her at a run.

Kara saw at least four men move out in pursuit of him. What had been their plan? Had they meant to grab Niall and escort him into the bank? Take the lockets before he even left the building? Or had they intended to accost him once he came out?

All four of them had been lingering on the bank side of the street. Cursing out loud, they followed, fighting against the flow of vehicles. They were still crossing when Niall, running away from her, approached a carriage sitting outside a linen draper's. Kara held her breath when Rob McRae stepped out from the shop, wearing an apron and carrying a high stack of fabric. Their timing was perfect. Rob opened the door, and Niall dived in. Rob stepped in close to place the fabric on the carriage seat as he praised the lady inside for her excellent taste. Kara couldn't hear Josie Lowe's response, but she imagined it was suitably autocratic.

The League men hit the pavement and started running for the spot where they'd last seen Niall, in the direction of the carriage.

Kara took up the sturdy black handbag at her feet and set out on her own mission. As the traffic ebbed, she set out to cross the street in the opposite direction the men had taken. She heard one of the League's men call out to his fellows, looking for Niall. A shout rang out, and Kara turned her head to see the flare of a long brown coat as a tall figure darted around a corner a good way further down the street. All four pursuers set off after the brown coat, as Rob, without the apron now, climbed atop the carriage and set off.

First step of the plan—complete. Kara walked right past another man posted outside the bank. He was too busy watching his compatriots and their chase to notice. She walked into Darrow's Bank without anyone taking note of her.

Her footsteps echoed on the cool marble floor. Darrow's catered to blue bloods and men of extreme wealth. They were known for their exclusive clientele and their utter discretion. If a man had secrets to lock away, he brought them here. Her father had done a bit of business with the place. She'd accompanied him a time or two, though she'd been but a girl. Nothing about the place had changed in the interim. It was still quiet, elegant, and imposing.

A clerk approached her. She smiled, greeted him, and asked to see the bank manager. With a bow, he led her to a sumptuous office, all fine wood, thick carpet, and the smell of leather. A high window let in the morning light.

Kara took a seat and set the black bag at her feet. After a moment, a man entered. She smiled up at him. "Good morning, Mr. Falkirk."

He stalled, caught off guard. He had a long face, with heavy-lidded eyes that nonetheless appeared to take in everything about her in a moment. "Miss Levett, is it not? Well. How lovely to see you again. It's been quite some time, I see. You've quite grown up."

"Indeed I have, sir, but you have not changed in the least."

He came around to sit at the desk. "Flattery from a pretty young woman? I declare it to be my new favorite way to start the day."

"I'm happy to oblige."

"How may I help you, Miss Levett?" Falkirk paused. "If I recall, your father closed his account some time before his death."

"He did, as far as I know. But I've come on an errand for a friend. Two friends, to be accurate. I am here on behalf of Mr. Niall Kier. Lord Stayme opened an account in his name when he was still small. His mother's name is attached to the account as well, but the lady has unfortunately passed on."

"I'm sorry to hear it," Falkirk intoned politely.

"Lord Stayme gave something into your keeping. Mr. Kier appreciates the care you've taken of his property, but he has now asked me to retrieve it."

Falkirk's face never changed expression. "Very good. Since it's been some time since Lord Stayme set up the account, I'll have to check the arrangements." He rang a bell, and the door opened immediately. Falkirk inclined his head at the young man who entered. "Bring me Lord Stayme's file, please, Baker."

"Of course, sir."

Falkirk eased a little as the door closed again. "May I offer you tea, then, Miss Levett? I dare not offer the sweets I used to tempt you with when you were a girl."

"No, thank you, sir." She grinned. "Although I do recall your chewy caramels with a certain fondness."

He nodded. "I have heard a bit about your success at the Great Exhibition. Such an extraordinary event. How did you find the experience?"

They had a lovely few minutes to chat about her time in the Crystal Palace before the young man returned with a thin file. He handed it over and departed. Falkirk was careful to keep it turned away so that Kara could see no part of what was written inside.

"Ah. I see the viscount has required that anyone fetching the item must produce a key."

Opening her pocketbook, she held up the key.

"May I check the number inscribed on it?"

"Of course." She handed it to him. He looked it over. "Thank you," she said as he handed it back. "I understand there is a password as well."

"Indeed, there is."

She leaned forward to whisper it. "*Mon chou.*"

He did not so much as twitch, let alone crack a smile. "Very good, Miss Levett." He stood and went to open the door. "Come in, Baker."

The young man returned, carrying a small chest. He placed it on the desk in front of her and bowed.

Falkirk stood. "We will give you a few moments alone."

"Thank you."

The door closed behind them, and she sat a moment in silence. After determining they were not going to rush back, she fitted the key and opened the chest.

A small, square box lay within. Taking it out, she drew a deep breath and opened it.

The breath went out of her at once. The two lockets lay within, sparkling in the light from the window. Picking up the first, she touched the portrait diamond with awe. Large and translucent, it allowed the image of a very young King George IV, then the Prince of Wales, to show through. More diamonds surrounded it, and together they made one half of the hinged locket. Being careful with the latch, she opened it and saw the portrait inside in more vivid color, mounted on gold.

She held a piece of history in her hand. A gift given by a king to the woman he publicly declared to be his one true love.

And next to it ... the last of the triple set. A portrait of a lovely woman with arching eyebrows and a sharp nose that Kara recognized at once. Her large, elaborate coiffure was tied with a ribbon, and the infant she held in her arms had grabbed hold of the ends. The child reached out, displaying the bright ribbons as if to show the viewer.

Anne. Niall's mother, as an infant.

Kara's heart clenched at the thought of taking these pieces out of here, of taking the risk that the League of Dissolution might actually get their hands on them. She'd hoped to come in carrying the counterfeits with her. She could've gone through the motions, left the real ones locked away here, and departed again with the fakes and a greatly increased chance of passing them off as genuine.

But the counterfeit portraits were not quite done, and Ansel Wells was fussing about being rushed. He'd sworn they would be ready in time for the switch tonight, but Niall had decided they needed to have the real ones nonetheless, both in case they were needed and because the League knew where they were.

Kara closed the box again and pulled a black scarf from her bag. Wrapping it up, she tucked the box in the bag and had just got to her feet when the door opened again.

"Thank you so much for your help, Mr. Falkirk. I've left the key with the chest on the desk." She gave him a curtsy. "It was lovely to see you again."

He returned the sentiments, and she took her leave. She was halfway across the marble floor when a loud, clattering bang startled her. It came from a closet at the junction of a side corridor. A woman stood there with the door open. She wore a floppy mobcap, faded skirts, and a patchy shawl. Several glass bottles rolled around at her feet.

Kara hurried over to help her.

"Oh dear. Oh dear. Now, don't you go staining your fine gloves with me bottles of cleaner, ma'am."

"Let me help you." Kara set the bag down and began to gather the scattered bottles.

"Oh, it's just me own special concoction. Takes the dirt right off any surface, I assure you! I brewed up a batch this morning and thought to deliver them to all the homes and businesses I keep clean."

"There you are." Kara stood with a smile. "That's all of them. And allow me to say that you do a fine job here. The place fairly sparkles."

The woman tittered, bobbed her head, and thanked her again. Kara left her and hurried out. No one stopped her or called her back, and none of the fine men working there noticed that her black bag now resided in the charwoman's storage closet.

DOWN THE STREET and around the corner, Niall peeled off the brown coat and donned a shorter, tighter one of green. He added a leather cap and pulled it low. At the horses' heads, Rob donned matching garments.

"Thank you for your help, Miss Lowe." Niall handed the young woman out from the carriage. "You'll be all right on your own?"

"Absolutely. I'll have to head out now or be late to rehearsal.

Good luck tonight, Mr. Kier. I'll expect to see you all tonight."

"We'll do our best to make it happen." He nodded as she set off, and then he grinned as two very young men careened around the corner and pulled up short in front of him. "Gentlemen," he said in welcome.

"We're here, right on time," young Harold said. The boy had been a street urchin when he and Kara had first met him, without a home or family. Kara had found him a place and Niall had begun to use him to run messages and errands. The boy was rapidly becoming a real asset. He was also, noticeably, trying to correct his language.

"You're sure you can handle the coach in this traffic?" Niall asked the other young man.

"Ye can trust me," Davey Dobbs assured him. "Ma's got a feller now. The bloke's a jarvey. He's been teachin' me to drive— when he's not makin' eyes at her, that is."

Niall chuckled. "Very well, then. Keep a light hand and take the long route around before you take the rig back to the livery. Be sure the horses are well cared for, too."

"Aye, sir!" Both boys sprang up onto the coachman's box. Rob handed up the reins as Niall took a long crate from the seat inside. The men took the crate up between them as the carriage moved off. Each holding a side, they started back around the corner and toward Darrow's.

They'd only gone a short way before Rob pointed ahead with his chin. "Here she comes."

The charwoman moved slowly, her back slightly bent. She carried a small black bag, held in front of her, half buried in the folds of her voluminous skirts and her large, patchworked shawl.

"Two of them," Niall muttered. "Coming up behind her. Moving fast."

They did not change their pace as they slowly moved nearer. The men from the League—Niall thought they might be two of the men who had chased him earlier—came up to the charwoman, pulling her to a stop. He could hear only the murmur of their voices and her higher, querulous tone as she answered.

One of the men snatched the bag. She started to screech at him in curse-laden Danish. The other man held her back as the first emptied out the contents, dumping out several glass bottles filled with vinegar-colored liquid. He held the bag upside down and shook it, before running his hand along the inside.

The other man started to move his hands along the charwoman's skirts—and she truly began to shriek in defiance.

"'Ere now! Let the old crone alone, ye 'ear?" Rob shouted in his best—not very good—Cockney accent.

The charwoman shrieked again and pulled away, trying to gather up her bottles.

The second man grabbed her arm and spoke low.

They were starting to attract other attention.

"Let her loose!" Niall shouted. He and Rob picked up their pace, keeping their caps low and the crate between them.

Another man stopped at the old woman's side. "Here now. Are these men molesting you, ma'am?"

"They're tryin' to steal me cleaner," she said harshly, clutching bottles to her chest. "It's me own concoction. I make it meself. You give it back!" she shouted. "Every last bottle!"

The two League men exchanged glances and backed away, setting off the way they'd come.

The stranger said a few soothing words and moved on as Niall and Rob approached. From beneath the drooping mobcap, Gyda grinned at them.

"Turner was coming into the bank as I was leaving," she told them. "He should have the box out of the closet by now and be on his way back to Josie's." She straightened, stretching out her back. "Now, where's Kara?"

Chapter Seventeen

S HE ALMOST MADE it. She'd passed the spot where Niall had dived into the carriage and gone a few doors further before she realized one of the League men was sauntering after her.

She did not change her pace. She kept close to a pair of gentleman walking together ahead of her and discussing import imbalances. When a larger group passed them, going the other way, she waited until they were between her and her follower. Glancing at the traffic, she darted out into the street. She was nearly at the other side when she saw another man eyeing her and moving toward her on this side.

Gritting her teeth, she kept going. Dash it all, it would be harder to lose them on this side, due to the proximity of the river. Her heart sank as she spotted another man ahead of her. This one grinned as he strolled toward her.

Kara turned abruptly onto Villers Street and started to run. Halfway to Duke Street, she ran past an alley that cut back east, instead of west, as she'd been moving. Sliding to a halt, she ducked in. A peek out showed her pursuers hadn't turned into the street yet. She pulled out her hatpin, tore off her jaunty hat, and tossed it as hard as she could throw, in the direction of the river. It hit a wall about ten feet further down Villers Street and landed with an edge of the brim tilted up against the wall. Briefly, she mourned it. It was one of her favorites. But if it gave her a chance to escape, then the sacrifice was worth it.

Ducking back into the alley, she ran until she reached a broken, discarded wooden box. Crouching down behind it, she waited.

Pounding footsteps. She breathed a sigh of relief as they hurried past the mouth of the alley before they paused. She imagined her pursuer taking up her hat and thinking she must have lost it as she ran. She heard nothing else for a long moment, then two more sets of footsteps thundered past. There was a murmur of voices as they conferred, then nothing more.

She waited a full minute before she stood and crept along the alley, heading east and being careful to avoid touching or stepping on anything that might make a sound. The lane ended when it met Buckingham Street. Pausing, she peeked out. No one, in either direction. Across the way, another lane led further east. She breathed deeply, checked one more time, then darted across and into the new alley.

No shouts. No sign of pursuit. Breathing easier, she kept going, making her way to the end of this lane. Dash it! There was no lane across the narrow street. To the right lay Duke Street and likely at least one of her pursuers. To the left, the street narrowed further, but she could see the outlet and realized it led back to the Strand.

She hesitated. There might still be League men on the Strand. But if she could get across the busy thoroughfare, there would be more streets and warrens to lose herself in.

Sucking in a breath, she turned left and ran. She'd just reached the narrowed bit when she heard a shout behind her. It spurred her to go faster. They were still a good distance away. She burst out onto the pavement on the Strand and headed east again, watching for a break in the traffic.

From across the Strand came another yell. Another of the men from this morning. He'd seen her. Behind her, two of the others poured out of the alley in her wake.

Cursing again, she started to run. She needed to cross, but the man on the other side was keeping pace with her.

The foot traffic was busier than it had been this morning. She had to dodge and weave as she ran. She was starting to attract attention. Pounding feet sounded behind her. She ran harder.

A hack, also moving east, slowed in the street. "Miss Levett!" A man's voice. She kept going, without looking.

The hack pulled over just ahead of her. She veered away. A man poked his head out. "Miss Levett? Is that you?"

Detective Caden. She pulled up short.

"I've been looking for you everywhere," he scolded. "Miss Levett, I've made some discoveries. I think you may be in danger."

She managed not to laugh. One of the men behind her gave a shout. She looked over her shoulder, then back to the detective. She had no desire to hear what he had to say, but ...

His gaze followed where hers had gone. "It appears you might be in some trouble now." He opened the door. "Come on, then." He sounded disapproving again.

Heaving a sigh, she ran over and climbed in.

He thumped the roof. "Drive on!"

Breathing heavily, she settled back. "Thank you."

He folded his arms. "I think it's time we had a conversation."

⟫⟫⟩⟨⟨⟨

"POUNDER, THESE ARE exquisite. Perfect in every aspect." Niall held the counterfeit lockets up and gazed at his friend in gratitude. "You have gone above and beyond, my friend. And no one has seen them?"

"No, one, though I 'bout busted a gut wantin' to show 'em off." Pounder held up a hand. "I resisted, though."

"Thank you. I'll throw in an extra fee for painful discretion," Niall declared. "If I weren't in such a tearing hurry, I'd take you out, get you roaring drunk, and weasel out the name of the man who does your paste." He shook his head. "It's genius, all of it."

Pounder grinned. "Finish your business, then come back and I'll take you up on that offer."

"It's a deal."

Niall shook his friend's hand and left the docks, rushing back to Josie's apartments. Gyda answered his knock. "Is she back?" he demanded as he came through the door.

"Not yet." Gyda looked serious. "Did you get them?"

"Yes. And the portraits?"

"Done. Let's put them together."

"You do it." Niall thrust the package at her. "No doubt your hand is steadier than mine right now." He moved into the sitting room and stared into Turner's worried face. "It's Friday. She's dropped out of communication. Where's your planned meeting spot?"

"The Screaming Eagle."

Niall pursed his lips. "It's not Thursday, so the crowd will not be as thick." The butler looked surprised that Niall was familiar with the pub's unusual schedule. He didn't elaborate on the night Kara had taken him to the place. "It's as good a spot as any to make the trade. What time is your planned meeting?"

"Four o'clock."

"Then let's send the League a message naming the back courtyard of the Eagle as the spot for the trade. If Kara doesn't show up here or there by four o'clock, the odds are high they have her. We'll set the meeting for five o'clock. Perhaps they'll bring her along."

"And perhaps they'll keep her somewhere in that damned labyrinth of theirs, as insurance," Gyda said.

"They might." Niall held his calm, though the thought set his blood to boiling in fury and fear. "And if they do, we will deal with it. Right now, all we can do is wait to see if she makes it back to us and make plans to see Stayme safe."

Turner cleared his throat. "Using the Screaming Eagle is a

good idea. There are a couple of features of that back courtyard that we can put to use. There used to be a magician that practiced his new tricks there on Thursday nights. He made several changes that could be useful to us." Sitting down at the table, he roughed out a sketch and marked the spots he meant.

Niall nodded. "Yes. Good. We'll use them. But perhaps we should manufacture a few of our own."

"They will be sure to scout out the place before the meeting," Rob said. "You should make your preparations before the message is delivered."

"Yes. What I have in mind shouldn't be hard to set up. The fence around the back courtyard, they'll be sure to post someone behind it, yes?"

"It's what I would do," Turner agreed.

"Then why don't we set up a surprise for them?" Niall described his idea and made appropriate marks on the map. Then he looked up and around at the small collection of his ragtag army. Turner, Gyda, and Rob. Kara's absence felt like an ache. "We need reinforcements. It might come down to a fight to get Stayme away safe."

"Stealthy reinforcements would be best," Turner mused. "The element of surprise is always an advantage. It would be best if we can make them look like part of the usual landscape of the tavern." He paused. "Tom is one of Bluefield's footmen. He's seen a bit of what's been happening. He could be disguised as part of the staff."

"Or a deliveryman," Niall said. "If he carries in kegs or crates, we could tuck weapons in them."

"Beth wants to help," Gyda said. "She feels a sense of responsibility for Sally's death. She wants a chance for redemption."

"She's in no way to blame," Niall replied.

"No. But you know you or I would feel the same," Gyda said firmly. "She deserves the chance to help."

Niall sighed. "Fine, then, but find her a task out of the way. She's a gentle soul."

"I think she might surprise you," Gyda said. "But I'll arrange something."

"We should ask Stayme's staff if they might lend assistance," Niall said, thinking out loud. "If Watts is recovered, I suspect he'll want a bit of his own back. And if I know Stayme, some of his other staff will possess some … unusual skills that might come in handy."

Gyda sat forward. "That's a good use for Beth, right there. If the League is watching Stayme's house, getting a message to them might be tricky. We can send Beth in the back, with a delivery to the kitchen."

"Perfect," Niall agreed.

"I'll take the message to the League," Rob volunteered. "They likely have a new watcher outside Boyd's Yard. I'll deliver it to him."

"Let's go to the Eagle first, the two of us, and see that our arrangements are made. I'll come back here, then, while you drop the message. Just be sure to get out of there quickly," Niall ordered him. "I don't want them to grab you, too."

"They won't," Rob promised. "I'll make my way straight back to the pub afterward and wait for you all, rather than risk being followed back here."

Niall looked around at his friends. "Thank you all," he said quietly.

"We'll get them back, safe and sound," Gyda vowed.

"All of us safe and sound," Niall added.

Rob stood. "Maybe we're worried about Kara for nothing. She might just have been delayed. Perhaps she'll be back when you return."

Niall nodded. "I damned well hope so."

"DETECTIVE FRYE STILL wants you nowhere near his case, Miss

Levett. I haven't told him about our little foray to visit Lady Marston."

Kara lifted her chin. "I have been nowhere near the viscountess since we left her home together, sir."

"That's well enough, but your name has once again turned up in my investigation."

"I don't know why it should."

"Bridget Carter."

She held her expression carefully blank.

"*Bridget. Carter.* We spoke to her. Lady Marston's maid."

"Oh, yes."

Detective Caden sighed. "The maid left the lady's service the same morning that we questioned her."

"I heard as much."

"The girl returned to her uncle's establishment to work in his taproom. *You* were seen there, looking for her, that same night."

She said nothing.

"Why were you there, Miss Levett?"

Kara relented. "I thought her answer to your questions about the knife was carefully crafted to hold back information. I wanted to ask her more about it."

"Despite my orders to stay away," he said on a sigh. "Well? Did you? Ask her?"

"She didn't wish to speak with me. Someone had already been there before me. They frightened her."

"Someone?"

"Some men, was all she said of them." She raised a brow at him. "I suppose it wasn't you, then?"

"It was not," he ground out. "But no one has seen Bridget Carter since that very same night."

"Oh no." She sank back against the squabs, her mind racing. She wasn't ready yet to share anything else with the detective. "Do you believe those men found her? Took her? Who are they?"

He leaned forward. "Have you seen Bridget Carter since that night?"

"No. That poor girl." Her eyes widened. "She's as good as dead, isn't she?" *And long live Mariana Smith.* "Yet you mocked me for wishing to question Lady Marston. And here's another of her maids, possibly in mortal peril."

"That's what I'm trying to discover. If the girl is in danger."

"Well, someone should warn her ladyship's next maid. It appears to be a dangerous position."

"It's no joking matter, Miss Levett."

"I am not joking, Detective Caden."

Sitting back, he blew out a breath. "Listen. These men … they are dangerous. They weren't the same ones who were just chasing you, were they?"

"I should hope not. Street ruffians? I swear, they hunt like a pack of wolves. They waited until I was separated from Turner, then closed in on me. Two behind and one ahead. But why would they be the same men who were looking for Bridget? It doesn't make sense. Why would they want me?"

"Perhaps they also discovered that you spoke to the maid that night?"

She drew a breath. "Do you think so? Heavens, what must that maid know about them, that they would be so desperate? To chase so slim a connection as me?"

"Another thing I should like to discover."

"Well, I'm sorry you have all wasted so much time and effort. I cannot help any of you find Bridget Carter." *Carefully crafted to hold back information.*

He met her gaze, searching her expression, for a long moment. She held her own gaze steady until he looked away, then she glanced out the window.

"Wait!" She scooted closer and stared out. They were moving across the river on the Westminster Bridge. "What is this? Where are we going?"

"We are on the way to my rooming house," he told her. "I have something I want you to see."

"No. I am sorry. I cannot." She had to get back. "I have an

appointment that I cannot miss."

He rolled his eyes as if he didn't believe her. "I can assure you, I have no designs on your person, Miss Levett."

"Such a flatterer you are, sir. But I meant what I said. I have an exceptionally busy day today."

"You cannot spare a few moments? Not even to help your friend, Mr. Niall Kier?"

"What has Niall got to do with this lost maid?"

"I'm thinking more that he has something to do with the men who are after the girl."

She snorted. "Ridiculous."

He sat forward. "I think we both know that Niall Kier is not in Oslo."

She cast him another look of disbelief. "Has he been seen in London? I highly doubt it." When he said nothing, she sighed. "And your lack of answer is an answer, sir."

"These people seem to operate in the shadows. I wish to know if he is hiding there with them. I want you to take a look at something and tell me if you recognize it."

She let out a breath of exasperation. "Very well, but only if you *hurry*. And allow me to take the cab back right afterward. I really have to get back."

"Agreed."

They continued on the busy street for several minutes before the carriage made a turn and slowed. The scene outside had turned more residential. As they pulled into a neat and tidy avenue, the driver guided the carriage to the side of the street. Kara looked out at the respectable-looking rooming house, with wide stairs and a tiny garden in front, planted with shrubs and dotted with flowerbeds, empty in this season. "It might be best if I stay here in the coach. You can bring down whatever it is you wish for me to see."

"Nonsense. My landlady visits her sister every Friday. There will be no one to sneer at you." He paused. "And I'd rather this object stay hidden. The fewer eyes upon it, the better."

If he'd meant to pique her curiosity, it had worked. She glanced about at the empty street, sighed once more, and agreed.

She kept her head down as she followed him into the building. Caden had the rooms in the left, back corner, one flight up. He unlocked the door and held it open, giving her an ironic bow as he gestured for her to proceed him.

She looked about with a curious eye. They were comfortable rooms, with stuffed furniture and sturdy wooden accents. Large windows let in a good deal of light. Newspapers and books were stacked everywhere, as well as several dirty dishes.

"Forgive the mess." He strode to the bookshelf and took out a leather-bound ledger. With a glance at the closed door, he held it out to her. "Have you ever seen this symbol?"

"No." She had only heard it described. Her heart began to pound. It was the map of Europe with a series of cracks imposed over it. She looked up to watch Caden's face. "What does it mean?"

He shook his head, giving nothing away. "Again, something I hoped to hear from you."

Kara began to feel uneasy again. He was as cagey as she was, stating facts without revealing the truth. But he was a detective with Scotland Yard, for heaven's sake. What had he to hide?

"I fear you give me too much credit, sir."

"I doubt that." He frowned at her, then appeared to come to a decision. "I'll tell you the truth, Miss Levett. I think this is part of something far larger than a maid's death in the woods."

She stilled. "There is nothing small about Sally Doughty's death."

"One maid, without even one person to mourn her?" He dismissed Sally with a toss of his hand. "I'm talking about the rise and fall of nations. Intrigue at the highest levels."

"Where did you get that?" She nodded toward the ledger.

"It was passed to me with a cryptic note."

"You haven't shared it with Detective Frye or anyone else at Scotland Yard?"

"I cannot go in empty-handed, spouting about plots against the government. I need *evidence* before I take it in. I was hoping you would have something for me."

It made sense. Still, there was something ... She still did not quite believe him. She shook her head. "I'm sorry."

For a moment, he looked furious. She took a step back. His brow cleared then. He ran a hand over his chin. "I can't help but feel you might have made yourself into a target, though. We must do what we can to ensure your safety. Here. Let me ..." He reached into his back pocket.

She didn't see what he pulled out until he grabbed her wrist and locked one end of a pair of cuffs around it.

"What are you doing?" The metal was cold on her wrist as she tried to pull away, but he dragged her relentlessly to an iron ring embedded in the side of his sturdy desk. "Release me at once!"

He hooked the other end of the cuffs into the ring. "I cannot."

She gasped in outrage as he put his hands on her waist and began to feel all the way around.

"Do not touch me! Let me go at once, Caden!"

"I've heard of your penchant for wearing a belt full of tools. I'm just making sure." He held up his hands and backed away. "I apologize. I need you to stay here while I see to several things. I am only trying to keep you from getting yourself into worse trouble."

"You cannot do this!" She drew herself up. "Do you forget Inspector Wooten? Do you doubt I could get an audience with the commissioners? I am not without friends, Caden. You will lose your position for this!"

He strode to the door before turning back to her, hesitating as the sun picked out red highlights in his hair. "Not if I break this case." He pulled his hat on. "It won't be for long. I'll come back and let you loose soon."

He just ... left. Kara heard the door lock behind him. Still in shock at this swift turn of events, she stared after him.

Chapter Eighteen

IT TOOK KARA a minute or two to recover from the extreme absurdity of the situation. The feeling of disquiet in her gut was growing. Caden had a smooth explanation for everything, didn't he? He even had a logical reason for *this*. But there was something ... It all struck a wrong chord.

She looked down at the metal cuff around her wrist and scoffed. Standard issue to every London policeman. Child's play. She'd practiced getting out of these a hundred times. And though she wasn't wearing her tool belt or even her specially modified skirts, she'd been busy with most of her wardrobe. This bodice featured stiff, round piping on the fluted edges and on the collar. She turned the right side of the collar up, picked out a flap in the edge, and slid out a thin lockpick. She had another on the left side, but the cuffs wouldn't even require it. It took less than a minute for her to be free. She considered taking the cuffs, but with a sneer, she left them hanging. Let him find them like that.

She started for the door, but then stopped. There was something not right about the detective. Beyond the feeling he gave her, what sort of policeman installed an iron ring to his desk at home? It was practically designed for keeping a prisoner. Detectives could not interrogate suspects at home. She wouldn't doubt the man was ambitious, but it seemed like something more sinister might be going on here.

She turned back to the desk. Taking a seat, she went through it all. Every drawer, even the secret one, which contained nothing more than some flowery love letters. Someone *else's* love letters. Was he blackmailing someone? She wouldn't be surprised.

Nothing else. Disappointed, she went to the window for a quick moment's thought. There was nothing to see but a functional back garden. She did notice there was a woodshed situated below, and just a few feet to the right of his windows. Likely near the kitchen doors. She couldn't help but consider he might use it as an alternate entrance or exit.

Turning back to face the room, she let her gaze run around it. The bedroom, perhaps? But she spotted the stuffed easy chair, with a matching ottoman. The ideal place for a man to sit and relax with his feet up. The greatest number of books, journals, and dishes were piled around it, on the floor and on the table next to it. His favorite lounging spot?

She went over and sat down. Put her feet on the ottoman. The chair was situated so that she could easily view the door and the windows. Coincidence? Crumbs littered the table. The book on the top of the stack was a treatise on the historic Congress of Vienna, after the end of the Napoleonic Wars. She put her fingers between the cushions. Nothing. But as she was tilted away from the table, the light hit the side of it. Her eyes widened. Was that a seam in the wood?

She explored. Yes. She pulled with her fingernails, and a false panel fell outward, leaving a shallow space built into the table. A folded paper lay inside.

She pulled it out. It was marked with the same image he'd shown her on the ledger. The symbol of the League of Dissolution, if Niall was right. Under the image, someone had scrawled something.

The spheres of influence will shatter and collapse.

What in heaven's name did that mean? Kara folded the paper

again and tucked it in her bodice. Not until then did she realize there was something else in the shallow hiding spot. More than one. Small, shining objects. She reached in with a forefinger and pulled one out. It was a small, translucent gem. Like a diamond, but not a real gemstone, surely. Why would Caden have diamonds hidden away? She ran a finger over the top ... and her heart stopped. There was a pattern carved in relief at the top of the jewel. A starburst. Or the rays of a sun ...

Her hands shaking, she pulled out the rest of them. With a sudden certainty, she knew what she was looking at. Nine in total. Two parents and seven sisters. The Pleiades. Apparently pried off the knife that Gyda had constructed for Beth. Presumably so that it wouldn't leave a distinctive mark the next time it was used.

The next time. Kara looked up at the door. Saw, in her mind's eye, Caden standing there, looking back at her with the sun searching out the red highlights in his hair. What was it Bridget had said? The big man Malina had given the knife to, he'd turned away to hide his face when Bridget encountered him, but the fire had picked out the red tint in his dark hair.

Malina had given *Detective Caden* the knife. The knife used to kill Sally Doughty. She started to tremble. He'd done it. He'd killed that poor maid and then stood right in front of Kara today and trivialized her murder. He was investigating his own crime!

Kara clapped a hand over her mouth. She'd taken him to question Malina, when he'd been the one in collusion with the viscountess all along! How amused they must have been.

Flushing, her hands still shaking, she poured the gems into her pocket and stood. Turning to face the table at the side of the chair, she held her breath and pulled out the drawer.

It was there. The knife. Beth's knife, with its curved blade and blue-stained handle. And marks on it where those stars had been pried off. She willed her hands to stop shaking. Carefully, she picked it up and gripped it tight.

She had to get out of here. The rustle of paper at her bosom made her pause again. He wasn't trying to break this case! He was trying to cover it up. He'd wanted to see how much she knew. He wasn't going to let her go. She had to leave. Now.

Moving silently to the door, she began to crack it open, but stopped when she heard low voices in the corridor. Moving over and peering out the crack, she saw Caden down the passage at the top of the stairs. Fury flooded her, and her hand tightened on the knife as she saw it was Malina he was whispering furiously with.

"You have to do it," Caden said, his tone fierce and low. "I have to find out how much she knows before I can turn her over. And who *else* knows. She won't talk. She doesn't trust me."

"And you think she will trust me?" scoffed Malina with a low and bitter laugh.

"No. She despises you. But her anger just might make her careless. You can taunt her." Caden sneered. "You're good at it. Make her angry enough and she just might grow reckless."

"And how am I supposed to explain my presence in your rooms?" Malina asked.

"Pretend to break in. Tell her you are looking for information on where Bridget Carter went. You heard I was looking for her and might have found something. The Levett woman is trapped and already riled up. You can shake her up a bit and get her to say what she knows about where that damned girl has gone."

"I cannot believe you have let that little maid outsmart you. Now I have to come in and clean up your mess?"

"It's *your* mess, if you care to recall!"

Malina tossed her head. "That girl is a loose end that needs to be cleaned up. Before it all begins."

"Do you think I do not know that? They've already taken over the acquisition of the miniatures. That was supposed to be *my* contribution!" He sounded furious—and worried. "I'm getting squeezed out. Now I have to find a new way to prove my worth. If I don't, then I'll become a loose end. And you know what that means."

"If you had been the one to find Niall, none of this would

have happened!" She flung the whispered accusation at him.

He glared at her. "*They* didn't find him. He found them!"

"It doesn't matter."

He whispered a filthy curse. "I should have taken him when I had the chance."

"If only you hadn't been so determined to preserve your precious reputation."

Malina's voice had begun to rise, and Caden shushed her. "It was too big a gamble. He's slippery, that one, and if he'd somehow got away, he would have revealed everything I've been up to. I would have lost my career."

"You are going to lose your *life*, if you don't fix your relationship with them."

"That's exactly why I need you to do this! Unlike you, I cannot seduce my way into the inner circle."

He spun on his heel and walked away a few steps. Kara froze, but he turned back again and moved in close to Malina's upturned, glaring face.

"Listen. This just might fix it. Fix it *all*. I'm balancing on a knife edge here, but if it works out, if they are successful and I have been a part of it, then it will be worth it. My star will rise. They will see to it. And the damned ladder I'm stuck on will turn to stairs I can sprint up. Maybe even all the way to the top! I just need to turn the Levett woman over. They have decided they want her. But first I have to understand who knows what, so I can clean it all up."

Malina was shaking her head. "It's too dangerous. She's wily too. And devious. You cannot turn her over to them. What if she turns them against you? Takes your place? I think you should kill her, as well as the maid. Convince them she was a threat, and they will appreciate you removing her."

"No! I cannot. She wants her. God knows why. And I have to deliver her. But I'm afraid it still won't be enough." He leaned over the railing and moaned. "Just go in there, Malina. See what you can get out of her."

Malina gave him a crafty look. "If you expect me to do your dirty work, then you will owe me. I want—"

"Owe you?" He snorted. "I killed your damned husband for you!"

"For me?" she spat. "You didn't want him getting the glory of finding the lockets before you did!"

"And you didn't want to stay leg-shackled to a man who wouldn't fight for you to gain acceptance in his family or Society! Enough! You get in there and you do as I say, or I'll contact Marston's family and tell them your pregnancy is nothing but a charade! That you plan on finding some unwanted brat to pass off as your own!"

Kara eased the door closed. Anger roiled inside of her. She didn't need to hear any more. She needed to get out. But she'd never make it past them both to get to the stairs. She headed for the window.

A sudden thought had her veering to the settee, where she grabbed up a discarded neckcloth. She wrapped it around the knife, stuffed it in her pocket over the paste jewels, and hoped they would all stay safely inside.

Slowly, quietly, she raised the window. Throwing her legs over, she sat, balancing on the sill, then jumped to land on the roof of the woodshed. From there she went backward, hanging over the edge and jumping down. A quick glance around and she headed for a gate leading into a lane on the side of the house.

She'd just rounded the corner when she heard a shout of anger echo from the open window. She put on a burst of speed and dashed across the avenue in front of the house, skirting between two homes on the other side. Behind them lay a mews lane. She followed it, searching her brain, trying to work out the way back to the main thoroughfare of Westminster Bridge Road. It should just be a short distance, ahead and to the left, if she'd calculated correctly.

The distant ringing of church bells brought her up short. Three bells? Three o'clock? Already? She broke into a run once more. Dash it! Turner might be waiting for her at the Screaming Eagle, but she'd never make it there before four o'clock. Damn Caden for taking her so far away! Would Turner wait? No, they likely all thought the League had her. And he would want to help with the arrangements for the meeting. They had to make it before sundown. But where? Had the League sent word? She had to make it back to Josie's apartments. Quickly, too, before they all left to make the trade for Stayme and she was left behind.

⋙⋘

GYDA AND TOM, Bluefield's footman, were arguing over who should don false facial hair and disguise themselves as the tapster behind the bar. The owner of the Screaming Eagle had agreed to clear the place of his own staff and customers. *Private Party,* said the sign on the door. Niall paid the man for the loss of the afternoon's business and would count it a bargain, as long as he got Stayme and Kara back safe.

For Kara had not come back to Josie's rooms. Nor had she arrived at the Eagle at the appointed time. Niall conquered the panic growing in his gut by ignoring it, seeing to the arrangements they had planned, moving like one of Kara's automatons, and speaking only when he must.

It was Beth who had found a little case of theatrical makeup in Josie's rooms. It also contained assorted hairpieces and accessories. She'd brought it along. "I helped run some of our village church's reenactments," she said with a shrug. Her gaze kept straying to Rob McRae as she held a couple of faux mutton-chops and waited to see to whom she would be applying them. "You would look fine with these," she told Niall's friend. "And they are a good match for your hair."

"Thank ye, lass, but I'll be stayin' by Niall's side," he told her.

"Oh, of course." She turned away, but not before her eyes filled with tears.

"Here now!" Rob said, dismayed. "I didna mean to make ye cry."

"No. No. You didn't," she said thickly. "I'm just not used to people acting so *dedicated* to one another."

Rob looked to Niall, his panicked gaze asking for help, but Gyda moved in to enfold the girl in a hug. "Get used to it, my dear, for you are here, are you not? You are one of us now."

Beth only cried harder then. Gyda patted her and gave Rob a nod. "Don't worry. They are happy tears."

Rob, an uneasy look on his face, backed away. "I'll just go double-check the setup in the courtyard."

"The whiskers match my hair, as well," Tom declared. "And Miss Winther fits in the cask easier than I would."

"Fine, Tom," Gyda said with bad grace as Niall followed Rob outside.

"Are we ready, do ye think?" Rob asked.

"We will be soon," Niall said. He was watching one of Stayme's young footmen, who had volunteered to help, as Watts was still suffering vertigo after the blow to his head. The boy was shuffling around the chairs and other odd pieces that served as seating during the Thursday night performances out here. They were all stacked haphazardly against the wall, and he was rearranging them, making himself a hidey-hole among benches and buckets and behind a large stump. Niall walked over to him. "Hide yourself well. They will likely come with a number of men. You stay in there as a witness. Watch it all and report to Miss Levett, or Scotland Yard, or whoever comes afterward, if we don't make it."

The boy looked serious. "Aye, sir."

Molly, Stayme's kitchen maid, had come as well. She was in the tavern's kitchen, sorting through knives, looking for the right ones to hide upon her person. "Just in case," she'd said.

"Gyda," Niall called.

She walked out, tying up her braid as she came.

"Is Tom ready?"

"Beth's tying his apron on now."

Turner beckoned her from the dilapidated stage set up in the corner. On one side of it, he lifted up a fence board that had been loosened at the bottom and hinged halfway up.

"That magician must have been tiny," Gyda said. "It's a good thing Stayme is not a big man."

Turner handed her a small pot of glue and a flyer advertising a comedic act at the Empire Theatre, similar to others posted around the fenced courtyard. "Cover the hinges on the other side with this and hide the pot," he told her.

"And get yourself settled comfortably in that cask," Niall said. "You might have to wait in there a while." He made a face. "In truth, the odds of getting Stayme up there and in reach are low, but we'll try. If the lane back there is clear, time your moment, pull him through, and get the viscount out of here—especially if fighting breaks out. But Gyda, be careful. They'll likely post at least one man back there."

"I know. That's why that cask was an ingenious idea. The panel you made removable is utterly silent. I fit in there, even with my trusty axe." She held up the weapon. "Don't worry, I'll take care of anyone that ends up back there."

"Be careful," Niall told her.

She ducked through, reached back for the flyer and the glue, then popped her head back in to grin at Niall. "It won't be a problem. Chin up. We'll get them both back."

Beth came from inside, tucking a towel into the waist of her apron. "Get ready! They are outside."

"How many?" Niall asked. "Do you see Kara or Stayme?"

"Two carriages. And only men spotted, so far." She looked sober. "Quite a few of them."

Niall watched her duck back in. He stepped up onto the small stage and exchanged glances with Rob and Turner. Together, they turned to face the coming trouble.

Chapter Nineteen

KARA POUNDED UP the stairs to Josie's apartments. Relief rushed through her when she found the door unlocked. She pushed through and rushed down the hall to the sitting room, only to find it deserted.

"They were already gone when I arrived, just a few minutes ago." Josie came in from the bedroom, carrying a fine woolen coat.

"No!" Kara slammed a fist onto the back of the sofa. "No! They've gone already to make the swap for Stayme?"

"I assume so."

Kara looked around frantically. "Did they leave word of where they were going?"

"No, but they wouldn't, would they? It wouldn't be wise."

Kara knew Josie was right, but she *hated* the feeling of helplessness descending upon her. "I can't miss it! I've already missed the appointment with Turner, and he's likely gone with them. How can I find them? They might need me! They will likely need all the help they can get!"

"I'm very sorry." The actress gripped her arm in sympathy. "I would have helped myself, had I been here in time." She sighed. "But it's just as well. My patron, the man who pays for all of this ..." She waved her hand. "He's summoned me. And I really should answer."

"Of course. Thank you for everything you've already done, for giving us a safe space ..." Kara's words trailed away. Frustration swamped her. "I can scarcely stand the thought ... I cannot just wait about for it all to be over! I have to contribute something!"

So many images were running through her head. All the things that might happen. The things that might go wrong. All the players of this dastardly game gathered for this monumental move, and she wasn't—

She stopped. Her brain veered off in an entirely new direction. Everyone likely would be at this swap. All of her friends and allies. The leaders of the League, and likely a great many of their men. What better time to find out more about them? Perhaps this was the perfect time for her to—

"Wait!" She rushed into the bedroom. Turner had brought her things ... Yes! There it was, folded neatly along with a couple of other gowns. The outfit of ivory, scarlet, and gold that she'd worn to Malina's home. "Josie!" She rushed back out. "Do you have a heavy veil I can borrow? Not black." Kara highly doubted Malina was wearing her plain widow's weeds when she went to visit her lover in the League, whoever it might turn out to be.

"I do." Josie brightened at the thought of being useful. "I have one in off-white, I do believe. You are welcome to it."

"Excellent! And thank you so very much. Can I ask you to help me into this gown? We'll move quickly, so as not to hold you up."

"Nonsense. I see you have come up with a notion." Josie smiled. "Let's get you dressed and then I'll drop you off. My gentleman friend is sending his carriage." Her mouth twitched. "It will do him good to wait a bit."

"Yes, thank you!" An idea struck Kara, and she embraced it, even if it did carry a bit of a snide tone with it. "And if you don't mind, might we make a quick stop along the way?"

THE FIRST TO stroll outside was the clerk. Niall watched as he was followed by two men. They moved to stand on either side of him as he faced Niall, Rob, and Turner on the stage. More men filed out, six more, in fact. They fanned out behind the first three.

"Where is Stayme?" Niall asked.

The clerk gestured. "Inside. Sitting at one of the tables. Under watch."

"Bring him out," Niall ordered him.

"Not until I have the lockets in my possession. Where are they?"

"I have them. But I want Stayme out here before I turn them over."

The clerk didn't answer. For a long moment, they all just stood and eyed each other. The man on the clerk's left wore a gentleman's clothes and a long, heavy coat. But the effect was as if they'd dressed a bull. He was broad, with a short, thick neck that made it look like his head rested squarely on his shoulders. And on his head was a snug woolen cap. It looked like something his grandmother had knitted for him.

The man on the clerk's right was his opposite. Shorter and slender, he was dressed like a prince, with a sable-trimmed coat, fine leather gloves, and a hat that must have cost enough to feed a family for a year.

Suddenly, Niall sighed. He let his shoulders fall. "Why am I talking to the League of Lackeys?" he demanded. "Where is she?"

"She?" The clerk scoffed. "Have you lost your woman?" He looked around. "Both of your women, it would seem."

"I think you know who I mean. She. Her. The one who is in charge of you boys."

The broad one spoke up. "No one is in charge. It is the point of a league. We are a coalition. Equals." His accent was thick and German.

"A coalition of dissolution?" Rob said scathingly. "What in bloody blazes is that supposed to mean?"

"The League of Dissolution is chaos," the thinner man said, and his English was tinged with an obvious Russian accent.

"The League is retribution," the German growled.

"The League is a pain in the arse," said Rob.

"Good." The German seemed satisfied with this.

"Nice hat." Rob snorted.

The Russian snickered.

The German glowered. "England is always so relentlessly *damp*."

"Ha! If you think London cold and damp, try traveling north a bit to Scotland," said Rob.

"You are weak like children," the Russian scoffed. "You do not know cold until you have wintered in Russia."

"Enough," Niall and the clerk said together.

"I cannot even see the old man," Niall said. "Do you take me for a fool?"

The clerk jerked his head, and one of the men behind him broke away to go inside. He came back to the door, hauling Lord Stayme by the arm. The old man's wrists were bound, but his back was straight. He narrowed his gaze at Niall and shook his head before he was yanked out of the doorway again.

"Thank you." Niall inclined his head. "But I would prefer to turn the lockets over to the woman in charge."

"No one is in *charge*," the German said again, aggrieved. "Do Englishmen never listen?"

"Quiet!" The clerk took a step toward the stage. "You will give me the lockets or the viscount will die. Do you understand?"

Niall looked around, sighed, and pulled the box out of his coat. The clerk snatched it and opened it. He held his breath, but the man's eyes grew large. He seemed to find nothing to question. "Magnificent," he breathed. Looking up at Niall, he grinned. "A bastard heir to the throne is one thing, but a bastard heir with gold and diamonds and a story of star-crossed lovers?

Oh, my dear Mr. Kier. You are about to become world famous."

The German chuckled. "And England, so proud, so mighty, so determined to expand its empire, and so arrogant as to poke about in the affairs of other nations—she is about to find she cannot even control her own populace."

Niall opened his mouth to speak, but the men were moving out from behind the first three and coming around to approach the stage. Immediately, Turner pulled out a pocket pistol. Rob crouched into a fighter's stance, the blade from his boot at the ready. Niall pulled out his own blade, reached out, grabbed the clerk by his neckcloth, and hauled him in close.

The clerk raised his hands, spread wide. "No. There is no reason for these dramatics. I have triple the number of your men, and more waiting in reserve. You cannot win. You can only see your friends harmed." His voice lowered. "You wanted to meet her. She wishes to speak with you, too. Tell your companions to lower their weapons. My men will only subdue them. No damage. You will come with us. You can have your questions answered, at last."

Niall stared, weighing the options and outcomes. "Stayme stays," he rasped. He wanted to ask about Kara, but he didn't dare tip his hand.

The clerk hesitated. "Very well," he said at last. "For now."

Niall let him go. "Stand down," he said clearly.

"But Niall—" Rob protested.

"He's right," Turner said. They had discussed this probability. He pocketed his pistol again, and one of the League men stepped up to pull his hands behind his back.

"No harm comes to them!" Niall barked as one snatched Rob's blade and another took a hold of him.

"No harm," the clerk agreed. "At least, we don't expect any. The effects we've seen with the usual substance have been mild. So far."

"Effects?" Niall asked, suddenly alarmed.

"Forget all that," the German suggested. "I'd rather see it

done the old-fashioned way." He glared at Rob. "This one could use a few bruises."

"I promised we would try it out," the clerk said.

"And I wish to see if it is as useful as the girl says," the Russian added. "Let's see how it works."

One of the men was securing Niall's arms, binding his wrists before him, even as another held a bottle of clear liquid over a cloth, sprinkling it liberally.

"What is he doing?" he demanded as the man went to stand before Rob. Restrained from behind, Rob could only struggle as the cloth was pressed to his face. He thrashed, his eyes wide, but he was held fast. It took only seconds before he stopped fighting. He blinked once. Twice. Then his eyes closed and he slumped down in his captor's arms.

Niall looked around wildly, but Turner was in the same state. The men laid them down across the stage. Niall stared in horror. "Are they ...?"

"Asleep," the clerk answered. "For a short time only. Let's go."

Niall was dragged to the taproom. He gasped to see Beth curled upon the floor and Tom being stretched out atop the bar by two League men.

"They will be fine," the clerk said as Niall stumbled to a halt. "Move." But he paused suddenly and turned to his men. "Where's the old man?"

They both glanced around in surprise.

"I ... He was right there," one said, gesturing to a table.

"This one resisted," the other said, indicating Tom. "It took both of us to put him out. The old man must have scarpered while we were busy with him."

"Then find him! Get going. He must have gone out the back!" The clerk gave Niall a harsh look. "He's coming back to the labyrinth, do you hear? Find him quickly!"

The men scrambled toward the back of the tavern as the clerk motioned to the men holding Niall. "Get him out there. She's waiting."

Niall was dragged outside. More men waited in the street and around a carriage, which sat with the door open.

The clerk gave him a push. "Get in."

Chapter Twenty

KARA, WEARING MALINA'S colors and carrying a small, square box, made it a good way into the labyrinth before she had trouble with a guard. They must have taken no small number with them to meet Niall. The thought did nothing to help her already rollicking nerves. But all she could do was hope her friends were all right. That, and discover all she could about their enemy.

She went in through Boyd's Yard, following the original path she and Niall had traveled the first time they chased a fugitive in here. She already knew where the traps were located on that way in. Avoiding them, she made her way to the odd internal warehouse constructed at the intersection of several buildings.

Niall had reported it had been emptied of the supplies they saw on their first foray, but now she noted that another stockpile had begun to grow.

She'd met a couple of yawning guards on the way in, but they nodded and let her pass. It was here in the makeshift warehouse, though, that she met her first challenge. A man moved to intercept her as she headed toward the elegant stone staircase on one side of the space.

She stopped, glared at him through the veil, and spoke in Malina's terse, disdainful tones. "I truly don't think you are so unwise."

The guard hesitated.

"Are you?" she demanded.

He stepped back, and she continued up the stairs.

Her eyes widened at the top. Here she reached the lush reception room Niall and Rob had described. The glass dome ceiling was spectacular, leaving it as bright as day in here, even so deep in the maze of buildings. Her destination was to the left. She passed through the ornate door into the counting room, avoiding the hinged panel of spikes lying beyond. Continuing on, she went straight through the more ornate office and into the parlor.

Here. She'd listened to Niall and Rob's description of the place and agreed that there must be a hidden door in here. She suspected it must lead to the real seat of power—the hidden lair where the leaders of the League lived and worked.

Setting her box on the small table near the window, she moved to the far wall and began her search. Surely the hidden door must be here? The wall behind her butted up to the office. The window wall had a narrow outside space before the next building began. The wall to her left contained the massive fireplace. So, must it not be here, ahead of her? She began to run her fingers along the wood trim, searching for a trigger.

"Well, this was a bold move."

She spun around to see a woman examining the contents of her box. "Miss Wilkes."

The lovely woman inclined her head. "Miss Levett. Oh, yes, I know it's you under there," she said in answer to the thought Kara had not even voiced. "You don't move like Malina at all. And she did describe your offending gown in great detail." She gestured. "I must say, it looks far better on you than she led me to believe."

"Thank you." Kara removed the veil.

"You are welcome. Malina does allow her petty jealousies to rule her. It's a shame, really. It will hold her back. It already has, if we must be honest. I just don't have time for all of that." Miss

Wilkes turned back to the box. "Yes, this was a bold move, merely showing up here. But you are alone, I assume?"

Kara didn't answer.

"Alone, then. Bold, but perhaps not wise."

"But you are alone here too, are you not?"

"Not really. We are never really alone in the labyrinth."

Kara decided to bluff. "Well, it seems we have a bit of privacy, in any case. Perhaps we can talk. I was hoping to see your laboratory. And perhaps you can come out to see mine?"

The other woman's eyes widened. "I almost believed you. You are rather better at this than Malina, aren't you? But I know why you must be here, Miss Levett, and you didn't expect to find me." She gestured toward the box. "These butter biscuits? They make a statement of their own. You are announcing without words that you know who you meant to find here."

Kara gave up the pretense. "And who leads here."

Miss Wilkes gave her a strange, wistful smile. "Ah, but what if you are wrong?"

"I'm not wrong, though. Am I?"

The smile now was not entirely pleasant. "No. You are not." Miss Wilkes picked up the box. "Well. You've come all this way. You might as well come all the way in."

Kara took a step back. "Thank you, but I think I'll just leave the box and go."

"No, no, my dear. It's too late for that. You're here. Presumably, you came for some answers. It's time you had them." The look on Miss Wilkes's face became positively predatory now. "And in any case, a shout from me and a dozen or so of our men will be on your heels. Some of them are quite ... uncivilized. You've already made fools out of a number of them. I can't guarantee they won't wish to take their revenge."

Kara watched her, weighing the chances that she was telling the truth.

"It takes a great many men to run a project like this. They work in shifts, you know, so we are never vulnerable. Just a shout, that's all it would take to rouse them." Miss Wilkes shrugged. "Much safer to stick to your original course." Beckoning, she stepped up onto the low hearth of the large fireplace, bent her head, stepped in—and disappeared.

Blinking, Kara followed. She paused at the hearth and peered inside. Logs were laid in anticipation of a blaze, but the firebox was utterly clean. And otherwise empty. It was so large that she barely had to duck her head to step in. But once she did, she understood. It was an illusion of perspective, the stones laid out to look, from the outside, as if the firebox was enclosed, as one would expect. But from here, she could see it was a mirage. To the left, a passage led out of the box. She ducked her head, stepped in, made a sharp right turn, and stepped out into another space.

"Oh my." It was a richly decorated space, elegant and lush. A fire burned merrily in a smaller, more functional hearth midway down the room. And here was another raised glass ceiling, this one in rectangular shape instead of a dome. Kara could tell the hour was advancing by the dimming light coming through. What time was it? How long until the other League members returned?

But Miss Wilkes was watching her expectantly, clearly waiting for a reaction.

Kara let her amazement show on her face. "You lot do well, don't you?"

"Indeed, and all earned by the might of our own brains," Miss Wilkes said proudly.

"And other people's fists," muttered Kara.

The other woman laughed. "Well, I'm sure it doesn't hold a candle to your great pile. Bluefield, it's called, isn't it?"

Kara took another step in. "I don't have a Rubens, in any case," she said, staring in fascination at the priceless painting hanging above a mahogany sideboard.

"Yes, well, Petra figured if it was good enough for Buckingham Palace, it was good enough for us."

"Petra?"

"Miss Scot, as you'll know her." Miss Wilkes set the box down on a low table in the midst of grouped seating that included a settee and some lovely Queen Anne chairs of walnut and ivory damask. "She truly did enjoy those butter biscuits, and she will appreciate the audacity of your statement." One of those fine, arched eyebrows rose. "How *did* you know it was her?"

Kara laid her veiled hat down on a table painted with a country scene, the surface covered with a glass overlay. "I caught a glimpse of her the night we all escaped your warehouse. It was from a sizable distance, but I thought I recognized a certain ... something in her manner."

"Yes, she does wear a haughty demeanor like a cape around her shoulders," Miss Wilkes said with a tinkling laugh.

"In any case, she watched us go without raising a fuss, without a word or deed. I knew, then, that only the leader of the League would make such a move."

"On the principle that the rest of us would be too afraid to take such a risk? You're not far off."

"Does she rule so harshly, then?"

"Strictly, not harshly. And we don't rule the League, but we do demand strict obedience."

"Is there a difference?"

"There is. Good pay and the chance to be a part of something."

"A part of something," Kara echoed. She knew how compelling such a thing could be.

"Yes. I know you understand. For you've done it yourself, haven't you? With your heroic butler at first, then with Niall Kier and Gyda Winther. A family. Created, not born."

A little unnerved at how much they knew about her, Kara started walking about the space, touching a shelf here, a table there, admiring the tasteful selection. "Are you a family, then? The League?"

"The leaders are. Those few of us who conceived of and began the League. We are a true family, though we were definitely created, not born."

"Who created you?"

"Well, a number of people, I suppose. The blood parents who turned us over. Mr. Matthew Hanlin and his wife, Anna, who took us in."

"Us?"

"There were five of us, to start. Infants. Unwanted. Gathered from all walks of life and given into the care of a radical-thinking educator and his wife, to raise as part of a social experiment."

Kara turned to look directly at her. "Experiment?"

"No, nothing so drastic as I can see you are imagining. No bloodletting or purges or isolation. Just a simple theory, with a simple premise and uncomplicated execution, although it did require a long and serious commitment."

"What was the theory?"

"Matthew Hanlin was one of a group of radical thinkers who advocated for educating the poor. Actually, he believed in universal education. He wanted to prove that blood and lineage don't matter at all when it comes to a young person's potential. Given equal circumstances and an equal education, he believed all will perform equally as well, despite bloodlines."

"Different bloodlines?" Kara asked, beginning to understand.

"Yes. Unwanted, natural children of nobility, of the merchant class, of factory owners, and me—the mulatto child of a slave."

"That's only four."

Miss Wilkes's mouth twitched. "Very good, Miss Levett. We were raised together. Educated together. We were meant to turn out equally smart, capable, and talented."

Kara was fascinated. "And did you?"

Miss Wilkes laughed again. "Absolutely not. We utterly destroyed their theory. Two of us dazzled in the fields we were suited for and interested in. Two were mediocre at best. At everything."

"And the fifth?"

The other woman shrugged. "The fifth was exceptional, but

volatile."

Kara turned away to wander again. "At least you got your family out of it," she mused. "And a solid education."

"A first-class education," Miss Wilkes corrected her. She looked about suddenly, as if realizing the room was growing dimmer. "Goodness, where has the time gone? The others will be returning soon. I don't know where that maid has got to, but let's get some light in here."

She went to a table drawer to fetch a taper and lit it at the fire. She moved about, lighting lamps.

"There now, that's better." Miss Wilkes gave her a satisfied smile. "It's nearly teatime. The tray should come at any moment. I think we should leave your gift of biscuits until Petra returns, but I do hope you'll join me." She moved past Kara and crossed all the way to the end of the long room, to a door crafted to look like another framed panel of wall. She opened it and peered down the passage behind it. "Ah, I hear the girl coming now, I believe."

Kara moved further into the room, making note of the furnishings and looking for something that could tell her anything about the League. "Do you need assistance?"

"No, thank you. Do take a seat at the table, though."

Moving slowly, Kara started back toward the seating arrangement, where the box still waited, going along the opposite wall. She paused near a dainty desk. It held several of the ledgers marked with the League's symbol and a map of England, marked with multiple bold red circles. Glancing back, she noted Miss Wilkes was occupied with the maid bringing the tea tray. She stepped closer. The circles on the map were around cities, across the island. York, Manchester, Birmingham, Bradford, Newcastle. She had no idea what it meant, but no doubt it was trouble. She started to move on, but her eye was caught by a gleam of glass.

Darting another glance back, she leaned in. A large and leafy plant graced the corner of the desk, and nearly hidden beneath its fronds was a small rack, filled with several vials of clear liquid. She snatched one up and took several steps away, hiding it in her fist, deep in the folds of her skirts.

Miss Wilkes moved past, trailing the tray-laden maid and beckoning her. "Come, I shall play mother and pour for us."

Kara stepped in behind them, but quickly opened the vial. It smelled sweet, but also ... industrial. Puzzled, she tucked it in her bodice as they reached the table. She took a seat as Miss Wilkes fussed with the tray. Hadn't Niall mentioned a lab in the corridor beyond the reception area? And a sweet aroma hanging over it?

She took a seat and the dish of tea that the other woman handed over. "I suppose you did get at least one other gift from your unusual upbringing, didn't you? Your love of chemistry and the chance to explore it."

"Indeed. It is my passion. The others tease me because I spend so much time alone in my lab, but in many experiments the timing of the thing is as important as the ingredients. It's no hardship to me, in any case. I get so caught up in my work quite often. I'm sure you know what I mean. I saw the complexity of your automatons."

"Yes. Sometimes hours pass but it only feels like minutes."

"Exactly. And I am happiest here in my laboratory. It is harsh out there in the world."

"Indeed, it is." Kara tilted her head. "Is that why you were left behind alone today? Am I keeping you from your work?"

"No, no. Today is the one time I was actually tempted to accompany them all on their escapades. They are testing one of my latest projects."

Kara stilled. Images of explosions flashed in her mind. Poisons. A chemist could cook up any number of dangers. She swallowed. "What is it that you've been working on?"

Miss Wilkes perked up, as if she was not often encouraged to speak of her work. "Oh, it is most interesting! First, let me ask you, have you ever attended an ether frolic?"

"I ... No. I'm afraid I'm not familiar with the term."

"You are likely too young. They were popular for a while, a few years ago. They were all the rage among some of the merchant class, but especially among medical students. The Americans were more than passing fond of them, as were the Irish, who viewed it as an alternative to alcoholic spirits. The revelers would inhale the substance, or sometimes drink it, as a recreational act. It made them quite giddy. It induced laughter and tears, often fighting or impromptu dancing. Eventually, some medical students in America noticed that when they stumbled or fell in their frolics, they scarcely noticed. They felt no pain, even when they developed bumps or bruises."

"I've never heard of such antics." Kara frowned. "Although I think I've heard ether mentioned as useful in surgical procedures?"

"Yes. Ten years ago or so, American doctors remembered their experiences and wondered if the painkilling properties of ether might be put to use. They began to experiment and successfully used it in terribly invasive or traumatic procedures, such as amputations, removal of growths, or even childbirth. It took longer for our medical doctors to embrace the idea, but in the last three years, ether has been put to practical use here in England." Miss Wilkes sat back. "So interesting, is it not? And it made me wonder what else might be done with such a useful substance."

A shiver went up Kara's spine at her tone. She suddenly understood what was in the vial in her bodice. "Such as ... what, Miss Wilkes?"

"Oh, do call me Clémence. Are not the possibilities obvious? Imagine being accosted. Threatened. You could have a capsule in your hand and break it under the villain's nose and he would slump down, asleep."

"Good heavens."

"And think what might be accomplished if you could pipe the vapors into a parliamentary committee meeting or a competitor's boardroom?"

Kara's eyes widened. "Those are completely different examples," she protested.

"That's not all. The fluid is volatile. Very flammable. Conceivably, you could craft explosives from it." Miss Wilkes laughed. "Goodness knows, I've dealt with an explosion or two working with it."

Kara stood and began to pace back and forth. "Miss Wilkes! Personal defense is one thing, but making weapons from a scientific discovery? Scheming to harm others for profit or political gain? It's not ethical. It's monstrous!"

"Nonsense. It's been done since the dawn of time. What is monstrous about using your skills to thwart your enemies? Or to line your pockets?"

"When it means indiscriminately hurting people? Everything!"

Miss Wilkes laughed.

But Kara was suddenly connecting with something the woman had said earlier. "Wait! You said the League was testing your project today? Do you mean on my friends?"

The other woman frowned. "Yes, if those people with the lockets are your friends." She must have seen the horror on Kara's face. "Do not get into a lather! They are only using the usual method of inhalation, with the same sort of ether you could track down in some apothecaries. Just as the medical doctors use—a bit of cotton laced with the liquid placed over the mouth and nose. Once it's inhaled, it's off to sleep." She pouted. "Unfortunately, my other ideas are not yet ready. The complication lies in the weight of the vapors. They are heavier than air and tend to sink. I've been trying to come up with a resolution to the problem, but I have run into difficulties. And yes, two of the men I tested them on never woke up. But the third is nearly back to himself now." Kara gasped, and Miss Wilkes sighed. "I thought to try my latest attempt on Lord Stayme, but Petra and William refused to allow it. They insisted he was too old."

"Miss Wilkes!" Kara said in shock.

"Come now, Miss Levett. You are a scientist. You should understand that the advancement of knowledge sometimes requires sacrifice. And who better than a man who has already lived a long life?"

Kara only stared at her in revulsion.

"Oh, please. If I had tuppence for every time someone looked at me like that ..." Miss Wilkes stopped and suddenly looked at her with a new light in her eye. "Wait a moment. You *are* a scientist, are you not? You could be a most useful subject, able to aptly describe effects and sensations in detailed terms." She smiled. "Come along to my lab. Let's give this a try."

Kara took a step back.

"Don't be tiresome, please," the other woman begged. "I can have the men compel you, but it would so much easier and more useful if you cooperate. Aren't you the least bit curious?"

"To see if your latest concoction will kill me or merely push me over into unconsciousness? No, thank you." Kara decided to try a different tactic. "Miss Wilkes, surely you don't wish to use me as a test subject. I thought we were becoming friends?" At the woman's doubtful look, Kara huffed out an exasperated breath. "Well, at the very least, I am not your enemy."

"Are you not?"

"I—we—would not even be aware of your League of Dissolution, had you lot not targeted Niall."

"Well, that couldn't be helped."

"I'm sure it could!"

Miss Wilkes brushed a hand through the air. "Oh, I don't know. Those sorts of strategies are not my specialty. William and Petra handle that sort of thing."

"That sort of thing? I don't even understand what your League is hoping to accomplish."

"Well, you know. War. The toppling of governments. The rise of other governments. All that."

Kara stared. "But ... why?"

"Petra will explain it. She sees it all so clearly. I just tinker away in my lab and make her what she needs." Miss Wilkes drew a breath. "Come now. I'm quite eager to get started. I wish to know what you think of my efforts." She headed for the passage through the fireplace. "Please don't make me call the men. We'll get so much more accomplished if you just resign yourself to helping me."

Kara blinked at her for a moment, then she let her shoulders slump in defeat.

"Ah, good." Miss Wilkes beckoned and ducked into the passage. As soon as she turned the sharp corner, Kara yanked Beth's knife from her pocket, glad she had taken the chance and brought it along. She unwrapped it from Caden's stolen neckcloth and folded the fabric into a square before liberally dousing it with ether from the vial. She pressed herself up against the wall, and when Miss Wilkes stepped back out, looking for her, she pressed the cloth to her face. The woman gasped and began to struggle, but Kara held fast. It took only moments for Miss Wilkes to sag against her and slowly drop to the floor.

Chapter Twenty-One

NIALL WATCHED THE two foreigners walk off down the street together. The League men started to pile in another carriage, but the clerk gave him another push toward the open door.

He climbed in and sat down. A woman waited on the seat across from him. At last.

Her gaze took a measured, yet avid tour of his person. He eyed her with similar rampant curiosity. She was older than he by at least ten years, he would hazard. She had a long, hooked nose, expressive, dark eyes, and a high forehead. She wore a carriage gown and matching coat of quality fabrics, in a quiet fawn color. Her bonnet sat high, away from her face, and was framed with ostrich feathers.

The carriage started to move. "Your foreign friends do not join us?"

"I wished to speak with you privately."

"Who the hell *are* you?" he asked congenially.

She laughed. "I'm not surprised you didn't work it out. Who do you think I am?"

Niall shrugged. "That note you left, I admit it set to my mind to wondering." He looked her over again. "But you don't look at all like ... my grandsire."

Her smile faded. "No. I did say there was no shared blood. But our lives have shared other parallels that make me feel a strange sort of kinship with you."

"A strange kinship, indeed. Since I am unaware of any shared circumstances, I am left with nothing to even base a guess on." His gaze hardened. "The only thing I know is that you are at the head of this plot to explode my life for your own veiled agenda. A choice that seems arbitrary and unnecessary from my point of view, I might add. There are any number of scandals you could use to start the unrest you seem to be looking for."

She shook her head. "No. I'm sorry, but your scandal hits every mark." She gestured. "Look at you! A good-looking tower of a gentleman who has made a name for himself using his own talents and strengths, and despite being ignored by your royal relatives. An image of you in the newspapers alongside those diamond-studded lockets? And a tale of a woman left behind, her love abandoned for power and money? Her daughter hidden away so as not to cause trouble? My dear Niall—may I call you Niall?—your story will catch the attention of every man, woman, and child on this benighted island. Everyone will have an opinion. Everyone will take part in the discussion. You are the start. The spark. And once we have their attention, once we have given them such a fascinating example of how the powers that be acted in such an underhanded way, then we will give them another. And another. And more after that."

Niall snorted. "Does that mean you have been chasing other men and their secrets about Town? Killing and abducting the people in their spheres? How busy you must have been."

"No need," she said airily. "The government has provided plenty of injustice, unfair treatment, and downright corruption. All we have to do is to start pointing it out."

"And rousing people to a fever pitch over it."

She shrugged. "Many people are easily swayed. Quick to rise to anger and blame and judgment. If they allow themselves to be easily led, why should I not lead them down the path I wish them to take?"

"If you see such injustice, why not lead them to thoughtful examination and discourse, to ideas for solving problems, instead of just to anger and hate?"

Sitting back, she gave him a superior smile. "Where is the profit in that?"

Niall reared back. "So that is all it boils down to? I've seen the symbol of your League. I met your foreign friends today and heard their eagerness to bring England to her knees. But it doesn't stop there, does it? Those cracks on your chosen image spread all over Europe. Do you mean to bring unrest to all of those places?"

"Unrest? You think too small, Niall."

"War? You wish to provoke wars all across the Continent?" He studied her. "For *profit?*"

"The League is in possession of several manufactories that will bring a tidy profit, should war break out, it is true. It is one motivation. But it is not the only one. Not for all of our members."

Niall held up his hands and waited expectantly.

She settled back into the corner of her seat. "Do you know the Spheres of Influence?"

He thought a moment, but shook his head. "I don't believe so."

"It is a policy devised back in 1815, at the Congress of Vienna. A balance of power between Great Britain, France, Russia, and Austria. They divided Europe, and each took power over their spheres."

"I suppose it makes sense. They were the major countries left by the time Napoleon was defeated and peace restored in this part of the world."

"But not the only ones."

"Ah, thus why your German-speaking friend has joined your scheming?"

"My Prussian friend has many reasons to assist us." She tilted her head. "You were at the Great Exhibition. I'm sure you know that there was a Prussian party visiting as guests of the queen and her prince consort?"

"Yes, of course. They came early, I recall."

"And did you hear the rumors that the young Prussian Prince Frederick was very often in the company of the princess royal?"

"I did. I assume you refer to the rumors of a match between them? But the princess is a child. What must she be? Eleven or twelve years old?"

"Old enough, when royal betrothals are being discussed. And many in the Prussian court are not in favor of such a thing."

"You would think they would be," he said flatly. "Are they not engaged in a battle to see the Germanic states united under their rule, instead of Austria's? A marriage with Princess Victoria would surely secure English help in that."

"One would think so. The 'Coburg Plan' is apparently for uniting the German states under a liberal Prussia, governed by modern ideals."

"And your friend does not favor such a plan?"

"No. Many do not. There are factions in the court at Berlin who are determinedly anti-English. They despise our style of government. They find us weak. They feel they have more in common with Russia and their harsher, more ordered society. They do not wish the heir presumptive's son to marry an Englishwoman, even a princess. They would prefer an alliance with Russia and one of their grand duchesses, instead."

"Your friend is among them, I presume."

"He is. He is also incensed that, despite the queen and Prince Albert's enthusiasm for such a plan, English foreign policy has repeatedly failed to provide any moral or material support for unification in Germany. Lord Palmerston does not wish a strong, united front of German states to interfere in English interests. Or to throw an imbalance into the Spheres of Influence."

"One can almost not blame your friend for his frustration."

"Especially not when he hears whispers that our government sent men clandestinely in to interfere in the revolutions there, in

1848. To stir up the dissension that made it all fall apart."

He gave her a sharp look. "And who might be whispering in his ear?"

She laughed.

"Do you have any proof of that?"

"There is never proof of such things. There are only ever whispers, innuendo, and quiet confessions often made in questionable circumstances." She grew serious. "It was enough to convince me. And infuriate me, on their behalf." She shook her head. "Words in one direction. Action in another. It is the worst sort of betrayal."

"Fine, then. Your Prussian friend has reasons to aid your cause. But isn't your Russian compatriot guilty of exactly that kind of betrayal? Russia is entered into agreement with Great Britain and is part and parcel of the Spheres of Influence. You said it yourself." He raised his brows, waiting.

"They are. It won't go well for them in the end."

"But you are willing to use them for your own purposes in the meanwhile?"

She shrugged.

"But you must have a surface reason. One that they have offered to you and on which you have agreed to include them in your plans?"

"They have given us twenty thousand good reasons, all in solid English currency," she said lightly. "And as for the tale that they spin? Well, Russia has long been an ideological rival with England. They find us lax in keeping our classes separate. And honestly, they are Russia. They are always interested in growing *more* influential."

"I assume they have come up with more concrete reasons than that."

"They do have designs on expanding their southern borders, which the English do not approve of. It might upset our domination of the Mediterranean. And it could block the land route to India."

Niall nodded. "So you wish me to believe that your foreign partners are motivated by political beliefs, and you are the only one pursuing this grand, complicated, many-layered scheme for money?"

"It is a great deal of money."

"I don't believe you. Not for a second. You've been after me and those lockets with all the tenacity of a hound after a fox. There's a personal element here. I must assume it is related to these parallel circumstances that you mention but do not explain. I can only hope I have not offended or harmed you in some way."

"You have not." Her mouth twisted. "In any case, I thought you admired tenacity. You've certainly showed it yourself. As have all the members of your little band, I must say. I've been most impressed with them." She sobered. "Until today, that is. I was disappointed when my men mentioned that Miss Levett was not at your side."

He schooled himself not to show a reaction. "Were you?" Did that mean that the League did not have Kara in their power? Then where the hell was she?

"I do hope she did not abandon you, once she discovered your true background?"

"Never," he said low and forcefully.

She shrugged. "Perhaps the thought of the immense scandal hovering on the horizon was more than she could stomach."

"It's clear you know nothing about her."

"I hope you are right." She looked out as the carriage slowed. "I did try to warn her that such a betrayal would be in very bad form."

Niall stared at her as the carriage came to a stop. Warn her? Warn Kara? His mind raced until he recalled her story of the woman who spoke with her in the bakery. He nearly snorted. If that was the message that this woman thought to convey, he did not think she'd been successful—nor that it had been necessary.

One of the men who had been perched on the back of the carriage opened the door and handed the woman out. Niall saw another man approach her. She stood on the pavement and listened as he spoke low in her ear.

Niall stepped out. They were back in the rookeries, and they'd pulled up outside a gin shop. The same one he and Rob had discovered on their way through the labyrinth?

Another carriage had pulled in behind them. Several League men were gathered in a knot before it. The clerk separated from them and also went to speak to the woman who, despite protests, must be their leader.

She listened for a moment before holding up a hand. "Find him. Bring him in." She gave the order to the clerk, who nodded and turned away and started off. "Hold a moment," she called.

He stopped. She held out her hand.

"Oh, yes." He pulled the box holding the lockets from his coat and handed it to her. When she moved to take it, he held on to it for a moment. "Don't open it," he said, low and urgent. "Wait until I come back." His gaze bored into hers as if conveying a message that only the two of them could understand.

The woman nodded. Satisfied, he moved on.

She tucked the box away as she turned to look up at the shop, her lips pressed together. "I'm sorry to tell you, Niall, but your faith in Miss Levett may be misplaced. It seems she is cooperating in some fashion with your enemies."

He snorted. "I thought you were my enemies."

"Not in the same way that others are," she replied. She turned her displeased look upon the building. "Your enemies came to me, not so long ago. They offered me exactly what I needed, and so I made an alliance. But things shift quickly in a game like this. Allies change. These are enemies we both share now—and it appears one of them is waiting for us. Unexpected, to be sure. A curious move."

"None of this is a game," Niall growled. "Where is Kara?"

She gestured toward the shop. "Let's go in and see if your former lady will tell us, shall we?"

Chapter Twenty-Two

KARA STRAIGHTENED MISS Wilkes, stretching her out on the floor. Guilt swamped her at the sight of the woman so still. She went to fetch a cushion from the settee to rest Miss Wilkes's head upon. While she was there, her glance fell on the desk further into the room. Glancing back at the woman, she dashed over and grabbed the circle-covered map, folding it smaller and stuffing it into a pocket.

She started to turn back, but paused. The other vials. There were three left. Quickly, she snatched them up. She had to dance and twist a little, making adjustments to her undergarments, but she made them fit snugly in her bodice.

She hurried back to Miss Wilkes, only to find her already stirring. Wincing, Kara draped the ether-dampened cloth back over her nose and mouth. The woman instantly went slack again. Tucking the cushion under her head, Kara looked at the cloth, then shrugged, folded it, and stuffed it into another pocket. It might come in handy.

She'd just got to her feet when she heard a commotion coming from the passage through the fireplace.

"You lot stay here. Give us a bit of privacy. Unless you are called for, of course, but I believe that Mr. Kier and I can deal with his erstwhile wife."

Niall? Here? But what had happened? Where was Stayme? What of the others? Her heart hardened. Had the League demanded Niall trade himself for the viscount? On top of the lockets? Niall wouldn't hesitate to sacrifice himself to save his old friend.

She was still standing over Miss Wilkes when Miss Scot came through the passage, with Niall on her heels. The woman stopped in surprise. Her gaze went from Kara's face, to the ivory, gold, and scarlet gown, to the veil on the chair. Kara thought she saw a measure of respect in her face.

But Niall gasped when he saw her and pushed past the woman. "Kara! Are you all right?" Grabbing her by the shoulders, he pulled her away from the prone form of Miss Wilkes. "They haven't harmed you?"

"No, no. I'm fine."

"On the contrary, I think she is the one doing the damage here," said Miss Scot. "It's a very clever disguise, Miss Levett. And I am oddly relieved to find you here, instead of the viscountess. I was very much afraid you had betrayed your friend."

Kara grasped his arm. "I'm sure Niall knew better."

"He did. I am glad you have justified his faith in you. I take it you walked right in?" She glanced down at her friend. "And somehow managed to give Clémence a literal taste of her own concoction?"

"I just wanted to drop off a token for you, Miss Scot." Kara nodded toward the box on the low table.

The other woman walked over to look inside. Her expression had gone blank when she looked up again. "How very clever you are. You are several steps ahead of where I thought you might be. But my men have only just told me you were seen leaping into a carriage with the good detective. You can see why I feared you had done Niall wrong."

Kara frowned. "No. I don't see." Suddenly she understood. "Oh. You thought I might have run away from all of this, with Caden?" She laughed. "No."

"He is an attractive man."

"He is a liar. And a killer." She looked at Niall. "He killed Sally Doughty. Not that I knew that when I climbed into that carriage." She glared at Miss Scot. "But your men had me cornered."

"He took you, then?" Miss Scot asked. "Fooled you into trusting him?"

"He tried."

"And he didn't turn you over to us," Miss Scot mused.

"He likely would have. Eventually."

"Wait." Niall was looking between them. "You lured a detective into your scheming? A detective from *Scotland Yard?*"

"That hesitation will cost him," Miss Scot declared.

"It already did. I got away," Kara said.

"He was already a disappointment. Another failure has sealed his fate." With a shake of her head, Miss Scot dismissed Caden. "So, you escaped, and then you ..."

Kara could see her running the scenarios through her head.

"Ah." She'd decided on one, it would seem. "You were too late to make the meeting to trade Stayme." She looked Kara over again. "So you decided to play at being the viscountess and bluff your way in here? To find out what you could while we were occupied?" She laughed. "An audacious move, Miss Levett. I applaud your quick thinking."

"Thank you." Kara decided she'd had enough of the woman controlling the conversation. She stepped in front of Niall. "That is exactly what I did. And I found Miss Wilkes, who gave me an educational and entertaining lecture on the uses of ether, but an even more fascinating tale about a grand educational experiment. One that included a noble's bastard, an infant from the streets, a factory owner's unwanted, illegitimate child, as well as a slave's. And one more."

"That's right."

"And she was what sort of child?" Kara asked pointedly.

"A royal bastard," Miss Scot answered quietly.

Silence reigned for a moment.

"But you said—" began Niall.

"*Not* George's," she spat, suddenly animated. "My mother was the much maligned Queen Caroline."

Kara was stunned into silence again. Niall stood beside her, absorbing the words like a blow.

"As I said," Miss Scot continued. "Similar circumstances. Not exact. But still, both of us refuted, despised, and ignored."

"We are not the same," Niall said.

"No. You are not," Kara agreed. She eyed the woman closely. "Who was your father?"

Miss Scot lifted a shoulder. "Hard to say, isn't it? Knowing my mother's proclivities? But I know whom she convinced. One of her most trusted advisors. A man of the law. A good man, by all reports. He believed in fairness and felt she was treated most unjustly. But my mother was famous for saying that men and women could not be friends. There must always be a sexual element between them."

Niall was frowning. "I've never heard a whisper about you. I heard she'd adopted a boy and kept him with her. There were whispers that he was hers. A bastard hidden in plain sight."

"She tired of him soon enough. She was not maternally in-clined or in any way fit to be a mother. It was why Princess Charlotte was taken from her and raised elsewhere."

"Your half-sister," Kara said quietly.

"Yes. I often wonder what might have been, had she lived."

"All of England and half the world must wonder the same," Niall murmured.

"In any case, Caroline adopted eight or nine children in all. She fostered them all out. How many were hers? Who can say? I came along much later. After the wars were over, the great delegation of visiting dignitaries came to celebrate. She was left out, even though some of the visitors were her relatives. She was excluded and humiliated."

"I recall the story," Niall said. "One of a heap of indignities she suffered."

"I've often wondered if she was left out because she was with child—with me—and already showing."

"It makes sense of something that otherwise doesn't," Kara mused.

"In any case, after that she petitioned the foreign secretary for a generous allowance, and in return promised to go abroad. She left in August of that year, and I was born in Switzerland early in the next. She went on to travels and revels. I was sent back to my father."

"Who promptly turned you over to Matthew Hanlin and his wife for their experiment," Kara said.

"I see Clémence was generous with her telling. But yes. My father was married with his own family. He is a radical thinker, too, you see. He believes in universal education and still fights for education of the poor."

"So you became a part of the experiment," said Kara. "Given equal education and upbringing and meant to be equally intelligent and mannered. Five peas in a pod. But you were not, were you?"

Miss Scot laughed. "No. I surpassed them all. Turned their theory upside down. But I was a difficult subject, in their defense. For on the one hand, I was of royal blood. But on the other, my mother was notoriously lazy and uneducated. And I insisted on causing my own difficulties, for I excelled at nearly every subject."

"You were not the only one, though, were you? Two turned out average in every way, she said." Kara looked toward Miss Wilkes, who was beginning to stir again. "But she was extremely skilled at her scientific endeavors."

"She was and is, but it is her only interest. William, on the other hand, is a genius with numbers and mathematical equations and is more versatile with it. He can chart the course of the planets, but more usefully, he can create a new accounting system with a built-in, utterly invisible way to scrape a percentage off the profits, and have it done before teatime. Fill him up with tea, brandy, and jam tarts and he'll invent another the same evening. He can do the opposite, as well. Give him a set of books to look over and he'll find the waste, the mistakes, and the spots where someone else has been skimming."

"I take it, then, that William is the man who met with me this afternoon?" asked Niall.

Miss Scot gave a nod.

"The clerk," he said in an aside to Kara. Turning back to the other woman, he wore a thoughtful expression. "An extremely useful man to have when you own several companies that will make fortunes off the wars you mean to stir up."

Kara blinked. "War profits? That's what this is all about?"

"No," Niall said grimly. "It is about betrayal. It's the theme she keeps coming back to."

"It is the theme of *life*," Miss Scot snapped. "Mine and yours, yes. But nearly everyone else's, as well."

"What happened?" Kara asked, not without sympathy. "Your story is bleak, yes, but it seems someone else must have hurt you. Betrayed you. Did the school try to stifle your growth when you proved more advanced than the others?"

"No. No. They were truly dedicated to the idea of education. They encouraged me, even when I began to outstrip the others. They made sure I had what I needed to learn more, as long as I was interested. They even brought in expert tutors when I needed them."

"That was generous," said Kara.

"So I thought, as well. I was grateful. I was also determined to pay them back. It was when I went looking for the costs of those extra lessons that I discovered the truth."

"The truth." Niall sounded wary.

"We were raised simply. Five of us to start and more added in later. We shared rooms, books, supplies. The food was humble. Never in short supply, but never plentiful, either." She glanced at the box on the table. "No butter biscuits."

"Perhaps it was a factor in the experiment?"

"That was what they claimed when I found the very large sum of money they had been charging our parents for our upkeep, all those years. It didn't quite ring true. I set William to investigating, and he found they had been using the money to make investments. In cargo, on the 'Change, in property. They were set to cut us loose as young men and women, planned to send us out into the world with the fine education they'd given us and naught else, while they lived like lords on our money."

"How terrible," Kara whispered.

"We had always known our own true parents had abandoned us. It was a blow to find such perfidy in the family we believed in." Drawing a deep breath, Miss Scot tossed her head. "But that was the true start of the League. We searched their records and found who our true parents were. We took the money that was left. Managed to get back several of their investments. The three of us pooled our resources then. We found a set of rooms. We decided to use our skills to begin to address some injustices."

"As long as you could make a profit?" asked Niall.

"Exactly. We started with our parents and grew from there. Until here we are."

"Yes. Here you are, and now you are the ones perpetrating the injustices," Niall said bitterly.

"No, no," Miss Wilkes said. Kara had nearly forgotten her, but the woman was awake now and trying to sit up. "Petra, don't. They don't need to know any more."

But Miss Scot's ire was growing. "He deserves to know, Clémence!" She rounded on Niall. "You've been the good, quiet boy your whole life, and what has it got you? What have they done for you, for keeping their great secret? Nothing! Not even a pat on the back. Just a thunderous shadow hanging over your head and their pet secret-keeper Stayme, sent to keep you in line!"

Niall snorted. "You don't know as much as you think you do."

"Oh, I do. I know so many of their secrets! How do you think

I knew about their secret forays into the 1848 revolutions? And the German states are not the only ones they've interfered with. And lest you think I tried to hide my own secret from them, I shall tell you different!"

"No, Petra," Miss Wilkes called. "Please. There's no need to hash anything any further. Don't get worked up again. You *know* what happens!"

But Miss Scot was as primed as a locomotive with a head of steam. She tossed off her coat and began to walk back and forth behind the settee as she continued. "It was long ago, but it still makes me furious to recall it. I was young. Twenty years old and sure of myself. I believed I did deserve something for keeping quiet about my background. I marched down to Whitehall and demanded to talk to someone close to the king. I wanted to talk to your grandsire."

Her eyes widened. Grabbing up the coat again, she drew out the box with the lockets and tore off the top, tossing it away from her. "Look at him. Still young and thin and handsome in this. Not the bloated slug he would become later. But he was not innocent, not by any means, when this was painted. He'd already secretly married your mother, left her, then married mine and left her! Abandoned her. Pushed her out. Made her life a misery. Pushed her onto the path that led her to spawn me. This man who could have—should have—been my father. He should have had her crowned at his side, made her Queen of England, as she was meant to be. I wanted him to see my face, hear my story. I wanted him to feel the shame he should have, for leaving her so miserable and alone."

Niall looked fascinated. "Did you speak with him?"

Her lip curled. "I couldn't even get past the lowest lackey. No one would see me. When I finally forced some lickspittle undersecretary of something or other to hear me, he went to fetch someone higher. He came back with a man who looked at me as if I were a worm under his shoe. I told him. All of it. And do you know what he said?"

"I can guess," Niall answered quietly.

"He told me to go ahead and tell my story. Sell it to the papers. I wouldn't be getting a farthing from the king, who would be happy to see my tale make the rounds. I would only embarrass myself and further stain the memory of my mother."

"That's what I expected you to say," Niall said sadly.

"I'm so sorry," Kara whispered.

Miss Scot took a seat on the settee. She took out the lockets again and stared at them.

Kara looked uneasily at Niall. She couldn't see how they were going to resolve this. Miss Scot had clearly been hurt. More than that—damaged. Kara doubted whether the woman could be persuaded to stop the plans she'd set in motion.

Miss Wilkes was on her feet now. She wobbled over and sat next to Miss Scot. She tried to take her hand, but the woman jerked away. Miss Scot held the portrait of Maria Fitzherbert close to her eye, then turned an astonished look on Niall.

He straightened.

Miss Scot deliberately held the locket at an angle and scraped one of the diamonds over the glass layer on the low table. She tried it again with the other locket. "Not even a mark," she said in a deadly quiet tone. "Paste. Quite good. But paste."

Miss Wilkes looked alarmed.

"You are just like them," Miss Scot accused. "Liar. Betrayer."

"Now, Petra," Miss Wilkes cautioned.

Niall's gaze narrowed. "You are willfully destroying my life in pursuit of your own plans. You abducted and threatened the man who is my only family, of the heart if not blood. You have endangered the woman I care for. And you expect me to just play fair and follow along?"

"I would have looked a fool," Miss Scot said. "Bringing fakes to the attention of the Crown, the public. Yes, the story would have been true, but the proof would not be. You would have cast doubt upon me. Made me look a charlatan." She shook her head. "You are the same as them. Willing to cheat and lie. Just as I found they would do anything, hurt anyone, lie, scheme, and steal to keep all the advantages where they already lay." She stood, and her voice rose along with her. Her anger was clearly growing again as well. "You are the fool. They keep their claws tightened around the money and the power, for that's all that matters to them!"

Reaching down, she grabbed the edge of the low table and flipped it, sending teacups, saucers, and butter biscuits flying. Snatching the teapot from the floor, she threw it. It flew through the air and shattered against the wall.

"Petra, no!" Miss Wilkes cried. "Stop now! You must. Breathe, Petra. Think! You do not wish for the men to see you like this again." She tried to grab her friend's arm, but the maddened woman shook her off.

"It's all so perfectly clear! Why can no one else *see*? Why do they not *listen*?" Miss Scot picked up one of the Queen Anne chairs and began to bash it against the side of the overturned table until it started to come apart in her hands.

"Stay back," Niall warned Kara. She watched as he stepped carefully closer to the furiously out-of-control woman.

"What is it? What's happening?" The League men had clearly heard the commotion. Two of them had come through the passage. They stared in horrified fascination as Miss Scot continued pounding the chair.

Miss Wilkes reached over and grabbed Kara's arm. "I'll try to calm her, but please, get the men out of here. It's not good for her or them to see her like this. There is always trouble afterward. Gossip and dissension and dereliction." She paled. "And worse. Please! Send them out of here."

Kara stared. Did Miss Wilkes think that Kara wished to help them keep their hold on their treasonous gang of thugs? But then it struck her ... She nodded. "Leave it to me."

Miss Wilkes threw her a grateful look and crossed to take a hold of her friend's shoulders.

Kara crossed to the avidly staring men.

"What's set her off this time?" one of them asked.

"It's bad," she said, using Malina's harsher tones again. "Extremely bad news. The queen's men. They are coming."

The men exchanged worried glances.

"A large force. Hundreds."

"How much do they know?" one asked.

"I knew this was bound to happen," the other one added.

"You must get away. Tell all the men to scatter. Everyone who is here. They must clear the labyrinth, or be caught. If they are not shot on sight, then they'll be hanged for treason."

"Damnation." One of them took a step back.

"What of her?" the other asked. "I'm not touching her. The last time she got like this, they asked for help in subduing her. The poor sot who put his hands on her had them whacked off after she recovered. His hands!"

"I'll get her out," Kara said. "You get yourselves away. Tell them all to go underground. Wait for word. But to save themselves now."

"All right. Good luck." The first man shoved the other. "Let's get out of here, quick-like."

As they left, Kara headed back. Miss Wilkes still grasped her friend's shoulders and was speaking to her, low and fast. Miss Scot had stopped shouting, but she was still wide-eyed and twitching, trying to get loose from her grip. "No," she said, growing loud again.

"Yes!" Miss Wilkes insisted. "You will. Do not put everything in jeopardy again."

"I? *I* put it in jeopardy?" Miss Scot knocked her friend's hands away, but she grabbed her in the same hold. "Do not cross me, Clémence! Not you too! Do. Not. Betray. Me." With each word she gave the other woman a shake, and at the end, she pushed her away. Miss Wilkes stepped back, stumbled on a broken piece of chair, and fell. There was a stomach-turning *thud* as her temple struck the side of the table.

Kara gasped in horror. She rushed to the fallen woman, but

Niall was there before her. Miss Wilkes moaned. Her eyes blinked open. She looked past Niall, searching for her friend, finding her as Miss Scot moved closer, her hand over her mouth. "No," she breathed.

Miss Wilkes tried to smile, but her eyes went wide and unseeing—and then she was gone.

"Oh no," Kara whispered.

Niall laid the woman gently down amid the rubble.

Miss Scot started to scream a denial. She went down on her hands and knees and shook her friend, as if she could wake her. "Absolutely not, Clémence! Do you hear me? Do not do this! You cannot leave me. I won't have it!" She struck the dead woman in the face.

Kara gasped, but Miss Scot struck again, and again.

Niall reached down and gathered her in his arms. She screeched in protest, but he held her pinned against him and pulled her away. "Enough!" he shouted. "That is enough!" He lowered his voice. "I am so sorry for all that has happened. For everything that has harmed you and everyone who has left you feeling alone and abandoned." He squeezed her tight for a moment. "But you must regain hold of yourself. You have a right to your anger and your sorrow, but you cannot use it to burn down the world."

Kara flinched when the woman threw back her head and laughed. The sound was wild. Utterly ungoverned. It made all the hair on her nape and on her arms stand up on end.

"Can I not?" Miss Scot yelled mockingly. "Can I not?" She wriggled furiously and dropped out of his hold. Darting to the table along the wall, she grabbed up an oil lamp and dashed it down onto the floor. The glass shattered, and burning oil spread across the carpet. "I can absolutely burn down the world. And I can reshape it according to my own needs." She glared at Niall with cold fury and hatred. "Watch it burn, then!"

She headed for the next lamp, but Niall grabbed her again. Leaning down, she bit his arm and held fast.

He shouted in shock and pain and tried to shake her off.

Miss Scot only bit down harder.

Kara, fury blazing, stepped close. She struck the woman on the side of the head, forcing her to let Niall go. As Miss Scot snarled at her, Kara grabbed the ether soaked neckcloth from her pocket. "Hold her," she told Niall, and pressed the cloth over her face and held tight.

Chapter Twenty-Three

NIALL LET THE madwoman slump to the floor. Grabbing his arm, he cursed. "Odin's *arse*, but that hurts like hell."

"I'm so sorry." Kara slipped into his arms like she had been doing so all of her life.

Holding her close, he felt relief flood him and hoped she never stopped. "You scared me to death today," he told her. "I had no idea where you were or who might have you. I've never been so glad as when I stepped in and found you here before me. Even though we were in trouble." He looked her over with a scowl. "And even though you wore that getup."

She laughed and nestled in. He pulled her closer. "I swear, I'm going to burn it when I take it off."

"Please do." Looking down over her shoulder at Petra Scot, he sighed. "What are we going to do with her? I confess, I feel some sympathy for her, but she is a true menace, in her rational mind or out of it. We cannot leave her here. But how do we get her out past all of those men?"

Kara stepped back to look up at him. "Actually, we may be able to just carry her out." She explained what she'd done, sending the men of the League scattering.

He stared at her, dumbfounded, and then picked her up and twirled her. "Kara, that was brilliant!"

She pushed away. "Careful! I've got a bodice full of ether!"

Setting her down again, he shook his head as she pulled one out. "Why?" He held out his arm and shook it. "Never mind. Tell me later. Damnation, but that hurt."

"Oh dear. Roll up your sleeve. I think I saw a drinks cart … Yes, there!"

He went and picked up the lockets where they had rolled near the settee while she fetched a bottle of brandy. He examined them, thinking sober thoughts as she doused the bite mark with brandy and tore strips from her petticoat to bind it tight.

"We need to get that seen by a doctor," she said, tearing more strips.

He gave her a questioning look.

She nodded toward the unconscious woman. "I want her bound. I don't truly know how this ether works, and I don't want to take the chance of her getting away, even if I would rather keep her asleep until we get her …" She stared up at him. "Where?"

He stared down at Miss Scot. She looked harmless now, but he'd heard enough to know better. "If she wakes up in the hands of the government which has treated her so ill, the one she hates so much …"

"It just might drive her truly mad," Kara finished. "The rest of the way."

Niall rubbed a hand over his mouth. "Let's get her to Stayme. He might know of an alternative."

"As long as it involves locking her away," Kara agreed. She looked at the still-smoldering carpet. "I suppose we should put that out."

She went on tearing strips, and he absently took them as he stared at the embers on the carpet. "Should we?" She raised her brows in question, and he gestured toward the carpet. "Or should we finish what she started and burn it all down?"

She stopped, her eyes wide. She glanced around, and Niall knew she was seeing the entirety of the labyrinth in her mind's eye, as he had.

"The warehouse. All of those supplies," she said.

"Let the Crown come in and take those. Let them deal with the apothecary and the gin shop and all those who cooperated with the League." He looked around. "But this? This is their lair. They hatched their plans here. Blackmail and intrigue, treason and abduction. If we destroy this, will it send a message?"

"To their men?"

"To any of them who might think to step in and take over."

"To their foreign conspirators, too." She nodded. "Yes. Let's do it." Handing him the last strip, she climbed to her feet. "Oh, but Niall, people live in the top floors of that building that lets out into Boyd's Yard. Might the fire spread so far?"

"It might. I hope it does, in fact. The mold and filth and squalor of that place is likely killing them all, just at a slower pace." He took her hand. "We'll clear it first."

"We can find them cleaner, safer rooms afterward."

He grinned. "It's the perfect excuse to meddle. Let's do it."

"Bind her tight, will you? I am going to dose her again." She gave a shudder. "I hope we will never have to converse with her again."

Niall bent to work, but he nodded toward Clémence Wilkes's still form. "What of her? Shouldn't we pull her out? So that she can have a decent burial?"

Kara's face hardened. It surprised him. "Gyda would say a burning is a warrior's funeral. I say it's more than she deserves."

"I did wonder if something had happened when I saw you had put her out. What was it?" he asked. Kara would not harden her heart against the woman without reason.

"She tested her experimental attempts on their men. At least two of them died at her hand, in the name of her warped science. She wanted to use Stayme in the same way. After all, he had already lived a long life. She had to be persuaded otherwise by the others." She lifted her chin. "I was to be her next test subject, on the basis that I could provide scientific observations on the effects.

That is, if I survived."

Niall tied the last knot and stood. "Leave her," he said flatly. He helped make a torch with the last strip of petticoat and a chair leg. "For the quick lighting of fires," he said.

Kara pulled out a vial of the ether from her bodice and smashed it into the embers on the carpet, setting them to burning higher. "It's volatile enough to act as an accelerant. We'll go to the laboratory and see if there are more. And we'll start the next blaze there."

Bending over, Niall hauled Miss Scot up and over his shoulder. "Check to be sure there are no men out there," he said.

Kara peeked out of the fireplace passage, into the parlor, and moved through the two offices. "All clear," she pronounced.

They moved quickly then, setting fires in the lab and several more in the makeshift warehouse at the bottom of the stairs. As smoke began to fill in the space, they moved through the corridors of office rooms and through the passage to the filthy building that led into Boyd's Yard.

Niall stopped to prop Miss Scot into a corner. "Dose her again—I can feel her starting to twitch awake."

Kara sprinkled more ether on the neckcloth and looked at the rickety staircase. "I'll go up and make sure everyone leaves. You stay here and wave them outside—and keep an eye on her."

"Hell and damnation, be careful. That thing looks like it's ready to come down on its own accord."

She nodded and took a deep breath. "Fire! Fire! Everyone out!" she yelled.

He added his voice, and between them and the thickening smoke, the occupants were convinced to take the threat seriously.

"That's it," Kara said, descending at last. "I knocked at every door and opened them all, too. Nary a lock in the place," she said. "Everyone is out."

They tossed the torch onto the decrepit stairs, along with a vial of ether. Niall took Miss Scot up again, and they stepped outside just as an explosion sounded somewhere far behind them.

"The lab?" she asked, as the crowd cried out in fear.

"Or a hidden cache of gunpowder," he answered grimly. "Let's go!" he shouted to the waiting occupants, standing in their nightclothes and clutching their belongings. "We'll be safer if we move out of the yard and into the street!"

They came at the rear, making sure no one stayed behind. A young girl helping her grandfather move down the alley called out in encouragement to the others and gathered them together when they emerged out onto Queen Street. Kara looked at him and nodded toward her. "I'm going to recruit her."

He nodded and watched as Kara convinced the girl to take charge and to keep all the occupants together. She promised transportation and temporary food and shelter. "You have a good head on your shoulders. Tell them I'm going to arrange for them all to be fed and bedded down for now. We'll start to sort through and find new, safer places for everyone, tomorrow."

"Let's go," Niall said. "She's heavier than she looks. We might find a cab closer to the center."

They set off.

"Davey Dobbs has a cart," Kara said. "I'm sure he'll let us borrow it. I'd thought to send them all to Rachel in her coffee shop, but the pie shop is closer, and Maisie will lend a hand."

"Her new beau drives a hackney, too," Niall told her.

"Excellent! We'll get them all moved and settled, and then we'll need to send for someone from Stayme's to come and take Miss Scot and—"

The rest was lost as Niall was struck a great blow from behind. He stumbled forward, fighting to stay on his feet and to keep from dropping Miss Scot.

"Niall!" Kara moved to help, grabbing the woman and helping to ease her down. "What—?" She stopped, staring over his shoulder. "Watch out!"

She shoved him, and he continued on with the movement, stepping quickly aside and into the street as a man lunged for him. Catching himself, the attacker reached out, grabbed Niall's coat, and spun him, slamming him into a wall.

"Is this your doing?" The man shoved a blade against Niall's throat. "Scotland Yard is streaming into the underground warehouse right now, and a large part of the operation is *burning!*" He paused as another distant explosion sounded. "It's the pair of you, isn't it? Interfering fools!" He pressed the tip of the blade harder, and Niall felt it break the skin. "I will kill you both for this! You've ruined everything!"

The man gasped suddenly, and Niall looked down to see Kara pressed up close behind him. "Ruined?" she snarled. "Everything you lied and schemed for, Caden? *Killed* for?"

Niall felt the man's back stiffen.

"Sally Doughty suffocated to death, did you know that? Just one thrust, up through the kidney and into the diaphragm, the coroner told me. *With this very blade.*"

The man holding him tried to jerk away, but Kara was still pressed in close behind him. "Move again and you'll feel the same," she vowed. "She couldn't breathe. She never drew another breath. Would you care to die the same way? Because you are going to, unless you drop that blade away from Niall. *Now!*"

Suddenly a hand reached in from the side and forced the knife away from Niall's throat before snatching it. "That won't be necessary, Miss Levett," someone said calmly. "Step away from him. We'll take him from here."

Kara moved back, her mouth open, and Caden was yanked away from him. She stepped in close to Niall, and together they gawked. "Wooten?" he gasped.

"*Now* you show up?" Kara griped.

"In the nick of time, it would seem," the inspector said. "Apologies for our late arrival."

"Wooten!" Caden called from where two men in police uniforms had dragged him. "Thank goodness you are here! These two have been consorting with conspirators against the Crown. Treason! They've burned down half of Seven Dials! Take them up, quickly, before they—"

"Someone has definitely been conspiring," Inspector Wooten agreed. "We became aware of the League a few weeks ago. I was tasked with finding out who has been working with them. I found a surprising number of them in Whitehall, most of whom had been blackmailed or forced into giving them information or aid."

"Not Caden, I would guess," Kara said bitterly.

"No. It appears his betrayal is entirely voluntary and motivated by greed and ambition." The inspector looked the detective over with distaste. "It took me longer than it should have to find we had a traitor in our midst. The signs you left indicating it was Detective Frye were cleverly done. It slowed me down a bit, I admit." He made a motion to the policemen, and Caden was dragged away toward a waiting van.

The inspector turned back. "We have taken the Viscountess Marston in for questioning as well," he told them. "As for you two ..." He paused and ran a glance over the slumped figure of Petra Scot. "Or three, I should say."

Kara stepped before the woman. "You can leave her to us. We're taking her to Stayme."

Wooten sighed. "I'm sorry, Miss Levett. I know who she is—who she truly is—and what she's been up to. I'm afraid I must take her into custody."

"Inspector, she's ... unstable. I'm afraid it will damage her beyond repair, to be treated callously again. To have her and her secrets brushed aside again."

"I see." Wooten gestured for his men to take her up. "Carefully, please," he instructed them. Sighing, he nodded toward Kara. "I will ask that she be treated gently, but we cannot allow the story of who she is and what she's been planning to get out."

"The sensation it would cause would be nearly as damaging as what she planned to set in motion," Niall said quietly.

"I'm glad you understand." Wooten's gaze spoke more than his words. "Let the secrets lie," he said. "All of them."

Kara's shoulders slumped.

"I have a carriage waiting," Wooten said. "Let me take you to my office. We'll get some coffee into you and you can tell me how you got mixed up—"

"No," Niall and Kara said together.

"Where is Turner?" she demanded. "Is he well? Gyda and Rob?"

"They are all fine and leading my men into that underground warehouse right now."

"I need to speak to Turner. He'll see to the people displaced by the fire. And then I am going home. To Bluefield. To sleep. For days, perhaps."

Wooten hesitated, but then nodded. "Rest. You've earned it, I suspect. And then we will talk."

"I should—" Niall began.

"No." Kara reached out a hand to him. "Come with me, please. Come with me."

He put his hand in hers.

Chapter Twenty-Four

WOOTEN'S CARRIAGE TOOK them to a warehouse around the corner and down the street from the apothecary's shop where Josie Lowe had put on her magnificent performance. Kara climbed down and spotted Turner standing near the large, open doorway. Running to him, she hugged him tight.

Gyda and Rob soon emerged, and hurried stories were exchanged.

"Stayme called in the cavalry," Rob said, indicating the mass of policemen and government officials swarming inside the warehouse. "We led them in the way we knew, but they soon found a couple of false walls and a wide stairwell leading up here."

"But what happened to Stayme? When they led me out of the Eagle, he had disappeared from the taproom," Niall recalled. "The clerk sent men in pursuit."

"Molly happened," Gyda said. "His maid, the one who volunteered to help. She cut him loose and snuck him into the kitchens while the League men were occupied with Kara's footman. He put up a struggle when they tried to dose him with the ether. They would have had a bigger fight, had they allowed *me* to play the role of tapster, but Molly got the old man out and hid him in the dumbwaiter."

"He's still complaining about the crick in his neck," Rob said with a grin.

Kara took Turner aside and explained about the fire and the group of newly displaced people she'd pledged to help. She sketched out the ideas she'd had to start.

"I will get on it right away," Turner said. "It's nearly dawn. The Dobbs family will be up and at work in the pie shop. We'll see them settled there for now and worry about sorting them out permanently soon."

Kara reached over to touch his arm. "You are well, Turner? Truly?"

"I am well," he said quietly. "I promise."

"Good." Tears threatened. "For you know how I get after these adventures." She sank down onto a crate. "The strength and stamina that all the anxiety lends disappears, and now I find my legs are shaky and I feel as if I could sleep for a week."

"Then that is exactly what you should do."

Kara looked up and saw Niall look over at her. A moment later, he was there and lifting her into his arms.

"I'm taking her home."

Kara gave Turner a smile, then closed her eyes and melted into the incredible comfort of Niall's arms. She barely noticed when he deposited her into the carriage. She just snuggled in when he sat next to her and sighed in relief.

SHE AWOKE NEARLY twenty-four hours later, alone in her bed at Bluefield. She was in her shift, and there was no sign of her ruined petticoat or that dreadful gown. The sky was just beginning to lighten, and the birds had begun to chirp a sleepy morning chorus.

Rolling over, she luxuriated in the warmth of the bed for a moment, but her busy brain soon had her pushing back the covers and ringing for her maid. There were a hundred things to do, loose ends to tie up, but first ... first she would see to the most important.

"Niall?" she asked as Elsie came hurrying in.

"Asleep in the loft over the forge," the girl answered. "I daresay he's been as dead to the world as you have been, miss."

Kara sighed in relief. "A bath, please? Quickly?"

Elsie gave her a knowing nod. "And that deep violet gown with the leafy embroidery?"

Kara had been saving it for a special moment. "Yes, please."

An hour later she slipped downstairs and sent word to the stables before leaving the house. She struck out across the grounds, heading for the forge. The sun sat just over the horizon, and the sky blazed brilliantly pink and orange. She walked slowly, breathing in the fresh air and wondering—

"My God."

She looked up from where she'd bent to examine a patch of clover.

"You look like springtime come to life," Niall rasped.

She flushed. "It's autumn," she reminded him.

"Perhaps for the rest of the world."

She stood straight, and neither of them moved. "I came to invite you for a drive. A bit of time away from everything. Just the two of us."

Stepping close, he held out his hand. She took it, and they walked to the drive, where her little chaise waited. Niall handed her up, and she took the reins from the groom, who was trying unsuccessfully to hide a grin.

She drove them through the village and past Wood Rose Abbey. Kara did not take the first turn that led to the trail to the pond they'd renamed Lake Nemi. She continued on, following the curving road and turning the chaise onto a smaller, barely-there trail that allowed her to drive up quite close to the water.

Niall climbed down and secured the horse, then reached up for her. She leaned in and let herself slide down the front of him, reveling in the heated contact, in the flutter in her belly and the pounding of her heart. When her feet touched the ground, she looked up at him and hoped he saw the invitation in her eyes.

He did. His hands came up to touch her jaw, to tenderly cradle her face, and to slide over her shoulders to pull her in for his kiss. It was soft and sweet, until it grew languid and exploring and at last hungry and demanding. She savored it all, relished in the sheer relief of it until her heart swelled—and until the horse snorted loudly and stamped a foot.

They both jumped a little, separated, and gazed at each other. At last, she drew a breath. "I brought a blanket," she told him. "It's under the bench."

He reached for it, and she led him a little way to the small cove carved into the shore of the pond.

"It's warmer in the sun." He spread it out near the edge of the water, where they could watch the dragonflies darting across the water as well as the bees buzzing in search of late blooms.

"I wanted to come here and tell Sally Doughty that her killer has been caught," she said quietly. "She has justice. I hope she's also found peace."

"I hope so, too."

She sighed, drinking in the beauty and the calm. Kara let her head fall back so she could feel the sun on her face.

"I feel as if we could be at the beginning of the world," Niall marveled quietly.

"We are, are we not?"

"The beginning of *our* world."

She leaned her head against him.

"My friend Ansel loves to paint diptychs," he said quietly. "Do you know what I mean?"

"The two-paneled paintings? Meant to hang together? I've seen one of his."

"I feel like it's what we are. Both of us complete. Functioning and effective. Creative. Whole, in and of ourselves. But place us together and the world expands. Everything becomes bigger, more beautiful and powerful."

"Infinitely happier," she whispered.

"Yes. I mean to make you my wife, Kara. I never want to go back to a life without you."

She smiled. "Good. Because I mean to be your wife."

"But I must go back to my rooms at the White Hart."

She sat back. "That's not what I expected you to say."

"I want this done properly," he said earnestly. "Without gossip or stain upon your reputation. You have friends in a multitude of worlds. I don't want you to lose any of them. You might need them all, if word of my background gets out."

"If it comes out, or if it doesn't, I'll always be by your side."

"I know." He took her hand and placed it on his chest. "It's why I feel so incredibly light and free. Thank you."

She moved into this arms again.

"As much as I am enjoying this, I think we need to go back. Rob will wake soon, and he'll be hungry as a bear. He always is in the mornings."

Kara sat back in surprise. "Oh, I should have thought! He's in the loft?"

"Yes. When he came in, he said Wooten intends to come out today, to question us."

She nodded. "All right. Let's go back and make sure Cook knows we'll need a large breakfast."

Cook was miles ahead of her, as usual. They arrived to find a huge buffet set out, and Rob and Gyda preparing to make a first pass. They all sat down to eat and catch each other up, while Turner and Tom kept the buffet full and the tea, coffee, and toast fresh.

They had barely started when Stayme entered. Both Kara and Niall hurried to make a fuss over him.

"Enough, enough! You are as bad as my staff!" he grumped, trying to hide a smile. "No, I've already eaten. I just wanted to hear all the gritty details from you two."

"Wait a moment, before we begin," Kara said. She looked to Turner. "Has Cook fed the pair of you?" She nodded toward Tom, the footman.

"Magnificently, thank you," Turner replied.

"She treated the whole staff to toad-in-the-hole, in our honor," Tom said, flushing.

"Remind me to raise her salary," Kara said. "And Turner?"

"Miss?"

"I'm very much afraid I'm going to need you more in the laboratory in the next weeks. There is still a backlog of orders to be filled after the Exhibition." She glanced at Niall. "And there may be an event to plan, before long. I'll need assistance there as well."

Turner bit back a smile, and everyone else exchanged delighted glances.

"In due time," Niall said, clearing his throat.

"Perhaps two events," Gyda said, jabbing Rob with her elbow. "I've seen the way little Beth looks at you, McRae."

Kara spoke over the general laughter and Rob's blustering. "In the meanwhile," she continued. "I thought perhaps you would not object if we promote Tom to underbutler? He can learn some of your duties in the house, freeing you to help me."

"I would not object in the slightest, Miss Kara," Turner replied.

"Excellent."

They sat then, and filled Stayme in on their harrowing adventures and heard the tale of his abduction. "I think they were glad to be rid of me," he said, chortling. "I kept hearing snippets of conversation and deducing their plans. I was quite critical in my evaluations, too."

Niall laughed. "No one is surprised there, old man."

Inspector Wooten entered as they were finishing. He declined breakfast. Looking sober, he asked to see Niall and Kara in private.

Kara took them to the ivory sitting room and closed the door.

"Petra Scot has escaped the Crown's custody," Wooten said immediately. "I am very sorry."

They sat in stunned silence.

"How?" Niall demanded.

"I don't know. I warned them. It shouldn't have happened. A couple of our people are missing. I don't know whether they are dead or bribed." Wooten shook his head. "I'm sure it entailed a great deal of money and a great deal of effort by her last compatriot in the League, William Barnstaple."

"That damned clerk," Niall swore.

"And Caden, too?" Kara asked.

"No. He's still safely locked away. He keeps shouting that Napoleon was right and England is nothing but a nation of shopkeepers. That he was passed over and held back because of the Irish in his blood."

Niall sighed.

"She left you a note." Wooten handed Kara a folded bit of thick paper.

"Me?" But she saw her name and started to read.

Miss Levett,

I am told that you argued against letting the Crown take custody of me. For that consideration, I am grateful. You were right. They should have listened. You were correct, also, in believing that had I been obliged to stay here, under their power, it might have been beyond bearing. Your Stayme would likely have made it far more difficult for me to escape.

You must know that I am at a very low point. My work of twenty years or more is disintegrated. Our men have deserted us. My foreign partners have given me up and fled for home. My home is destroyed. My friend and sister is dead.

I know you will think most of these tragedies are of my own making, but I am writing to let you know that I lay part of the blame on your shoulders, and on Mr. Kier's.

And so I warn you. Do not presume that I am finished with

you. Do not believe you have seen the last of me. Do not grow complacent or even too comfortable, for I will be back. Perhaps not right away, but someday, I will come for you both.

Until then,
Petra Scot

Kara breathed out and handed the note to Niall. He read it and cursed.

"I am very sorry," Wooten said.

"Do not be." Kara took the letter back and shoved it in a drawer. "Niall has had a secret hanging over him all of his life. I have lived with threat on the horizon since I was eleven years old. And we have lived on. Thrived. Created. Loved." She raised her chin. "She has underestimated us separately. How much worse will she mistake us when we are together?"

"She's right." Niall stepped close. "We defeated her once. If we must, we'll do it again."

"Petty threats will not steal our contentment in our work, our friends, or the joy we find in each other." She took Niall's arm and beckoned Wooten. "Come, Inspector. There is much to be done, but today is for celebration. Please, join us."

The inspector hesitated, but then nodded. "You are always a surprise, Miss Levett."

She laughed.

Niall grinned. "May that never change."

They made their way back to the others, and as they entered, Gyda stood. "Wait!" she called jovially. "There's one thing I must know, Niall!"

"What is that, Gyda?" he asked. Kara could see he was smiling despite himself.

Gyda pointed at Rob. "Who the hell is Great Bruce, and what is you two find so fascinating about his balls?"

Rob's jaw dropped, then he roared with laughter. Everyone joined in.

And as Niall tried to explain, through bouts of laughter, about the village bull they tormented as boys, Kara squeezed his arm. She knew they were more united and determined than ever. They would face what came, fight when they needed, and take joy where they could.

Together.

ABOUT THE AUTHOR

USA Today Bestselling author Deb Marlowe grew up with her nose in a book. Luckily, she'd read enough romances to recognize the hero she met at a college Halloween party – even though he wore a tuxedo t-shirt instead of breeches and boots. They married, settled in North Carolina and raised two handsome, funny and genuinely intelligent boys.

The author of over twenty-five historical romances, Deb is a Golden Heart Winner, a Rita Finalist and her books have won or been a finalist in the Golden Quill, the Holt Medallion, the Maggie, the Write Touch Reader Awards and the Daphne du Maurier Award.

A proud geek, history buff and story addict, she loves to talk with readers! Find her discussing books, period dramas and her infamous Men in Boots on Facebook, Twitter and Instagram. Watch her making historical recipes in her modern kitchen at Deb Marlowe's Regency Kitchen, a set of completely amateur videos on her website. While there, find out Behind the Book details and interesting Historical Tidbits and enter her monthly contest at deb@debmarlowe.com.

Printed in the USA
CPSIA information can be obtained
at www.ICGtesting.com
JSHW011231090823
46199JS00004B/46